Ropewalk; Rebellion. Love. Survival

Ropewalk, Volume 1

H D Coulter

Published by H D Coulter, 2021.

This is a work of fiction. Similarities to real people, places, or events are entirely coincidental.

ROPEWALK; REBELLION. LOVE. SURVIVAL

First edition. February 22, 2021.

Copyright © 2021 H D Coulter.

Written by H D Coulter.

For Andy and Mina.

My love, my world.

Chapter 1

Late March 1831

Ulverston, a small town crammed on to the side of an estuary, stood shielded by ancient fells. Whilst the growing high tide covered the last few remaining pieces of the decaying disused pier, a time before industrial advancement branded its mark on the area.

Bea sat alone on the old harbour wall, the sun barely visible behind Cartmel Fell and embraced the silence, the peace of the fresh crisp morning as the dew soaked into her old evergreen woollen dress. This was where she was at her happiest, waking before the family, with only the morning larks serenading her before she became bombarded by the mayhem of home. She watched the restless ships stretch out along the bank, waiting for their turn to enter the canal. The tide was already at its highest and in an hour, it would be gone again. Her Da had taught her the design of most of the ships - what they traded in; whether they were local, where they were going. Now and again a new ship would appear, hailing from a distant land, and she yearned to sail away, and to escape from her reality and the foreseen path ahead.

She had imagined a life outside her home, the moment her father had given her a copy of *Gulliver's Travels*. In those rare moments of free time, late at night, he had taught her a few words on top of the basic letters she had gained from school, and the rest she memorised herself in secret. Her Mam didn't believe that a girl should read; it gave her airs above her station. But Bea loved books, understanding how and why the changes in the human and natural worlds manifested themselves, letting herself believe that one day she might use her letters for other purposes. It allowed her to discover that the world was larger than this small town.

Over the last few years, the sea air had become thick with tales of travel and adventures; newspapers and books describing recent discoveries by some new explorer. Ulverston even had its own pioneer in the way of Sir John Barrow. Stories flowed through the streets about his most recent travels around the world, passed down through gossip and rumours, stemming both from letters to his family and town chatter.

As she gazed at the ships in the distance, Bea saw they were to dock at Lancaster and Liverpool, not Ulverston. All Ulverston traded in was iron ore, slate and linen brought down from the fells. *Nothing exotic about that*, she thought. Every day the sailors would go about their jobs, preparing to come into port, fixing down the masts and bringing in the rigging. Their voices would carry across the stillness of the morn, animated at the prospect of spending their two days of freedom on shore before they became trapped once again on the open ocean, usually for weeks or months at a time. Ulverston was often full of the ebb and flow of sailors, and of girls of a certain age dressing to impress them, as they paraded up and down Market Street.

If Bea's Mam had her way, Bea would do the same, exhibiting herself to gain the interest of a potential husband. But Bea didn't want just any man or sailor, and she certainly wasn't interested in the examples her Mam had indicated as being suitable for her. She wanted to meet someone she could admire and learn from, to be their equal in every sense of the word. The suffocating knowledge that she could do more, be more, drove her towards a forbidden hope; that leaving Ulverston with someone worthy and interesting would allow her to truly become herself. And yet, what possibility was there to make a new life halfway across the world. It was just as likely as if she'd find a fortune buried on the shoreline; she thought ruefully.

To pass the time whilst watching the ships being dragged past, she and her Da had, on many a morning, taken turns at guessing if it was their own rope strung across each rigging below. The simple game never became old: it was a comfort, and a playfully competitive side shone through their banter on both sides. A smile would spread across her Da's face every time he explained his victories, pointing out the colour of the hemp, and the even twist. He knew each length of rope he created, like she knew every piece of lace she made. It became a part of them both, the act of watching something blossom from nothing. The proud, accomplished feeling they enjoyed at the end of their labours. But for her Da, it came from somewhere deeper, in his bones, and in his blood. Rope was the Lightfoot trademark, a reputation her great

Granda had built up and continued through to her Da, and on to her brothers.

As Bea listened to her Da's tales, she found it difficult to picture Ulverston the way he described it in years past: a slow trudging town. To her, after every season that came and went, Ulverston grew bigger and louder thanks to the canal. If it had not come to be, would things be as they were now? Would the pier still have rotted away through lack of use? Would her Da still be a master at his craft? Would she have grown up in the workhouse instead of her family home?

And yet, Ulverston advanced before its time. Ships able to sail into the town centre doubled the amount of trade and business, bringing with it merchants, mills and the gentry, along with the promise of new jobs, and more workers than the small collection of buildings could house. *One of which is ours*, thought Bea, smiling with just a touch of irony as she turned to head home.

BACK ACROSS THE FIELDS, an array of four miscellaneous cottages stood at the end of a muddy track, forming the small hamlet of Outcast. Amongst them was one which had become particularly tired looking, with its sea-ravaged lime-washed cob walls. The neat edges had been smoothed and polished away. Even the windows had become opaque and milky in their small square lead boxes, as the relentless sea battered, blasted and bleached everything that came within its reach.

In the corner, a small wooden cow barn and a neatly ploughed vegetable patch waited patiently for spring to start, whilst hens roamed freely nearby. Ten yards away, a long narrow building signalled the start of the Ropewalk, housing the Lightfoot's rope-making business. With the fires already lit, the smoky smell of coal and wood filled the air, blackening the newly formed clouds above. Bea opened the gate and slowly trudged up the muddy path towards the cottage, bracing herself for an onslaught from her Mam.

Bea steadily placed her hand on to the iron door handle and with a deep breath, she gave the door a slight push.

"Beatrice, is that you? Where have you been? Have you been down to that harbour again?" In one breath Mrs Lightfoot bawled her three questions at Beatrice above a harrowing cry from her youngest sister. Sighing, Bea wandered reluctantly back into her suffocating home.

"Well, have you? Your father and I 'ave been over this, it's not *becomin'* of a young woman to be alone at such an hour down there. D'you want there to be rumours about you, about your character? How are you ever meant to get yourself a husband, if y'have a reputation of giving it away for free?"

Bea glanced at her Mam hopelessly and nodded; she heard this lecture most mornings. Over the years, she had learned to switch her mind off from the endless, biting noise emitted by her more outspoken parent. Through her teenage years, the arguments became more frequent, and Bea fought back. But that only ignited her Mam further, using it as an excuse to seek comfort from Mr Lightfoot, and make life at home unbearable for her daughter, who noticed the enjoyment her Mam got from her angry reactions. So, Bea, storing up her rage and frustration, instead sought solitude in smaller acts of rebellion.

She placed her shawl on the back of one of the chairs and glanced around the room. Her family home had not changed internally in the last hundred and fifty years. The thick earthen walls were painted in a light blue lime, reflecting the glow issuing from the large open hearth which dominated the living space. They positioned the original table her great Granda had built in the centre of the room with an assortment of chairs, each one eventually added as and when the previous one broke. Holly, her second youngest sister, was playing silently at the opposite end of the table, whilst Rowan, the youngest, stood in the pulled-out bottom drawer, grasping on to the sides, screaming for attention.

Mrs Lightfoot, perched at the head of the table, leant forward towards her visitor, a Mrs Dent, continuing to enjoy her role as overwrought mother. This morning she was using her company voice, a clearer, higher tone rather than her usual accent.

"D'you see Mrs Dent, how she doesn't care? How her selfish actions could bring this family into *dis-re-pute*, but does she listen to me? No!"

Mrs Dent lived with her young children in one of the handful of other cottages in the hamlet. A quiet, quirky sort of woman, she was a harmless creature who five years ago had lost her husband in an accident at sea. A large storm had raged over the Furness estuary, resulting in two ships crashing against the coast near Barrow. Mrs Lightfoot had taken her in like a beaten dog, controlling her every move, drowning her in charity to the point where she could not say no. Majority of the time, Mrs Dent seemed happy, grateful, and unaware of the games being played to gain an unnatural loyalty.

Bea, however, saw it all too easily, and felt sorry for her mother's companion. Somewhat under duress, Mrs Dent nodded her head in agreement at Bea, and glanced back at Mrs Lightfoot for approval.

"I hope you never experience this treatment from your daughters...?", her Ma finished haughtily, her words dripping with reproach.

"Yes, I do see, I..." Mrs Dent's meek voice barely audible.

Mrs Lightfoot interjected. "I am her better, her *Mother*..."

Bea wandered over to the far corner of the room to her sisters. Red-faced with tears, Rowan stretched out her little chubby arms.

"Oh Row Row! There, there...," Bea whispered in her ear as she scooped her up and wiped her hot, sticky cheeks. Automatically, Rowan placed her head into the nook of Bea's neck and clung on tightly with both arms. Bea ran her fingers through Rowan's fiery red curls and peeled off the loose strands glued to her cheeks.

"Beatrice, do not give her any comfort, she is only doin' it for the attention... she has been like this all morning! She must learn to never seek comfort in that manner, I won't be givin' to it, and neither must you. Poor Mrs Dent and I have not had a moment's peace with her wailing... put her down, I forbid you to mollycoddle her!"

Bea gritted her teeth and replied sternly, "I am just taking her to bed."

As she made her way to the foot of the staircase, Mrs Lightfoot bellowed across the room.

"Have you finished the lace off yet? The gentleman who commissioned the piece, is collecting it today, this afternoon. So, yes, *do* take your little sisters upstairs and make sure you have it ready."

Bea took hold of Holly's little hand and guided her to the door, continuing to balance little Row-Row on her hip. Without another word to her Mam, she silently made her way to the bedroom, trampling down her fury and frustration with each step.

UPSTAIRS, THE SPACE comprised of low beams and small windows, perched low just above the oak floorboards. The two rooms sat side by side; one for herself and three sisters Beth, Holly and Rowan, the other held her younger brothers Matty, John and Peter.

The sun was barely visible over the top of the trees in the distance. A single lead-lined pane of glass was pushed open, allowing a funnel of a salty breeze into the room. Staring out through the milky glass, Bea gazed at the fields in front of the cottage, reaching out to the salt marsh as it merged with the sea, a scene unchanged for generations.

Once Rowan and Holly were safely cocooned in the patchwork blanket on their shared bed, Bea sat on the floor and nestled a padded footstool between her legs. It was covered in a reddish-purple calico which she had dyed last summer, using the rotten berries, so that she could see the ivory threads clearer, making it easier to create a more detailed and intricate lace. Bea was building a modest reputation around the local area for her lace by selling her pieces at the dressmaker's in town. Her Mam had taught her the craft at the age of six to help bring in money for the family, but by ten she could match her on skill and design. By fifteen she had overtaken her entirely and taught herself skills and techniques, creating new designs in her own distinctive style.

This new piece was one of the best she had created, with its long, detailed panel of roses and leaves, designed for a proud young lady. She examined the lace. She felt the rise and fall of the design, the pins and smooth wooden bobbins sitting patiently at the end of the delicate threads. Like an old friend, she knew every intricate detail about her pieces; they held no secrets, giving her advice on where she had gone wrong, and how to remedy the problem. In the end she was sad to see them leave, as though bidding farewell to a loved one, never to be seen again. Bea stretched out her back and pushed her two palms together with only the back of her fingers touching, praying for a blessing from the angels of lace. She braided her hair back, weaving her long auburn strands in and out, as if it was practice for the threads. The lace was awaking from a deep slumber, and their conversation continued as if no time had passed. Her fingers moved without thought or conscience to the rhythm of the bobbins. She carefully placed a pin in the correct position, and under her hands her roses grew.

THE LAST PATCH OF LATE afternoon light highlighted the glowing crown of Rowan's head. She gazed down, watching Bea's fingers weaving in and out whilst she played with their ginger cat, who also loved to watch the bobbins move, trying slyly occasionally to paw at them herself. To help focus her thoughts, Bea sang some of the ballads her Da had taught her. Unable to pronounce majority of the words, Rowan loved to add her own, clapping and humming along. They repeated the same songs time and time again:

"As I walk'd thro' the meadow
to take the fresh air,
the flowers were blooming and gay:
I heard a fair damsel so sweetly singing
her cheeks like the blossom of May.
Said I, pretty maiden, how came you here
in the meadows this morning so soon?
The maid she replied: For to gather some May,
for the trees they are all in full bloom."
"Said I: Pretty maiden, Shall I go with you,
to the meadows to gather some may?
O no, Sir, she said, I would rather refuse,
for I fear you would lead me astray.
Then I took this fair maid by the Lilywhite hand;
On the green mossy bank we sat down;
And I placed a kiss on her sweet rosy lips,
while the small birds were singing around."

Rowan, clasping her little hands over her mouth, began rolling around on her back and giggled so hard her entire body shook, scaring the cat in the process. Not fully understanding the meaning behind the words the first time they heard it, she and Holly had asked Beth to explain. Beth hastily informed them it was naughty to kiss boys, and not to do it. Now each time Rowan heard the song, she thought it was hilarious.

"And when we arose from the green mossy banks,
To the meadows we wander'd away;
I placed my love on a primrose bank,
while I pick'd her a handful of may.
Then early next morning I made her my bride,
That the world might have nothing to say;
The bells they did ring and the birds they did sing,
and I crown'd her the sweet Queen of May."

"Again, again!" Rowan pleaded, giggling.

"No, that's enough for today, lovey."

"Please Bea." Rowan cast her big brown eyes with false sorrow towards Bea, who tried to distract her by holding up the lace for her to see. Downstairs, she could hear their small mantle clock chime out the hour.

"There – done – just in time. What do you think? Do you think it will be good enough for the gentleman?" Rowan smiled brightly.

Downstairs, a loud banging noise ricocheted through the cottage, causing the girls to jump and the cat to go flying with a disgruntled meow. Rowan descended into a second fit of giggles.

"Beatrice, come down at once," her Mam called up a couple of minutes later in a sickly sweet tone, "and bring the Lace!"

Bea knew the gentleman buyer must have arrived. Her Mam's tone placed her on edge; she had become almost embarrassed for the way her mother flirted with some clientele, and their indifference towards her in return.

"Coming!" she shouted back. Rowan, knowing already in her short years it was best for her to stay out of the way when there were visitors, instead sat playing with the cat, with Holly still sound asleep. Bea delicately picked up the lace and made her way down the stairs. The sooner she got this over with, the sooner she could go outside with the girls, she thought.

THE GENTLEMAN STOOD leaning against the door frame, silhouetted with the sunlight peering round his coat tails. Mrs Lightfoot was standing rather close by, making flirtatious gestures, her best lace cap balancing on top of sagging curls. She turned mid-sentence and faced Bea.

"Forgive me, ma'am, I didn't mean to interrupt. I was just bringing the lace down, as you asked."

Bea drifted towards the centre of the room, holding out the velvet pouch. On closer approach, she saw the man had a handsome face, with hazel eyes and brown hair. The sunlight warmed his neat side-whiskers, transforming them to a golden red. His tall, broad stature filled the door frame, and his weather-worn tanned skin and uniform told her he was a sailor, and an officer of some sort. He had lost his youthful bloom, instead he was a man in every sense of the word.

He stared at Bea with an enormous smile on his face, and humour in his eyes. The stare made Bea uncomfortable. Awkwardly, she averted her gaze, her eyes skipping around the room, not knowing where to look. The gentleman chuckled gently at her response.

"Beatrice, this is Captain Hanley. 'E is the gentleman who commissioned the lace," Mrs Lightfoot interrupting, bringing the sailor's attention back to herself. "Captain Hanley, this is my eldest daughter Beatrice, to whom I learned the craft."

Captain Hanley broke through the gap Mrs Lightfoot had just made and stood in front of Beatrice. Instead of holding out his hand for hers to fall upon, he tilted his head with a slight nod. More customary amongst the working classes.

"Miss Beatrice Lightfoot, a pleasure to make your acquaintance." His voice was strange, a mongrel of accents stemming from the lakes and Lancashire, all the way out to the Caribbean, instantly making him a great deal more interesting than anyone else Bea could think of in the locality.

"A pleasure to meet you Captain Hanley."

His sight lingered for a moment on her face.

"Was that you I heard singing outside before?" Bea hesitated; she felt attraction building between them. "I must admit, I took a moment to stand and listen."

Bea felt her cheeks become hot and flushed at his gaze fixated on her face. "Yes, sir, that was I, - I was singing to my sister upstairs, whilst I... finished the lace."

He took a couple of steps closer to Bea. He seemed taller now, standing before her, his scent a distinctive perfume of smoke and spices. He had a presence about him that Bea had never encountered of arrogance and power.

"Would you be so good as to show me the lace?"

Aware of her Mam's gaze, she held out her hand in front of her with the small parcel on top. Gently, he placed his hand on top of the lace and slid it from her hand, the tip of his finger caressing the inside of her palm as he slowly pulled away.

Bea pulled her hands back towards herself, placed them behind her back and swallowed hard. The Captain, without waiting for an invitation, dragged out a chair, and sat at the table. He pulled the lace out of the velvet pouch and explored the ridges of the delicate threads.

"Very impressive Miss Beatrice; truly, it is a beautiful and creative design. It is a match for any I have seen in Manchester, possibly even Boston. Your reputation is not exaggerated."

"Thank you, Sir." She had been remarked upon for her gifts in Ulverston, but never compared to Manchester lace-makers, never mind the Americas. She knew he was a traveller.

"There you go Beatrice; didn't I say she were talented? Manchester indeed! Taught her everything she knows, Captain Hanley." Mrs Lightfoot took the compliment for herself, delighted.

In one move, he pushed back his chair and stood up. "I don't doubt you did, Mrs Lightfoot," he muttered, throwing a second glance her way. He delicately placed the pouch into an inside pocket and leant towards Bea: "Thank you Miss Beatrice... I look forward to watching your gifts continue to blossom, with great interest."

Chapter 2

April 1831

Hemp had an undeniable smell, and even at ten feet away from the building Bea could pick it out from all the others in the morning breeze. As it was spun and stretched, it filled the air with a warm earthy scent, herbal, sweet, and pungent. Men's voices, calling to one another as they worked, grew louder as she approached the building.

Her Da's voice stood out above the rest, the Master giving out his orders to the workers and their boys. Her father kept a stern but fair set-up. Bea had loved to get away from the house and come to the Ropewalk to watch her Da and her Granda work the rope ever since she was a little girl. Before her Granda had passed, there had been three generations working together on the same shift. Her brother Matty, the newest recruit, had begun to learn the trade aged six, and when her Granda died, her Da became the rope-master, and her Uncle John his second.

Bea walked through the large door and took a seat on the bales of raw hemp, which were stacked high against the wooden wall. The century old building showed its age. The wooden panels were peeling at the edges, the murky sun casting bars of light onto the earthen floor, loose strands of hemp glinting as they floated to the ground. The hazy light made the narrow building, which already spanned three furlongs, seem even more vast, and the figures at the other end like distant toys.

Studying the movements of old Jack, she watched as he effortlessly hackled the rope. Old Jack had worked here as long as her Granda, and no one could hackle like him. To hackle, her Da had explained, was to take the raw hemp, and feed it through an old board which contained long, razor-sharp teeth set into it. This combed out the tow and the matted fibres, leaving a trail of clean straight hemp. Old Jack would then take these fibres, tuck them into his worn belt behind his back, and wrap it around his body. Once he had finished hackling, he would finish holding an enormous mass of free fibres with which to start the spinning process. Under his instruction, Matty spun the large, well-seasoned wheel as he twirled and glided from side to side, a form of a dance down the long walk, feeding the hungry contraption the straight hemp a handful at a time. The old man would then attach the four yarns to the whirls at either end of the walk, where he would meticulously twist and rotate them in the opposite direction. Bea watched her Da and Uncle John, using the same process in parallel with the small ropes, twisting and rotating a group of six in the other direction again, to reinforce the strength of the rope. Finishing the operation, her younger brothers oiled and sealed the ends, before transporting them off to the shipyards.

Bea enjoyed the peace and tranquillity of the place. The familiar routine, sights and sounds were all a comfort to her. The walk was a place where history and time stood still. If she had been born a boy, she would work here, learning the trade, and one day she would have become Master - but she had been born a girl, and that meant a life at home. She enjoyed creating lace, and remembered how, the first time she had shown her Da her finished product, he had been proud, and said she was born to use her hands. But it didn't establish her freedom; instead she felt cornered, forced to wait for a man - any man - to come and claim her before she became too old to know any other life.

Lost in thought, half in the past and half in the present, her eyes glanced across the long narrow building and found her Da, a tiny speckle in the distance. As he grew closer, he noticed Bea perched like a small bird on top of the hemp bales, bringing a broad smile to his worn face.

"What brings yer 'ere lass?" his warm, welcoming tone showed a hint of hesitance, cautious for the news she might bring.

He held out his hand and supported her as she climbed down from the stacks.

"Mam says she wants you home for noon today. I'm heading to town, to Johnson's."

"Aye, lass."

The reply was acutely tired; the smile had faded from his face. As the years had passed, he spent as little time at home as he could. Whenever Mrs Lightfoot had challenged this, he simply blamed it on the amount of work he had on. Bea, on the contrary, saw the difference: at the Walk, he was alive and fulfilled, whilst at home he was careworn and silent.

"I'm off Da", Bea smiled encouragingly, and kissed him.

"See yer at tea, lass..." his distant voice responded. Still holding on to her hand, he gave it a light squeeze and let her go.

AFTER TWENTY MINUTES of walking along the bleak, muddy track with the biting wind on her back, Bea arrived at The Ellers, a narrow street off the primary hub of town. The clean air had turned thick with soot and grime, spilling out of the tall chimneys. She placed her scarf over her mouth and stepped further up the road. It consisted of a row of cottages and two mills. It was also home to another, smaller rope-making business, which had popped up after they built the canal.

Passing the raucous sound issuing from the Corn Mill at the bottom of the street, Bea ambled upwards. The thin street seemed to be vacant of life; the tenants either in the mills or working down at the canal. The only sounds came from the washing billowing on the lines behind the houses and the monotonous ticking from the cotton mill ahead. Bea paused for a moment, staring at the large overbearing building with its foreboding wooden gate. The one thing she was always grateful for was the fact she had never needed to work in the mills. She had heard stories around town of the conditions there, how they employed the forgotten children from the workhouse to run the looms and trapped destitute families into service. Tales of children and adults developing cotton lung, or becoming mangled in the looms and machinery, now living on the streets begging for scraps or returning to the workhouse and a life of unbearable squalor, haunted her each time she passed.

If this was the sign of progress everyone talked about, she wanted nothing to do with it, she thought, shivering. Industry had brought people down from the fells to work in the town, with the promise of a better life, but now they had no home or work to go back to; also, the money had gone down, but the cost of living had gone up. A single loaf of bread cost them a week's worth of wages. Over the past six months, however, a restless feeling had gripped the working-classes across the country. She overheard hushed men's conversations in the street and learned of small closed-off meetings springing up in pubs and parish halls all over Ulverston. A few weeks back, upon entering the Ropewalk, she had heard her Da talking about it to her uncle, how the men were angry, and talked of change; demanding the right to vote, to choose a representative from their area to become their voice in parliament. Her Da had continued in a low hushed voice.

"And they're goin' to threaten that parliament with marches, riots and revolution, same as the French did forty year' since, if they do not meet our demands."

"It's not your business this time, not again. Think of what you have now," her uncle had replied.

The conversation had swiftly drifted on to other subjects when her brother joined them, and over the next couple of days the discussion had slipped out of Bea's head.

Standing there, looking at the smoking mills rising impassively before her, it all came back. What power would they have against this, to create change? None, surely. She gathered her woollen shawl tighter around her shoulders and trudged on to Market Street.

TODO WAS MARKET DAY, the same as every Thursday since medieval times, when Ulverston's streets were graced with stalls. Local farmers brought their meats, small time merchants brought their goods, and travellers made their daily living, selling small trinkets from one town to the next. From first light, the noise of chatter surged through the streets, and stallholders celebrated their deals across the square to attract customers competing against their neighbours. Bea had almost forgotten that all this went on. The town was another world to her small hamlet.

Meandering passed Thompson's, her stomach grumbled at the smell of freshly baked pies and breads. She gazed even more hungrily at the new copy of Mary Shelley's '*The Fortunes of Perkin Warbeck*' enticingly displayed in the window of Sutton's bookshop. A year ago, she had sneaked a copy of '*Frankenstein*' home without her Mam noticing, and spent three subsequent nights engrossed in the horrors within, wary of each shadow cast by the moon, dreaming of corpses and monsters. She was tempted to come back with her lace money and spend a shilling on a copy of the new book, but knew she had to be more careful with the disappearance of such a sum in one go, knowing each penny was counted out and placed into the old tea tin by her Mam.

Bea begrudgingly peeled herself away and stopped halfway up Market Street just outside Johnson's. The large windows were painted in a ruby red, framing the latest fashions from Paris or London. Women of all ages stared in, mesmerised as they discussed their opinions with their eager friends. Feeling for the package in her bag, Bea smoothed down her dress, making sure her bonnet was set straight, and opened the door.

Inside was packed full of animated women, and the occasional man who looked like they'd been sentenced to ten years' penal servitude. The women were engrossed in their joyous task of picking their next outfit or enquiring about haberdashery to fabricate a dress. Johnson's clientele came from the upper middle to lower-upper classes, supplying the ladies of the town and the nearby area with the ever-changing patterns and fabrics they needed as active members of the local society. Bea's eyes swam in the sea of alluring muslins, threads and ribbons placed delicately in glass cabinets, or draped over the display counter like an elegant waterfall.

"Miss Lightfoot? I expected you an hour ago!" came the politely vexed voice of Mrs Johnson.

Bea quickly turned on her heels and rapidly returned her hand to her side; she had been told off once too often for touching the goods. Mrs Johnson was poised behind the counter in her deep purple satin with lace trimmings. Her hair was delicately arranged in a simple design, a perfect balance between showing her distinction from the other shopkeepers, but still not as grand as her customers. Now in her early forties, she still held a sincere elegance in her countenance. She stared down at Bea, drumming her fingernails on to the polished wooden counter, irritated. Majority of the women knew the lace she sold was created by a cottage girl, but seeing the evidence of its origins was another matter.

"Sorry Mrs Johnson, I had an errand to run."

Mrs Johnson exhaled, her way of warning Bea not to let it happen again.

"Very well - have you got the six pieces I asked you for?" Mrs Johnson held out her hand delicately, as though disinclined to touch Bea's own. Yet it was these hands which produced the lace she requested. This had puzzled Bea at first, given her family's business brought in two hundred a year before costs, matching any other trade in the area. But a stigma of poverty still clung on to her hamlet and lingered above the cottage industries. Mrs Johnson opened the package, placed the contents on the counter and examined the lace with great intensity.

"Yes, they will do, I suppose... not as fine as the Paris lace, but we must get what we can," said Mrs Johnson.

Bea certainly knew straight away by looking at the women passing her in the town and at church whether the lace they were wearing was hers. More often than not, they were. Her jaw set.

"Here you go." Mrs Johnson presented Bea with three coins on to the counter.

"... But we had agreed on a pound, Mrs Johnson, since there was more work gone into these pieces?" The shopkeeper sniffed, and pushed the coins further towards Bea, who glared at her.

"I know how much you sell each piece of lace... for one of the simpler designs you charge up to two guineas. These six pieces are worth over ten pounds for you - this is all you want to give me in return?"

"Please lower your voice, Miss Lightfoot, believe me, you do not want to attract attention!" Mrs Johnson hissed at Bea, peering hastily round the crowded shop over her spectacles.

"We had an understanding Mrs Johnson, and, if you are not happy with the price, I could go elsewhere," Bea said in a low voice. "Two other shops in town have made me an offer to produce lace for them."

She allowed the words to hang in the air between them. This had been true a year ago, and probably still held today. But she prayed Mrs Johnson wouldn't call her bluff. She reached out and hovered her hand over the package, threatening to claim back what belonged to her. Mrs Johnson gave Bea a scrutinising look. The girl was too intelligent for her own good; if she didn't renege on her attempt to get a bargain, it would cost her in both price and customers. She put her hand in her pocket and placed two more coins on the counter.

"Do not be so hasty, Miss Lightfoot. I will pay you two more shillings for these pieces, and if you can deliver six more to the same standard by this time next month, then I will pay you a pound."

Bea knew when to keep fighting and when to stop. This was the time to do the latter.

"Very well, Mrs Johnson."

She lifted her head, holding her gaze, a new understanding lying tensely between them. Without another word, Mrs Johnson picked up the lace, turned her back and walked off in the opposite direction. Instantly engaging herself with a customer, she transformed back into her other agreeable, deferential self. Bea let out a breath and allowed her body to relax. She picked up the coins, which weighed heavily in her palm, and smiled wanly.

"I am impressed," a male voice breathed lightly into her ear.

Bea spun round to see Captain Hanley place his right palm to his chest and bow slightly. He was wearing a light grey woollen suit, the colour of the stone at the old harbour, with a long black overcoat and a black top hat. Today he blended in more with the other gentlemen in the shop, and she felt herself drawn in somewhat by his tall elegance and raw, handsome features. He stared down at her with a smile which Bea couldn't help but return. He in his turn noticed the same sweetness in her countenance as when they had met. But something was different with her today, a spark that illuminated her from within.

"Forgive me for startling you - good afternoon, Miss Beatrice Lightfoot."

"Good afternoon, Captain Hanley," she countered with a slight nod.

"My... sister, thank you for the beautiful lace." His broad shoulders and proximity inspired a confusing combination of attraction and defensiveness in Bea. Suddenly startled by her own thoughts, she felt herself becoming flushed. She smiled and took a step away from him.

"I am glad she liked it."

"What do you plan to spend your winnings on?" He inclined his head in the direction of Mrs Johnson. "I admire how you stood your ground."

"Thank you, Captain... I have to sometimes... she has tried it before."

A light-hearted smile spread across her face at the thought of her Mam's reaction if she ever found out how her daughter had behaved.

"Indeed, Miss Lightfoot?" his eyes lit up with interest. "So - is the money to go toward some of this beautiful fabric?" He stepped toward the glass counter, pointing towards the brightly shining rainbows cascading towards the floor. "This one in particular," he held a creamy muslin with flecks of gold, "brings out your eyes. No, this one, suits you better Miss." he simpered, doing an uncanny impression of Mrs Johnson as he grabbed hold of a golden silk fabric, reminding her of a winter sunrise.

For a moment she chuckled, her face bright with a smile. He smiled slowly in return. Then remembering where they were and with unfamiliar faces upon them, she straightened her face and took a step back.

"The money is intended for my family, especially," picking up the label and looking at the price, "with this muslin at a shilling a yard!"

"I assume you will attend the May Day dance attired in *something*?" he asked in a low voice.

"I'm not too sure I will attend this year, it depends." She couldn't help looking at the array of stunning fabric with desire before dropping her gaze. "I must be leaving; I have another errand and I'm already late".

"Of course, I have taken too much of your time. Until we meet again, Miss Lightfoot". He gave her what seemed like a genuine smile and lifted his hat to her as he bowed his head.

"And to you, Captain Hanley – good day." She gave him a small curtsey, turned, and headed towards the shop door.

"Good day, Beatrice," he murmured quietly as he watched her leave, pulling the door shut behind her.

AT THE TOP OF MARKET Street, Bea turned right and continued to Kings Street, onto the next destination. She pushed the last thirty minutes from her mind with an effort. The Captain was charming, confident and seemed interested in her, but something deep down made her cautious. She felt foolish at not being able to read the signs of men, so familiar to society women. The sky-blue paint and faded gold sign of the curiosity shop stood before her, making the smile return.

The tinkering bell announced her arrival as she stepped through the door. The walls were lined with shelves and cabinets full of old books, china ornaments and strange-looking objects Bea had never seen before. She loved to hear about other worlds and faraway lands, but here, the words became real, alive almost through the paintings and exotic stuffed animals. She squeezed past a table which took up most of the space in the centre of the shop. Scattered across it, in no apparent order, were the latest acquired items. At the sound of the door and the prospect of a customer, a man popped his head through the small archway leading through from the back room. His professional glance changed to a friendly countenance as he recognised Bea studying a strange artefact.

"Hello Beatrice, you are just in time for a cup of tea and some cake, come along through."

"Afternoon Mr Little, have you had many customers today?"

"A few... business is not what it was, but we get by - there is always tomorrow."

Mr Little did not tally with the proportions of his name, being over six feet in height, and a broad man. But Bea liked him; he was kind and surprisingly optimistic, despite having had his fair share of heartache over the years.

"Indeed." Bea weaved herself through the tables and cabinets full of treasures; she could spend happy hours in this shop examining all the wonders she found so fascinating, particularly on a day like today.

"Alice is in the back, she has the tea laid out." Mr Little turned around and ducked back through the archway, Bea following close behind. A sitting room, the same size as the front shop, contained a few pieces of furniture, stark in comparison to the room she had just left. A simple dresser housed a few treasured objects; small trophies left over from a bygone time of prosperity. A humble stove filled the fireplace where the whistling kettle signalled it was time for tea. Alice, not noticing the new arrival, sat hunched over the table with her blonde hair pinned back and her green eyes locked on to a fiddly piece of sewing. Bea smiled as she silently admired her friend, who was wearing another new creation of her own making, her tall slim figure hidden beneath layers of simple yet delicate emerald fabric. Her impressive skill at needlework was well-reflected in the tailored design of the dress.

"Hello Alice!"

As if she had just been woken from a deep sleep, Alice's head popped up in a startled motion. "Sorry. I was lost in this," gesturing to her embroidery, "I did not hear you come in." She beamed a welcoming smile at Bea. Alice was the last surviving daughter of Mr Little. Her Mother and her three younger sisters had died within weeks of one another eight years since, when an aggressive fever took hold of the region, claiming the upper and working classes alike, including Bea's uncle. Being the same age, Alice and Beatrice had known each other from childhood, attending the small charity-funded school together two afternoons a week until the age of ten, to learn their basic numeracy and literacy, with the added benefit of needlework classes thrown in. Girls were not permitted to attend school full time, as the authorities deemed unreservedly that their efforts were better spent at home or in the mills.

"Is everything all right? Alice asked, curiously.

"Yes, why?" Bea's tone sounded a little too bright as she tried to push away the image of the Captain who had suddenly popped into her head.

"You look a little flushed – distracted," said Alice, looking keenly at Bea.

"Oh - it has been a long morning, that's all!" Bea took a seat around the table next to her. Not fooled by her response, Alice refused to remove her inspecting gaze.

"I'll tell you about it later," Bea whispered under her breath.

Alice gave her a little approving nod and smiled. "Tea?"

The single word drew Mr Little's attention back from his daydreaming. He made his way to the side table, and all three sat sipping tea and consuming the simple cake whilst they discussed local events and developments. After half an hour, and feeling more refreshed, the shop doorbell rang out. "Excuse me, girls," Mr Little muttered, rising from his seat.

"So - now Da has gone, what is it you need to tell me?" Alice whispered.

Bea revealed the details of both her recent meetings with the Captain, leaving nothing unsaid. Alice remained silent and nodded her head occasionally. "So, what do you think?" Bea asked eventually.

Alice smiled. "Honestly, I'm not sure. - He is a gentleman of sorts and... you - we - are not. If he is interested, which I believe he might be, I think only time will show if his actions are honourable . . . or not. I think you should cast all this out of your mind unless he becomes persistent. There is no point dwelling on it as things stand." Alice gave Bea a knowing look. "But - I think you should act with caution. You have said yourself that something in him warns you away, somehow." Alice placed a comforting hand on her friend's arm. "Bea... I know you desire to leave home, and escape your mother, but I have also seen you turn down suitors. None, I agree, would have made you happy; nonetheless, you said no to all. Have you truly considered the options you have in life, now you are grown into a woman?"

Bea closed her eyes for a second and sighed "To be honest... I am lost. I need to leave home; I want to leave Ulverston, even, and see more of life before I hand over my choices to someone else ... but I'm a woman, and that is a man's way of things. My only means of escape is through what might, in the end, be the cause of a new confinement - marriage. My other choices are the mills, shop work – and that wouldn't pay enough for rent, or to continue just as I am."

They both sighed gently as one. Acceptance was often a woman's best way to whatever happiness was available to her. Squeezing Bea's hand tenderly, Alice changed the subject to the dance, and the latest round of gossip she had overheard in the shop.

"... I was there when she fell, you should have seen it! *The* Mrs Armstrong, in that hideous blue dress of hers, flying and landing in the muck... The horror on her face. But the worst was all the laughter, no one could stop."

"I am not sure how she will survive that, poor thing."

"Serves her right." Alice crumpled her face into a trout-like expression, making Bea laugh.

"Now on to more pressing matters; the May day dance is approaching. Have you decided if you will attend? A chance to see the dresses and the latest fashions?"

"I would love to spend the night dancing, like they do in the stories I've read, but I have nothing to wear, and *she* won't give me money for fabric. Say's I have better things to be doing than looking like a fool besides the ladies of the county. And if I wore one of my dresses, I would."

"I could do some work on one for you. Add some embellishment?"

"Thank you, but maybe she is right. I wish for one night I could be their equal, be amongst them and have all their opportunities."

"You *are* equal to those ladies, better than. Think it over and let me know. Speak to Beth." Alice placed her hand on top of Bea's and gave her a warm smile. "Another slice of cake before heading back, and a splash of tea?" She waited for a nod before standing.

"You will not believe what I heard about Mr Woodhouse."

"Mr Woodhouse, the blacksmith who owns a shop on Queens street?"

"That's the one." Alice turned back and saw the smirk on Bea's face.

"What of it?"

"He comes in twice a month and says hello to Da… after he fixed the sign a year back.

"Oh yes, and what of this Mr Woodhouse? What have you heard?" Bea grinned delightedly at Alice's blushing face. "Is he hoping your Curiosity sign might need a little work doing soon?"

Chapter 3

A disguised over-grown path sneaked out between the bare trees and gorse bushes, which ran parallel to the sea. Now used only by the local inhabitants on their way to the canal, instead of the tradespeople, fishermen and town folk of forty years ago. Bea breathed on to her fingers to warm herself, before quickly pulling her skirt up around her knees as the morning tide attempted to lick at its hem. In doing so, she smeared the inch-high collar of mud from around the edges of the dress onto her legs. Showing a glimpse of her grimy petty coat, she smiled; she never had given much heed to formality. The freezing stone touched the backs of her bare legs causing her to inhale sharply as they swayed free over the sides, kicking out a rhythm whilst the sea, two feet below, crashed under her boots. The sun attempted to peak out through the clouds as it rose behind the fells. She would need to head back earlier today, there were too many jobs to be done.

She readied herself to return home when she heard a hoof kicking up stones behind her. Startled at being caught on the harbour's edge at a time she could usually count on another hour of solitude, she turned hastily to see a horse and rider standing around ten feet away. Straddling the path from the canal, the newcomer looked like he belonged in one of the big southern cities in his fashionable caramel trousers, cream waistcoat and a high-collared woollen overcoat. He held her stare for a moment, seemingly as surprised as her to find the path occupied. He was undeniably handsome, with his short golden hair and bright features. And yet, a blank expression sat heavily over his face, betraying nothing. Confused about how to react, Bea lingered, awkwardly. A few moments passed with only the sound of the waves bashing against the worn rocks. She had no doubt that the working-classes probably did not register in his thinking. And yet, whether it was wishful hope, or simply a proud denial of this fact, she could not help but feel there was some sort of communication between them.

She met his gaze now purely out of cheek, a playfulness stirring inside her, and unwilling to relinquish her spot. At that moment, the light breeze transformed into a sudden furious gust of sea air, charging in and dancing around her, causing an enormous wave to crash on to the rocks below and soaking her shoes and legs. Her long auburn hair flew around her face like a veil of silk and she jumped involuntarily. Without thinking, she shrieked, and then laughed, delighted.

A slow smile crept across the young gentleman's face as he watched her trying to wrestle with her hair and clinging to her skirt all at once. Then, as though in answer to a call, he turned his head back towards the direction in which he had come, and gently encouraged his horse to trot. Bea watched him for a couple of seconds before heading home herself. Her future path had shifted slightly once again.

JOSHUA FOLLOWED THE overgrown track, past the hamlets and Low Mill, and raced towards Lightburn Park. He needed to gallop, to feel the surging power of the horse and rid himself of the burden of work before the morning began. He had been back for six months now and was missing the hustle and chaos of city life. After the suffocating academia of Cambridge, Liverpool had been a breath of fresh air; his home for nine years, where he had forged friendships and prospects with the burgeoning northern industries. Joshua had always known he would return to Ulverston one day, just like his father, but it didn't make it any easier; it didn't feel like somewhere he could belong. The town had changed over the last twenty years; there were more people, and more companies, and more life in the small market industries, even so, it wasn't Liverpool.

He breathed in the cool air as he felt his horse open up, and a flash of the strange, windswept girl entered his mind again. She had looked like some sort of spirit, how the sea spray and the wind had danced around her. She exuded an untouchable fearlessness as she watched the rolling tide coming in, unafraid of the wildness of the sea. Most of the ladies he had known in Liverpool had a confined, calculated presence about them. Always the same conversations, or what they thought he wanted to hear, always attempting to win some favour or make some step up on the social ladder.

He wondered who the sea-sprite was; she would certainly never be found in the close-cut drawing rooms of the society women he knew. An isolated encounter, more was the pity. He steered his horse back towards town. Soon he would be missed, and his father would expect an update on the previous day's inspections. He trotted through Queen Street, passing the early commuters as they bowed their heads to him, until he arrived at: "Mason and Son". Feeling the familiar heavy burden of responsibility return, he dismounted and entered.

The building was laid out with the clerks on the ground floor with his fathers, two other managers and his own office on the first floor. It was designed to intimidate anyone who stepped over the threshold. Clerks rushing round with too much to do, not enough hours and no waiting room. His father liked the idea of the businessmen and clients standing awkwardly, waiting for him to arrive. It was all a game of power, and Mr Mason always liked to win.

A burst of conversation spilled out of one of the clerk's office.

"He is in there right now and he ain't happy with Mr Mason. I heard him shoutin' about the prospect of losing money."

Joshua turned on his heels and made his way up the stairs, taking two at a time. He met the sound of voices as they flowed down the corridor.

"That's not good enough, Mason - I invested in good faith, and now I hear there are going to be strikes?"

"I can promise you, Mr Marshall, that there will be no strikes in my quarries, and I am sure, moreover, that there will be no strikes of any kind. The workers like to talk, but that is all it is: talk. They do not have the knowledge or the powers to act. They will be grateful at the chance of a job and leave it at that."

"They are a bunch of *un*grateful wretches, the lot of them. What is Forester doing about it?"

"Magistrate Forester tells me that unless he has documented proof that they are meeting above the limit, or take action, he can do nothing with regard to the law."

"What good is he to us anyway... his father was a worker; his loyalties will fall on their side. He is just another local social climber, if you ask me."

"You are indeed correct, Mr Marshall, but unfortunately he is also correct, upon terms of the law."

"So, what are you planning to do, Mason, to secure my money? Because if you don't do something, I will have no option but to withdraw my investment."

"Please Mr Marshall, allow me some time. I have men looking into the matter: we will find the ringleaders and put a stop to all this nonsense. You have my solemn assurances."

"Very good, very good... I will leave it with you, for now; but I want to be updated within the week."

"Of course, Mr Marshall."

"Good day, Mr Mason."

Joshua hurried back down the corridor to give the impression he had been coming through from another office when the door opened.

"Good day, Mr Marshall..."

For the rest of the morning, Joshua felt restless, too much had happened for him to concentrate with ease. His mind kept repeating Mr Marshall's words over anxiously, jumping from one question to another. What did they mean by a strike... and why would the men be striking? The pay was decent in the mines and on the ships, it was a decent job, and brought them into town and away from the workhouses. He himself hadn't heard the men talk of taking action. Not that they would communicate anything of that sort to him, their master. In that moment, he missed his friends back in Liverpool acutely; friends who understood the trade and understood him.

By lunchtime, he had completed less than half of his tasks for the day but had no more meetings to attend. He would come in early tomorrow and catch up, he promised himself. He felt the need for a long ride and a pint before heading home.

"AFTERNOON SIR."

"Thank you, Butterworth." Joshua handed the butler his jacket and made his way to the stairs.

"Mrs Mason would like you to join her in the parlour, Sir."

"Did she say why?"

"No Sir."

"Thank you." Joshua turned right and headed towards the familiar room on the left, positioned perfectly to catch the afternoon sun. He gave the door a slight knock before entering.

"Come in."

"You wanted to see me, mother?"

The late sun flooded the room in an orange light, highlighting the deep rose rugs, and a few pieces of fine furniture. It had always been the woman of the house's personal space, decorated always according to her taste and enjoyment. His mother was sitting in her usual chair, and had a companion, a young lady, positioned next to her.

"You're back early this afternoon. Forgive me, my dear - you remember Lady Dawn Richmond of Conishead Hall?"

Joshua remembered. She was the beauty of the county, elegant, slim and dressed in the finer gifts of life. Her blonde hair was pinned up with small braids draping in and out of wider loops, a neat picture of perfection. A fleeting image of the young woman from this morning came into his mind again; her mild auburn hair and playful laughter in stark opposition to the lady sitting before him.

"Of course - good afternoon, Lady Dawn." Joshua performed his gentlemanly duty and strode over to her. He bowed, took her held-out hand and hovered a kiss above it.

"It is good to see you again, Joshua."

"I did not realise you two were such good friends." Joshua smiled, throwing a swift glance at his mother.

"Lady Dawn and I sit on the board of a few local charities together and I decided it was high time I knew her better."

"Mrs Mason has been very good to me - passing on all her great wisdom when it comes to dealing with some of the finer details."

"Please, call me Clara, my dear."

"With pleasure."

"I will leave you ladies to it, then…"

"Will you not join us for a cup of tea, my love?" Joshua recognised the look from his mother all too well and made an instant and easy decision not to be part of her plan.

"Sadly, I cannot; I have an appointment with Max early this evening and I must change. I will speak to you later, mother dear. Lady Dawn, it was an honour."

"Very well." Mrs Mason smiled. "Very well."

Chapter 4

Bent over the old wooden table, Bea sprinkled out a second dusting of flour before pulling and stretching the stringy wholemeal dough to make the bread for the evening meal. The house was quiet; her brothers were out working with her Da, and her eldest sister Beth was a housemaid over on Southergate. Holly and Rowan sat playing with their wooden toys by the fire as Bea placed the dough in a bowl in front of the grate, covered it with a cloth and allowed it to prove. She made a start on the rabbit stew with the animal she caught yesterday in one of her Da's traps. She peeled the potatoes and chopped the cabbages she had dug out of the small vegetable patch earlier that morning, finishing with a handful of the dried thyme and rosemary which hung in bunches over the hearth, throwing them in to the pot.

With the stew bubbling away above the fire, Bea placed the bread in the small oven inset to the right of the grate. The front door rattled open, abruptly disturbing the peace, as Mrs Lightfoot strutted into the seat in front of the fire.

"Come on girls, move out the way." She kept nudging them until she could sit down. They looked up at Bea, who gestured with her eyes for them to play at the other end of the table.

"How is Mrs Dent faring?" Bea asked politely. Mrs Dent had a nasty turn at the same time every morning, roughly about the time Mr Lightfoot left for work.

"Oh, she is just fine now," her mother remarked with no interest.

"How's dinner comin' by? Anythin' else you need to do? Your father and brothers will be home soon."

Bea continued in silence, turning her back on her Mam and smiling towards the girls. This seemed to vex her Mam once more. She raised her voice a notch higher.

"Your Father can't be expected to always..."

A knock echoed across the room, putting a stop to her complaint. Bea let out the breath she had been holding in. Like a Greek player with two masks, Mrs Lightfoot quickly substituted her frown for a large smile. She stood up and smoothed down her dress, rushing hastily to the door.

"Good day, Captain Hanley! Please, come in!"

Without thinking, Bea ducked down and hid by the girls behind the kitchen table. She couldn't imagine what he had come for; it had been a week since their last encounter and the awkwardness she had felt then suddenly came flooding back.

"Good day, Mrs Lightfoot, forgive the intrusion," he greeted her as he stepped into the room, scanning his surroundings quickly.

"Tea?" Her Mam grabbed a grimy tin from the top shelf of the dresser and dusted off the small china teapot given to her as a wedding gift. She hovered over the precious leaves, counting out each spoonful.

"Please." He took off his hat and placed it on the table alongside a large paper parcel.

"If you don't mind me being so bold, Captain Hanley, what do you have there?" She offered the Captain a beaming smile, attempting to convince him it was meant for her. With relief, Bea realised, her Mam had no intention of making her presence known.

"Is Miss Beatrice around?" he enquired, ignoring Mrs Lightfoot's question.

Mrs Lightfoot paused. So did Bea, mid-breath. Holly looked down at her sister with a delighted smile and bellowed, "Here, Bea is HERE!" She covered her mouth for a second, and then descended into a fit of giggles. Bea's cheeks became hot, feeling like a child herself, caught hiding with the young ones. Rowan joined in with Holly's laughter. Bea stood up slowly, keeping her eyes low.

"Good day Miss Beatrice, I have brought you a little something, which I hope you will like." Hanley smiled, indicating the parcel.

"I... thank you...?" She hesitated, unsure how to receive such a gift, or if she should receive it at all. She stepped out from behind the security of her sisters and moved towards the Captain.

"Please - open it." His voice held a hint of pride.

The brown wrapping paper was closed with a golden ribbon. Without thinking, she stroked the satin material with her fingers, tugging at the tails, and in doing so, sealed her acceptance. The ribbon fell away gracefully on to the table, and the paper cracked as it gave way to yards and yards of stunning silk cloth which glowed like her beloved early dawns down at the harbour. A couple of seconds passed, and no one uttered a word.

"Do you like it?" Hanley knew it had already worked its magic.

"Thank you, Captain, it is beautiful... but I cannot accept this". She folded the brown paper back over, concealing the temptation inside.

"Now Miss Lightfoot, it is merely a simple gift - I came across it through a friend, for half the selling price, and thought you could make good use of it with the dance coming up."

He opened it up again, luring her in. She did not recognise it from Johnson's, she was certain of that. So where had he obtained it? From his connections with the smugglers, being a sailor? He might be a smuggler himself, for all she knew. Regardless, it must have cost him a shilling a yard, if not more, even at half the price. There must be at least twenty yards sat on the kitchen table. She felt a reckless tightness in her chest. The sound of his voice brought her back into the room.

"Will you do me the honour of accepting it?" His soft voice was low and clear.

"Sir – Captain - it is too much; I've done nothing to deserve..." Her heart was a marching drum in her chest. She had never, would never, be able to afford such a quantity of beautiful fabric in her life. It would give her the dress she wanted, allow her to attend the May Day ball which would please Alice - and herself, if she was honest. But what would she owe him in return?

"Forgive me, but I saw how you looked at the fabrics in Johnson's, the other day," he looked at her in a way that made her feel they were the only two in the room, "and by coincidence I came across this similar silk at a lower price only hours later. It was meant for you."

Bea felt the words pulling her in. His hand slowly crept towards hers across the oak boards.

"Isn't that lovely Beatrice?" Mrs Lightfoot exclaimed in a shrill voice, breaking the spell. "You didn't tell me you saw Captain Hanley the other day? And to think, 'e has bought you such a lovely gift!" Bea pulled back her hand

and took a step away from the parcel, looking at the door. She wanted to escape, to bring this ordeal to an end.

"What if we perform a simple exchange?" He felt her attention return to him. "If you accept this small gift, in return I ask for the first two dances at the May Day Ball?" Bea's eyes widened, and she looked at him earnestly, inspecting as best she could the meaning in his words, the truth behind the smile. She knew the implications if she said yes.

Glancing at her mother, she saw an unpleasant look on her face, a mixture of frustration, envy and resentment, her hands twisting her apron into a funnel, like a dishcloth. Bea's finger graced the top of the fabric. It reminded her of the creaminess of a rose petal. She would be a golden rose. It would make her beautiful. The equal to any of the other ladies, for one night only, to know what it was like to have opportunities. Her heart cried out for her to say yes; for the price of the first two dances, how could she refuse.

"Captain, I will accept your offer."

Hanley looked triumphant. "I am pleased to hear this. I look forward to seeing the dress you create from the silk, and to have the honour of the first two dances." He made his way without ceremony to the door.

"Thank you..." Bea nodded her head at no one in particular, dazed.

A wide smile filled his face, and he gave Bea a deep bow. Turning on his heels, he faced Mrs Lightfoot.

"Thank you for the hospitality, as always, ma'am," and tilted his head with a curt nod. In two steps he was out of the door, leaving behind a chipped cup full of untouched tea, and a silent kitchen.

"WELL, THERE'S NO GOIN' back *now*." Her mother sneered spitefully as the sound of the Captain's horse receded into the distance.

Bea did not want to discuss the matter any further, hoping to clear the fabric away before her Da came home. What could she do now, anyway? She had agreed; she had said yes. There was no going back; her mother, for once, was right.

"Beatrice!" Bea did not look at her, instead began stirring the pot and thought of the dress she could design with the help of Alice's talent for needlework. "You'll face me when I speak to you, girl!" her Mam spat haughtily.

Bea was taller and older now, no longer a child. She found herself able to meet her mother's glare at eye-level, using anger to make her brave. Holly and Rowan were silent at the other side of the table.

"Nor shall I go back on my word. The Captain asked for two dances, and I said yes. I will have a beautiful dress to wear, and that is it. Nothing more, nothing less." The words tumbled out of her mouth; she was unsure even she believed them.

"He's a man Beatrice, don't be a fool. He'll try for more than that, and you'd better be ready to aim for marriage - nothin' less than *that*!"

"I'm not bound to him for anything! Though," she raised her chin defiantly, "what if I did marry? You should be pleased for the chance – you tell me often enough how much you want rid of me! - I'm not like you, Mam! What if I want to change my prospects, what if I want more?"

"Don't you think *I* wanted more?" There was a note of anguish in her mother's exclamation. Her eyes were wide and staring. Suddenly, Bea saw the life she was in danger of falling into; the person she could become. Her mother was her mirror image – only twenty years, seven children, and a lifetime of regret between them. They were both silent. Bea gathered the parcel from the table, placed it behind the stairwell, and moved towards the girls.

"What say we go play?" she breathed deeply, balancing Rowan around her waist.

"You think you're better than me, don't you!" Her mother wasn't done. "You think that you're meant for better things than the life I've."

"*Enough*." Bea shouted, allowing her bottled-up frustration and anxiety to come spilling forth. A sound made them all turn to see Mr Lightfoot in the doorway, with his sons standing behind him. Suddenly the noise of the bubbling pot above the crackling fire seemed thunderous.

"After a hard mornin' workin', is this what we're to come 'ome to?" He made his way to the wash bowl on the sideboard before he took a seat in his usual place in the middle of the table. Bea moved the two girls back to where they were sitting before. Rowan, reluctant to let go of Bea and held on tight around her neck.

"Robert - if only you could hear the way she speaks to me sometimes. I'm 'er Mother; she can't be allowed to be'ave in such a way."

"Row-Row, let go love, I need to get dinner out," Bea whispered. Letting go, Rowan gave a brief nod in agreement, allowing Bea to quietly, move back over towards the pot.

"Robert... will you not do something?"

Mr Lightfoot slammed his palm open on to the table, making his two-pronged folk and plate jump.

"I want no more o' this." His authority filled the room. "Where's dinner?"

"Coming" Bea announced meekly. She pulled the bread out of the oven, which had become slightly charred due to recent distractions, and placed it on the table.

Her Da caught sight of her eyes and knew something had changed in his daughter, beyond the quotidian arguments and frustration to which he so often came home. She gazed at him for a second with an apologetic look, then turned away to fetch the pot. He let out a long sigh, knowing they would both have to practice the usual drill.

"Bea... if I hear yer have been speaking to yer Mam disrespectfully again, it'll be the strap for yer. Am I clear?"

"Aye Da." Bea heaped a spoon full on stew on to his plate and sliced off a chunk of bread in silence.

Chapter 5

"Can you tell Charlie; I have his rope delivery?"

The man investigated the back of Mr Lightfoot's cart and then back at him. "Aye."

"Tell him, its Bob." The man nodded before shuffling his hunched body up the narrow path toward the Master of the canal's offices.

A melody of sound surrounded him. Men busy at work in shipyards old and new, lining the sides of the basin, reaching deep within the canal, and dosing the area with the smell of freshly cut wood, tar and burning metal. At the top basin, two iron cranes broke up the view of the rolling countryside, a statement to what the town had become, with teams of men and boys, standing to attention, ready for the next load of cargo, their horses waiting patiently to guide the ships back around and down the canal. They docked a few scattered ships in some of the side ports along the water. They had already completed their early morning load, and now the tide gave them some much-needed respite before it came flooding back in again and forced their decks into action once more.

Bob Lightfoot jumped down from the cart seat and stretched his legs up and down the narrow path, gently stroking his old mare, and calming her own shuffling feet. He enjoyed coming here once a month to drop off an order or two for the shipowners, but over the past six months he had been too busy, sending another in his stead. And yet, that wasn't the only reason he had been missing the habit; he had wanted to avert the conversation he was about to have.

"Bob."

"Charlie."

Bob gave the oncoming man his usual nod. He was a small man, wider than he was tall, with broad shoulders formed by decades of working on the canal.

"Grand, you brought this month's order?" He peered over the side and dropped his voice. "Are you coming then?"

"When?"

"Tonight. You haven't been to the last few."

"Work has been busy."

Charlie gave Bob a questioning look. "The men look to you; your voice carries weight. You speak plain - but true."

"Aye."

"So, are you coming then?"

"What if they catch us? They would take my walk, my house - who would put the food on my table, and the tables o' the men? I have talked it over with my brother, and he agrees."

"Fear is what they are hoping for, to stop us again. We must stand united. Think it over, they need you. These responsibilities didn't stop you seventeen years back."

"I was younger and foolish back then - the rules have changed since, and there is more to lose." Bob moved round the cart and pulled at the ropes.

"I'll send some boys down to help, and I'll see you tonight for a pint, Bob." Charlie left before his old friend could refuse him again.

"Master," the hunched man saluted out as Charlie passed, nodding his head in respect; then moved toward Bob to help unload the ropes.

Bob Lightfoot started yanking at a stubborn one, stuck underneath one of the larger strands. Why didn't Charlie take no for an answer? He knew exactly how it would affect them all, and that was the problem. They could never win.

On the way back to the Walk, Mr Lightfoot took another portion of time to think. The arguments of the strikers made sense; in fact, they brought out a rage in him he kept well-hidden from his family and friends. But since that fateful day in St Peter's Field, over thirteen years ago, the government had quashed any chance of the workers rising again. What was the point in risking everything, only for nothing to change? To watch his men being slaughtered in front of him all over again.

As he twisted the bridle rope in his fingers, so the arguments became tangled in his mind. He thought of his eldest son walking the rope, whilst the two smaller ones sat in the far corner sealing off the finished product, and realised with a jolt, this wasn't just his fight, it would be theirs one day. When Matty became Master, what position would the workingman be in then? His Da had told him he had too much fire in him when he was young, told him to sack away his ideals, and to settle down and marry. So he did. Married a woman who would take him without knowing him, without thinking of the consequences, and they had created heirs to his small kingdom, and grown further and further apart. Sometimes, he heard that younger self calling out in anger once more. This was one of those times – this was his time again.

EVERYDAY CONVERSATIONS filtered out from the pub, welcoming him in. They wouldn't start the meeting until the door was bolted shut. He made his way straight to the bar on the other side, giving the customary small nods and acknowledgements.

"Haven't seen you in a while, Bob."

"Liam – work keeping me busy." He gave the tall man standing next to him a quick glance, trying to gain the interest of the landlord.

Liam leaned in a little closer. Twenty years younger, he had the reckless fire that the ropemaker used to have. "Good to hear, thought maybe you'd left us?"

Bob took a sip of his pint and leant his back against the bar. "Thought about it – don't get me wrong, it's a worthy fight."

"What changed?"

"Charlie."

"Aye." Liam let out a broad smile and took another gulp of his pint. "We'll it's good to have yer back."

"Alright Bob, family well?"

Bob turned to his other side to see a familiar face. "Aye Ian, yours?"

"One of the little ones ain't been well, had to spend five shillings on the doctor - 'e said it was a sickness going around, there was nothing more could be done, an' it was in God's hands. We don't have money to waste on crooks like that!" Ian shook his head as he lifted the pint up to his mouth, with his coal-blackened fingers smudging the side of the tankard.

"That ain't fair. How's the child now?"

A drip of ale dropped from his chin onto Ian's pitted shirt. Using the back of his hand, he smeared the residue from his chin, leaving behind a black mark. "Better - thanks be to god, - not the doc."

Bob couldn't help but laugh, and his friend joined in.

"Bob."

"Charlie – well, I'm here."

"Thought you'd come." He gestured for another pint from the landlord. "Are you sticking around for the meeting?"

"Might as well."

"Good man, talk after?"

"Aye." Bob nodded his head, as Charlie made his way over to a makeshift stage at the far side. His voice soon rang out, and the crowd grew still.

"Men: we risk a lot comin' here, gatherin' to speak about one thing - our rights. The government has banned us fer' doin' this, and so I understand why some workers shy away. We could lose everything: our homes, our businesses, and goin' on the mood of one or two o' them judges, our lives. But if we don't act, if we don't speak out, then we are risking something far greater - our voice.

For too long we have been the downtrodden; the forgotten men and women who build and make this land what it is today - but for what? Friends and family, our own, are butchered in those mills, in the quarries, even on the canal - and when they aren't able to work, they're left in the street like scraps for the stray dogs." A grumbling noise rippled through the pub in agreement.

"We are worth more than that, and we are stronger than they think. By comin' together, we become a powerful force, a voice that must be heard. Wages are droppin', but the price of living is increasin'. A loaf of bread is more than a week o' wages for a mill-family: why are we letting the government control us like this? They tell us from the moment we are born to the time we are in the ground, that we are not worthy, we are less than they. Well - I say we are not! Our work merits our voices to be heard. If we do nothing, then nothing will change. Our children will starve, and their children will face a future the same as ours. Is that what we want for them?"

"No!"

"What do we need to do to change that?"

"Fight!"

"Fight for change, fight for the right to be heard, fight for the right for a vote!"

"Aye!" The room exploded with noise from men championing Charlie's sentiment and slamming their tankards down on the tables and the bar: including that of Bob Lightfoot.

Chapter 6

May 1831

Sitting in their own puddle of wax, the small flames struggled to stay lit on the stub of wick remaining. Bea rolled her head from side to side and stretched out her back. She felt the lack of sleep in every ache of her body, but the reward was more than worth the pains. She leant back and studied her dress, constructed according to a new pattern from Johnson's. The neckline cut straight across the chest to the shoulders; the sleeves were extravagant, dominating the top part of the dress, and the waist was slightly lower than she was used to, drawing together a fuller skirt. It was a bold design, but she had been determined to do the fabric justice, perfectly complemented by the lace trim she had added, full of tiny roses, delicately draped around the neckline. She checked to make sure the positioning was straight, and hung it over the end of the bed, watching delightedly how the light material floated and fluttered in the early morning breeze.

She was ready. She had seen the Captain twice since that day he had presented her with the fabric, finding herself darting around corners, watching him march past, then taking off in the opposite direction. She smiled now, hugging her knees to her chest. Whatever his intentions might be, she knew she was looking at the only thing she wanted from their deal.

Her sister Beth stirred as the light glistened across the room. She yawned and then noticed the dress.

"Oh, Bea... look at it! You'll be like one of those society ladies in the pamphlets. You'll put my dress to shame."

Bea beamed at her. She knew Alice would be at the ball tonight, but knowing she would have her sister at her side meant just as much. They looked at each other and giggled.

Bea leant her head back against the bed, sighing with nervous, gleeful anticipation. Her eyes drifted shut, and without the will to fight against it, she fell into a dreamless sleep.

A HANDFUL OF LADIES and gentlemen stood gossiping in their finest outfits outside the Assembly rooms. Having been worried she would be overdressed, Bea soon realised hers was a relatively simple design compared to the majority of the ladies' present. They looked like they belonged at the palace amongst royal courtiers in their lace, feathers and pearls. One of the few nights a year, the classes of Ulverston might mix even a little. This was only the second time Bea had attended a comparable social gathering. The first had been at the harvest festival two years ago, but that was far less formal, and far less impressive.

Bea and Beth carefully weaved through the crowd to the main hall, the splendour of the illuminating light issuing from the candles as it reflected off the over polished oak panels, their honey-scented wisps of smoke smudging up the newly painted walls. The warm glow created a romantic atmosphere in the large open space, as the music of the small orchestra flowed sweetly over the dancers. They spun and swirled, every partner casting a glittering shimmer onto their neighbour's silk finery.

The sisters were happy to stand back and watch every interaction, absorbing every detail. They saw the disgust on some of the more gentile faces whenever a lower-born figure approached to pay their respects. Bea noted the awkwardness in some of the poorer ladies, attempting to hide in the corners of the room so that no one would notice their simple, plain dresses against the splendour of the county women. A few mothers scouted amongst the men for a potential husband for their meek daughters, pushing them on to the dance floor unashamedly, praying for a match.

In general, however, there was a gayness to the guests, and a constant flow of laughter circulating the room. People were taking advantage of the precious few hours of light merriment to forget their troubles, and enjoy themselves in the company of friends, and a mediocre punch. She noticed a few eyes glancing their way, but was too excited to register whether this should flatter or trouble her.

"Is this not wonderful?" she remarked to Beth.

Beth could hear the joy in her sister's voice. It was rare to see her this happy, and it pleased her to be a part of it. She deserved to have cause to smile about.

"Yes, it is, - look." Beth noticed Alice on the other side of the room and waved her over. Alice glided through the knotted crowd immediately.

"You look beautiful." Bea beamed at her.

Alice stood poised in a new dress of her own creation in soft violet muslin, with a velvet sash.

"You both look so wonderful. Look at that fabric, you did such a fine job."

They continued to analyse the surrounding crowd, remarking on the handsome men, and pointing out the most elegant women. All three failed to notice Captain Hanley making his way towards them around the edge of the room.

"Good evening ladies". A gut feeling, something inside Bea, twisted suddenly. It was time to pay up the cost of her evening of freedom. She took a large gulp of her punch and focused on her friends as she introduced them.

"Good evening, Captain Hanley. May I introduce my sister Beth, and my good friend Miss Alice Little," Bea gestured to each in turn. The girls curtsied. Beth gave her sister a puzzled look as she felt her squirm under the Captain's gaze.

In the glow of the low light, Bea had to admit the Captain looked handsome. Wearing a smart white cravat and deep blue tail suit, his smile was bright, but his dark eyes seemed to see straight into her revealing nothing in return.

"Miss Beatrice, may I say I knew you would create a beautiful dress, but I never imagined it would be something so superior to every other woman in the room." Bea felt the overly familiar compliment prickle her skin. She had imagined being noticed at such a ball by a handsome officer or gentleman ever since she was a little girl, so why did it feel so wrong now? She longed to be standing outside so that the cool evening breeze could take away the heat in her face.

"Thank you, Captain..." she trailed off. No reply sprang to mind. Hanley seemed pleased at her confusion.

"I believe it is time for our first dance." He held out his arm.

He positioned her opposite him on the dance floor, marking their space proudly. Bea felt only awkward and exposed, openly encountering the gaze of strangers. She was used to being invisible, standing on the side-lines, people passing by without giving her a second glance. In her usual clothes these people never acknowledged her, but this dress seemed to shed any disguise behind which she might have hidden. But that had been what she had wanted after all, she told herself, to be one of these fine ladies for the night, to shine like they did.

Bea recognised the music and sent out a small thankful prayer as her feet anxiously waited to trickle across the polished floor. Bea knew the common country dances upon which most of the motions were roughly based on but feared the more recent waltzes from London. Their first piece seemed to evaporate in a matter of seconds. They both smiled and laughed a little in the closing bars, his hand holding tight around her waist and a look of longing in his expression making her blush. By the time the last notes rang out, her muscles had relaxed into each graceful step as a natural child-like enjoyment took over.

As the second dance began, Bea found it harder to hide her smile and her excitement, taking a couple of steady breaths to compose herself. She looked down the line of other ladies as they waited, in an undulating sheen of elegance and demure gestures. Beth standing four couples down from her, looked a little anxious opposite an equally nervous-looking young gentleman. She glanced up at the Captain and discovered him gazing back at her with a reassuring smile. The pace of the violins eased; the tempo relaxed as the steps began. Rising and falling on the balls on her feet, she glided back and forth, greeting each partner at every turn, then twirling around the lady next to her, bringing her back to the centre, then back to the Captain. He was not forthcoming with words during the dances, and Bea found herself grateful for this fact; it allowed her to feel more at ease and enjoy her own simple movement.

Spinning around the lady next to her, Bea placed her hand out in front for her new partner, and this time was taken by surprise, feeling the gentle grasp and seeing the impenetrable face of the stranger she had seen that early morning on horseback, a month ago. Time slowed again in that moment as his face instantly delivered the same intensity of expression, and Bea became lost once more in a tangle of thoughts. Pausing back in line, they waited as the lady and gentleman standing next to them took their turn. Then the two sets of couples weaved in and out of each other, finishing side by side in a line of four, with the new gentleman standing next to her. She held her hand to her side, counting the half-seconds until it was enclosed in his for another brief moment. She stole a glance at his face and found him staring back at her with a surprised warmth in his eyes. He gave her hand a brief squeeze before letting it go, and smiled at her hesitantly, before moving back to his original partner, of whom Bea could not help but feel envious of; her tailor-made silk and pearls evidence of their mutual status and their conversation suggestive of friendship.

Standing opposite the Captain once more, she realised he had lost his occasion to shine in her eyes. He seemed smudged and distorted, somehow smaller. Her heart, suddenly absent from the dance, ached momentarily, without reason; she felt light-headed, breathless, and confused. How could her feelings possibly change so fast?

The music stopped, and the couples broke away from the group as new ones took their place. Bea used the opportunity to break away swiftly from the Captain and seek her friends. She felt a hand on her shoulder as she tried to negotiate the crowd and turned to see Beth smiling at her; in relief, she smiled back.

"I need some more punch! Shall we?" Bea managed a small nod and allowed Beth to guide her away.

ON THE OPPOSITE SIDE of the hall, Joshua watched Bea join the party around the punch bowl. "Max, do you know who that girl is? The one who just danced with the gentleman in blue; standing over there with two others at the punch bowl?" he enquired of his friend, who was engrossed in the women on his left.

"The one in the golden dress? No, I cannot say I do. I have not come across her before, dear boy..."

"Then how am I meant to be introduced to her...?"

"Steady on, Mason! That's easily accomplished." His companion finished his punch, bid an affectionate farewell to the women, and strode across towards the group with his empty goblet. Joshua Mason continued to gaze at the unknown girl, observing how she carried herself, which was markedly different to the ladies he knew, more at ease, open and relaxed. He remembered her sudden laugh on the shoreline that morning, unashamed and free. This time, he decided, he would not leave until he knew who she was. His friend returned, looking triumphant.

"I was trying to find someone who might know the ladies when I noticed the gentleman who has just joined them – that so-called gentleman is Captain Hanley; I know him from the card tables at the club. Come, we shall get you noticed, dear fellow."

"HANLEY, MY GOOD MAN - how are you this evening?"

Hanley seemed a little disgruntled at the interruption as he bowed his head.

"Well, thank you, Sir Elliott, and how are you enjoying the evening?" His voice held a hint of displeasure. Bea glanced over at the new arrival, who was smaller in build and height compared to the Captain, yet certainly wealthier, going by his demeanour and sharp tailoring.

"Yes, yes, pleasant enough, rotten punch... But I am forgetting myself - may I introduce to you and your companions; Mr Joshua Mason."

Joshua took a step out from behind Sir Max Elliott and cast his gaze over the three young ladies standing before him, finally settling on Bea, whose mouth opened slightly.

"Good evening Mr Mason, may I introduce Miss Beth Lightfoot, Miss Alice Little and Miss Beatrice Lightfoot."

"Good evening, ladies."

"Good evening," Beth and Alice chorused. Bea coughed a little, conscious of Captain Hanley watching her. Taking a cue from his friend, Sir Max

Elliot encouraged Captain Hanley to join him at the card table in one of the back rooms, refusing to take no for an answer.

Once the two gentlemen were out of sight, Joshua turned to Bea.

"Would you do me the honour, Miss Beatrice -for the next dance?" Placing out his arm.

"Thank you, Mr Mason." She held her hand lightly on top of his forearm and allowed him to guide her back to the floor. She could not help but catch her breath at the slightest touch of his person; she felt like another woman, someone she didn't recognise, but playing in a role that she wanted to embrace with both arms.

Couples took their places, forming the arrangement for a quadrille. This was one of the more fashionable dances of which she possessed little knowledge. She had seen it performed a few years ago, reminding her of a complex type of country jig. Noticing the nervous expression develop across her features, Mr Mason whispered, "I fear I do not know this dance too well!"

An instant wave of relief washed over her. "I... I've only seen it danced once before myself." His warmth tickled the tiny hairs on her neck as he leant in and murmured conspiratorially.

"If we make a pact and stick together, we should survive the fray." Pulling away again, he gave her a reassuring grin as he took his place across from her.

The music flourished as the other couple in the quad started the dance. Bea and Joshua studied the couple's feet closely, giving them a vague idea of where to begin. Once it was their turn, they both fumbled the steps, with Bea struggling to hold back the giggles. She felt oddly relaxed with her new partner. It made a lovely change to find a man who did not find the need for the usual pretence of formality, allowing her the freedom to disregard the crowd. After a couple of rounds of the same steps, they integrated properly into the dance. The laughter faded away as their eyes locked on to one another.

"That was you by the old harbour that morning, was it not?" he asked quietly.

So, he did recognise her then, as she had hoped he might have done. They were in the quad's epicentre rotating clockwise, and she felt as if they were the only two in the room.

"Yes, it was. I go down for the peace and quiet, to... to watch the ships". They changed counter-clockwise. She could see the distinct tones of blue blending together in his iris.

"I thought it was, I recognised your smile when we danced a moment ago. I often went back to the harbour..."

Far too soon the dance came to an end. Bea did not know if she would even see him again after tonight, and the thought made her numb and heady. At least she had this second brief encounter to cling to.

"Thank you, Miss Lightfoot, that was... very pleasant." He began to slowly guide her back to her friends.

"Do you think anyone noticed we were stumbling blind out there?" she laughed, a little breathless.

"I think we might have out-danced the room," he replied with melodramatic pride.

Bea smiled nervously, but said nothing further, not wanting to give away too easily the fact she had no social standing. Joshua stopped in his tracks and glanced sideways at her, tense and hesitant.

"Miss Beatrice, may -"

At that moment, Captain Hanley stormed towards them, and the opportunity had vanished.

"Miss Lightfoot, there you are. May I escort you back to your friends? Thank you, Mr Mason, I will safely return the lady; Sir Elliot is requesting your company on the far side." With few alternatives open to her, Bea let go of Joshua's arm.

"Mr Mason, thank you again."

For the rest of the evening, the Captain kept a close eye on Bea. Warning off any other suitor who might want to ask her for a dance, he purred something in her ear about feeling responsible for her honour that evening. Bea felt smothered, sensing something had changed in him, and there was no further sign of Joshua.

Bea surveyed the rest of the dancers with Beth and Alice, keeping close at their side. She sighed. One of the few nights in the year that a rope-maker's daughter might dance with a gentleman... as long as tomorrow everyone fell back in line. Bea felt the distance between Mr Mason and herself, their backgrounds, wealth and family. He was another creature entirely to her; in his circle she would be a mere insect... She allowed her mind to linger on him, wishing childishly for another dance, time to study the shifting colours in his eyes, and how his top lip curled upwards at the corners of his mouth when he smiled.

Throughout her life she had lamented many things, but never her birth. She had been proud to be a working-class girl, even with the accompanying restrictions. But suddenly she wished to be his equal, in both status and wealth. To find herself standing by his side and know there was the smallest possibility that he would listen to what she said with any measure of interest. Catching herself angrily as her thoughts strayed without warning towards imagining his mouth on her own, she coughed, took another sip of punch, and tucked a stray curl back behind Beth's ear. Her life left no room for such fantasies.

Chapter 7

Bea sat silently on the deep window seat, listening to the night creatures call out to one another. She pulled her woollen shawl tighter around her shoulders and tucked her toes into her thick cotton nightgown. The dancing stars shone brightly under the light of the May moon as it cast a silver shimmer on the grass and late spring flowers. There was no order to her thoughts. They spun from image to image as she tried to recapture the smallest of details from the night before. Realising her mind would not allow her the simple gift of sleep, she crept out of bed and gathered up her clothes.

With the dawn chorus echoing around her, her feet instinctively knew where to take her. The golden light reflected on the calm rippling waves of the softly groaning sea. She crouched down and took her usual place at the old harbour wall. She had missed coming here over the past month, and now she was back she could sense her mind relaxing with every crash of the waves against the rocks below. The air held a sharp, crisp bite, surprising for this time of year, as the growing wind carved its way towards her. Lost in thought, she did not notice the muffled sound of the hooves or the light footsteps approaching her from behind.

"May I?"

The words startled Bea and made her topple slightly as she quickly turned to answer. In that moment, feeling his proximity, breathing in his scent, she felt the numb, heady feeling she had at the dance, but this time she let herself go towards it, relinquishing control. Instinctively, he placed both hands on her shoulders to steady her.

"Careful."

His hands lingered, reluctant to move. He looked at Bea, staring up at him with a steadiness that made him swallow hard, and lose a little composure.

"I apologise, I did not... I- I called out as I approached, but you did not hear, I think . . ."

He looked like he had not slept much more than she had.

"May I?" he gestured to the ground beside her.

"Yes, of course Mr Mason – sir..." Crouching down to take a seat next to her on the wall, his heavy woollen overcoat brushed against her hand.

An awkward silence fell over them both, absorbed into the crashing sound of the first high tide as it encroached upon the old, battered rocks of the harbour.

"It is peaceful here."

"Yes, I've been coming to this spot since I was a child, watching the ships in the canal. Normally no one else..."

"Forgive my manners, were you wanting solitude? Would you like me to leave?" Feeling embarrassed, he shifted around, positing himself ready to stand.

She pondered the question for a half-moment. She knew what her Mam would say, what people would warn her about. It was not becoming for a young woman to be sitting with a strange gentleman alone, especially at this time of day.

"Please stay, if you like, Mr Mason."

He settled back down, the awkwardness of the past minute lingering as he hesitated over what he should say next.

"Joshua - my name is Joshua. Mr Mason reminds me of my Father." There was a brief pause.

"Well, you know I am Beatrice, but my friends call me Bea."

"Did you enjoy... did you enjoy last night's dance?" the young man asked, starring out at the horizon, unable to look at her.

"Yes, it was a good turn-out... the music was beautiful... And you?"

"I am not used to a country dance . . . but I enjoyed it more than I thought I would and the added gift of forming new acquaintances, which I hope in due time will...", he coughed, and clasped his hands with a clap, his forearms on his knees, staring out to sea. "Do you attend many dances, Miss Lightfoot?"

"No, not many; Ulverston doesn't hold such gatherings often. I enjoy them when they come around when I'm able." Her fingers fiddled with a long strand of wool that had fallen from her shawl.

"I myself am not familiar with the social calendar as of yet - I have been away from home."

"How long, if you don't mind me asking?"

"Almost fifteen years, only just returned from Cambridge and Liverpool. I am to take over the family business one day. They summoned me back so that I may now begin to learn the ropes here." Bea smiled at the turn of phrase.

"I believe I've heard your family name mentioned by my father, I... I understand he has done business for you." She noted his lack of reply with a sickening disappointment. But at least now there would be no doubt.

Joshua thought he had recognised the name and felt a small sinking feeling threaten to spoil their conversation. As if noticing her for the first time, the simplicity of her dress, and the holes in her shawl.

The howling wind gathered up tempo, the noise surrounding them making conversation harder. The waves swelled and rushed towards them as if the sea itself was reaching out to pull them down to the murky sands below. Bea felt as though she was standing on a greater precipice than merely the harbour wall, threatening to swallow her whole. She did not stir.

"Forgive me, you must be cold – Here, use my coat to keep you warm," he began to shrug off the garment from his shoulders.

"No, I thank you...I must get back, my family will wonder where I am." Bea looked to the sky for a glimpse of the sun, but it was hiding behind a mask of dark threatening clouds. She climbed to her feet and straightened her dress.

"But- but of course," a disheartened look spreading across his face. Following her lead, he stood once more in front of her, and then made their way back to the well-trodden path.

"We may stumble across each other again", she said flatly, with a sad smile. "Goodbye Mr Mason – Joshua".

"Goodbye Bea."

Joshua looked back at her quickly as he edged his horse away. Bea let out a long, shaking breath, and began the quiet walk back to Outcast.

She approached the cottage gate with the smallest of hopes that her parents were still unaware of her absence. She stood for a minute, contemplating her family home, covered in shadow, the sun still struggling to break the veil of cloud. More now than she ever had done before, she felt the grimy quality of her home. She knew already, as a woman it limited her future prospects, but she had never believed she would have had the chance to encounter a man like Joshua Mason.

Instead of going straight into the house, she walked over to the cowshed, telling herself that she may as well embrace her life gratefully, as she should. Clover the cow, waiting patiently to be milked, made a welcoming noise as Bea approached. She grabbed a small three-legged wooden stool with one hand, and the small wooden bucket with the other, and sat next to Clover. With the rhythmical movement of her hands rolling down the teat, she was glad of the distraction, allowing her aching mind a rest from the additional difficulties she had left herself to face.

BEA AWOKE IN THE GREY dawn, craving the sound of the waves and to feel the salty cool breeze reel around her, fooling herself that it was not Mr Mason she desired. The last few days she had hardly been present at home, trying to find reasons for her mother to be out whenever she was in, and to occupy herself with the girls as much as possible. Thought, and space to think, were her enemies. But not this morning. She was at the harbour wall before she knew it, and the aching in her heart resurfaced with a renewed strength as the spot lent her mind the vivid memory of his nearness.

"Miss Lightfoot, is that you?"

Turning the corner with her favourite place in sight, she observed a man dismounting a familiar horse. Automatically, she hid the light from her lantern with her shawl at the sound of a voice, and then sheepishly removed it again. She had kept away day after day, but that morning she had lost the battle. She had told herself surely he wouldn't be there today. The novelty of meeting her would have worn off by now, she would become a distant thought. So why was he here?

As Bea removed the shawl from around the lamp it flooded the path in front of her, highlighting the shadowy figure standing facing her, arms at his sides.

"Good morning, Mr Mason," Bea announced loudly and clearly, as though to set a formal tone for her own emotions, rather than anyone else present.

Cautiously, she approached him along the path, the lantern light spilling out towards him, and then over his boots. He stood wearing only his trousers, a dishevelled shirt and an overcoat. A wide smile spread across his lips with the usual curl in the corners of his mouth.

"Good Morning, Miss Lightfoot, I woke up restless and suddenly found myself here – truly, it is a place which draws one back time and again." Bea felt herself blush. She didn't know what to say, wanting to remark on something smart or amusing, but her mind went blank, leaving an uncomfortable silence between them.

"I should not have come, perhaps, but . . . You are a refreshing change, Miss Lightfoot, to my usual party – though that might be too bold of me." He took a step forward as she moved sideways. "Please tell me – is it purely a delight in childhood memories that you find yourself here?" Bea smiled, despite herself.

"I come for the sea, really, and the distance from everything – often that brings back the memories. And I suppose the ships remind me of stories I have read."

Bea moved to take her seat in her usual spot, Joshua following closely behind. A newfound nervousness made her clumsy; she crouched down to slide her legs over the side, with her right foot catching in her dress, jerking her forward. Quickly she placed her hand out to steady herself, but instead of feeling the damp gravel and moss laden rocks, her fingers were gripped tightly by his.

"Thank you." Their connecting hands caused her stomach to perform somersaults. He steadied her as she freed her foot and then lowered her down gently on to the harbour wall. "Thank you" she repeated, sliding her hand free.

"It can be hazardous, sitting down here." he smiled.

"Indeed, Sir."

"Sir... what happened to Joshua? I would count us as friends by now, would you not?" There was a light-hearted humour in his voice. Joshua steadied himself next to her, close, the tips of their little fingers almost touching. Her nervousness made it difficult for her to think.

"We are, forgive me, it's..." she paused, "it's a habit."

"Whether I was at school, or in the south, working; as long as I had some wild spot, I could call my own, I was happy." He smiled. "What else gives you pleasure in your quieter hours?"

"I love to read and when I'm not helping to look after my younger sisters...," she took a deep breath, and even the sea seemed to still: "I make lace to sell at Johnson's in town." She answered honestly, waiting for him to move away, but there was no shock, and no horrified change in his body language.

"You create lace to sell? Would you be the person who produces the local lace collars of which my mother and sister are in awe?" There was an interested tone to his voice, and a kind expression. It dumbfounded Bea. She had certainly not imagined this reaction.

"I could be, if she buys from Johnson's. The rose-work collars and narrow cuffs; I'm the only one who supplies to them from around here".

"Tell me, then, what does your father do?" he asked, with equal interest, knowing the answer already.

"He is a master ropemaker, we... own the Walk by Outcast... the Lightfoot's have had it for generations."

"I thought I had heard the name before! He must supply ropes for our ships - and that explains why you know so much about the ships and about the canal."

Bea knotted her fingers together tightly, and half-shrugged. Then she couldn't hold it back anymore.

"Forgive me – you see now that I am by no means a lady? That you... that I am low-born?" Her eyes lingered on the horizon, and the variety of intense reds creeping up from the sea. Fearful that she might have spoken wrongly, or taken too much of a liberty, she glanced at him. His face was inscrutable.

"I had a vague notion after the first time I saw you, and once I had learned your family name, it came as no surprise. I have not lived in Ulverston for years, but I do know that the women I usually associate with wear grander dresses and would not be seen sitting by the harbour as the dawn comes up, alone." He could tell the last part had insulted her. "And yet," he added, turning towards her, "they are nowhere near as interesting and gentle-hearted as I already believe you to be." He held her gaze and noticed the same fires of the sky reflected in her eyes.

"You are a gentleman... the son of a gentleman, and, I am a cottage girl". She cast her head down, letting the statement speak for itself, bitterly realising the meaning of the words fully for the first time in her life. Why did she feel so ashamed; she knew she had deceived no one and owed this man no particular efforts.

"You are more than that - I may be a gentleman but that does not mean I see myself that way, at least... Without your family's industry, our ships would not set sail to trade – and your work adorns the women I love most on this earth. Besides, I... hold you in high regard, Miss Lightfoot, who could not? I am simply a man and you are simply a woman, equal to one another, sitting side by side – starting to know each other." He spoke with a sincere tone in his soft voice as he gently placed his thumb and forefinger under her chin and lifted her head up so that their eyes could meet.

She felt the warmth of the early morning sun on her face and neck, as she allowed him to tilt her face upward gently. The contact was not intrusive, and Bea felt an unfamiliar ache in her chest as she tried not to take his words too seriously. His eyes met hers, drawing her closer, and the desire to kiss was overwhelming.

"I had not noticed the time, I- I must be going." Her movements and voice broke the trance. His hand dropped from her chin, and the clouds took away the rising warmth for a moment, as if the summer had given way to autumn and the last of the leaves had fallen away.

"Will I see you again?"

"I will try, if I can . . . but please think what you're asking of me." Bea deliberately backed away from him back down the path.

"Please hear me out, for just one moment." Bea stopped mid-step as Joshua quickly caught up with her. "I truly wish to see you again – purely to talk, do not mistake my intentions. Given our difference in... our differences in life, this is unlikely to be possible in any other context but an early morning stroll. If you feel you are able... I will be here at the same time in four days. I am fixed in a series of business meetings and commitments until then." He gently lifted her small working hand and held it for a moment. She wondered what he was thinking, whether his feelings were anything akin to her own. "I understand what I am asking of you but, I must ask all the same".

With the tingling sensation still rippling through her hand, it surprised Bea at the boldness and frankness of his demand. She took her hand from his.

"I will honestly consider it." There was a broken note to her tone which she had not meant to show him but felt keenly. In that second, she saw the same anxiety in his own expression. Surprisingly, she felt comforted by this, knowing that she was not alone in her fear of losing their connection. She hurriedly turned her back on him and ran back down the path, gripping her skirts, knowing with every panting breath of sea air that each time, it would get harder to leave.

Chapter 8

The coarse rope burnt against the calluses spread across his palms as he dragged in the heavy mast and tied it off. Captain Hanley, still feeling the effects of his drunken night before at the club, sought out the ever-faithful silver flask in his left pocket. Gratified, he took a mouthful, instantly extending the buzz and keeping his headache at bay. He smiled to himself. How pleased he had been with himself when he took ten guineas from the smug gentleman in a single play, winning a further fifteen guineas during the rest of the night. He took another swig of the delicious golden rum and inhaled the last puff of his pipe before knocking out the hot ash over the side. Spent by the previous night's celebration with a busty brunette and her smooth snow-white curves, the desire to call upon her again tonight made the idea of his forthcoming meeting a tedious one.

He strutted past a young seaman, crouched down on the deck, trying to collect the wooden bucket and brush he had accidentally knocked over.

"Have a care man or it will be the lash for you!" The young sailor kept his head down and nodded, cowering with fear like a dog.

Scrutinising the crew at their tasks, the Captain watched over them; a lifetime of evoking fear in those around him was useful for some things. He stroked the wooden railing, taking in every dent and notch underneath his hand. He was proud of his vessel, one of the largest ships the canal could accommodate. He would sneer at the gentlemen who came on board, issuing orders at him as if it was their ship. He saw himself as their equal, if not altogether their superior in experience and physical prowess. He had grown up scraping at the bottom of the barrel, but now it was his turn to choose his work.

"First Mate Gregson, I am expecting a gentleman shortly; when he arrives, show him to my quarters." The stout, simple man seemed confused by even the simple task.

"Ah... yes... very good Captain."

Leaning back inside his cabin, Hanley rested his feet on top of the desk and picked up a half-used match box to strike a match against the rough desk-leg. Drawing in deeply on the pipe, he relaxed again as the smoke seeped out from between his lips. With his head pounding, he swallowed another mouthful of rum and closed his eyes.

"Captain Hanley, your guest has arrived!" Gregson yelled through the thick oak door.

With a start, the Captain jumped up, smoothed down his hair and replaced his jacket.

"Very good man, show him in." Hanley leant over his desk as if he had been staring at his worn maps the whole time.

"Captain Hanley, Mr Mason," said Gregson blandly.

The Captain glanced casually upward.

"Morning Mr Mason." He waited until the heavy door was firmly shut before he continued: "A pleasure to meet you again sir, I hope you enjoyed the May dance last week?" He straightened up, moved around the desk and stood directly in front of the young gentleman.

"Likewise, sir – and, indeed, I did." Mr Mason found himself mirroring Captain Hanley's tone, and stood a little straighter to demonstrate his few inches' difference in height as well as position.

Hanley calculated how to play his next hand. He had seen how Mr Mason had looked at Beatrice Lightfoot that evening. How he had found them dancing, how she had smiled at him with a keen interest.

To this gentleman, Miss Lightfoot would merely be a plaything, nothing of note. He had heard the rumours about his true intended – a Lady Dawn, a county heiress. But he couldn't take the chance, either way, he needed to make doubly certain that Miss Lightfoot was his property. He wanted her - and on some level, in his own strange way, he believed that he cared for her.

"I must confess, I rarely attend - but I promised the first two dances to a sweet village girl – a Miss Lightfoot; I believe you danced with her also?" He paused, calculating, waiting for the nod as he studied the resignation spreading across Mr Mason's face, and his entire body sank momentarily before he straightened once more. He recognised the anger in Mr Mason, in his icy stare, as he fought against the requirements of a gentleman.

"Captain Hanley, I am in need of a ship. One of my own is docked for repairs, and Sir Maxwell Elliott informed me that your ship is currently vacant of cargo. Therefore, as I was doing the rounds this morning myself, I took the opportunity to enquire, is this correct?"

"It is indeed Mr Mason; can I ask what form your cargo takes?"

"It is principally composed of iron ore and slate, but this journey will be slate only. Is that an agreeable prospect?"

"Where is it your cargo needs to go?"

"To the Continent."

"The journey would be about four weeks in total."

"Yes, that is what I had expected."

"Well Mr Mason, I will not be able to provide you with an answer straight away as I am already in talks with another merchant in France, he wanted me to Captain his vessel you see, and I may be able to raise a higher price than usual."

"Of course, I am meeting with two or three other Captains today, so if you decide to take up this French offer, I understand, there would be no harm done. Thank you for your time today, Captain Hanley." He held out his pristine hand. He hadn't worked a day in his life. Not genuine work. Prancing around and interrupting other people's days was not work. Hanley placed his larger, tan skin hand in his and gave it a light squeeze before letting go.

"Good day Mr Mason, I will be in contact shortly."

The Captain felt drained. The last half hour with Mr Mason had wiped clean any buzz he had enjoyed about the morning. He went to light his extinguished pipe and stared at the battered match box in his hands. He needed to take the job with the French merchant, no question about that. Too much was hinging on his past and he needed the money. But what should he do about Miss Lightfoot before he left? There was an old feeling in his gut, of wanting her; not simply in the physical sense... of possessing her, claiming her, having her turn only to himself. This one would end differently, could change everything. This time he had behaved differently; with her he acted as a gentleman and she seemed to have responded to it. Perhaps with her it could stay that way.

He reached into the top drawer and pulled out a wad of paper. Grabbing at his quill, he dipped it purposefully into the black ink.

"Gregson... Gregson!" The crimson droplets pooled together, sealing in his unexpected secret. The cool golden crest plunged into the wax, raising his mark for everyone to see. The door was hastily thrust open even as the entrant gave a heavy knock for permission.

"Sir?"

"I need you to deliver this note. I am off to the club on trading business... I shall not be back again tonight."

"At once Captain." Gregson muttered, making sure he ducked his head as the Captain strode past.

Chapter 9

"Good evening Master Mason." Butterworth stood tall and firm as he offered to take Joshua's coat and hat in his usual dispassionate, faceless manner.

"Thank you - less than eventful - is my father about?"

"I believe Mr Mason senior is in the study, sir."

"Thank you, Butterworth."

Feeling unusually nervous made his way down the hall, he took a deep breath and as he exhaled, knocked three times on the beautifully crafted panels.

"Come in."

The golden light of early summer warmly illuminated the old leather-bound books lining every inch of wall space. Joshua glanced over toward his father's large solid oak desk on the right-hand side of the room, expecting to find him hunched over, scrutinising a pile of papers. Instead, Mr Mason was sitting in front of the enormous marble fireplace in his beloved Chesterfield, with only his crossed legs visible from the door.

"Do you have a minute, sir? I require your advice on a business matter."

"Certainly, come in my boy." Mr Mason's deep, measured tones seemed to absorb into the books which surrounded him, the room and its owner balanced in a familiar age-old symphony. The sweet scent of his father's pipe tobacco smoke, mingled with the distinct musty smell from the aged leather and the carefully bound tomes, gave Joshua a sense of refuge as he walked into the room.

"May I?" he gestured, standing in front of the decanters.

"Help yourself."

"Thank you, sir." Joshua poured out a large measure of his father's single malt and swallowed it in one. He felt the day's tension release as the dark golden elixir slid easily down his throat. He poured himself another.

Gingerly, he walked toward the fireplace and took a seat in the twin armchair opposite. His Father had a steely character; a respected business owner, whose name hailed back within the merchant circles from generations past. A stickler for traditions, and for routine. Mr Mason still belonged firmly to the Georgian era, often refusing to acknowledge the new industrial age, and the change it was bringing in all the trades.

Reflecting on the days' business, and the peace of the sanctuary surrounding him, he seemed almost oblivious to his son's presence. Joshua tried to relax into a similar harmony of mind with every sip he drank, watching his father's red silk house coat shimmer with the flickering flames below his perfectly tied cravat. He pulled out a cigarette from its silver case, tapped it twice on the end, as he had watched his father do often from a young age, and placed it in his mouth. Leaning forward and taking a thin shard of kindling from the fire, he lit it, and relaxed back into his chair, exhaling a large puff of smoke.

"What do you need to ask?"

"Sir Maxwell Elliott recently recommended I speak to a certain Captain Hanley regarding the matter of procuring a ship to replace the one in the yard, as he had heard he was in need of cargo, and subsequently I made his slight acquaintance at the May Day dance."

At the mention of Hanley's name, Mr Mason's interest seemed to pick up. He shifted his gaze from the fire onto his son. "I must admit, even on that first occasion... he seemed rather arrogant, but I thought to give him the benefit of the doubt, and speak to him in a business setting before I gave myself cause for doubt," Joshua continued. He ran this thumb over the engraved designs on the crystal tumbler. "I accordingly met with him yesterday to discuss the matter, and I regret to say that it seemed my first opinion was indeed correct. However, I sensed something more despiteful in his manner... What do you know of him? Is he a good sort? I do not wish to condemn any potential dealings simply because of an impression of unpleasantness, but..." Joshua leant back in his chair, glancing up at his father before taking another sip of single malt and reaching for a second cigarette. His father sighed.

"I have never met him - but I have heard of him, and from what I have heard, I would hope never to do business with him upon any account."

"Indeed?" Mr Mason took a long draw on his pipe, a greyness sinking over his face.

"Captain Hanley senior had charge of a slave ship which was part of the Guinea trade, and he held a bitter reputation for brutality. From the age of around eight, I believe your new associate, the son, joined his father on board as a seaman, and learnt to deal in the African peoples. Our family thankfully had our mines and our ships, though we were not untouched by the profits of that commerce. Unfortunately, selling slaves was the norm thirty years ago, as Liverpool harbour grew to be one of the largest in Britain. There were two scales of trading – what I shall refer to is the Guinea trade, which held the more lamentable reputation; indeed, it was only through the abolition in 1807 that the nation discovered the true extent of its shadow; but there are rumours it continues to this day."

Mr Mason looked in that moment as if he were a young man again, standing on the edge of the Liverpool docks, torn between conscience and ambition. He rose slowly from his chair, walked over to the decanters, and poured himself a double measure. Joshua sat in silence. Slowly approaching the fire, he balanced his glass, took a pinch of earthy pipe tobacco, and coughed quietly.

"I have heard that at fourteen years of age, he assisted in chaining the cargo, ankles to necks, in groups, in order to remove their means of suicide by jumping off the sides. He became an able seaman, one of the youngest to do so, under the guidance of his father." Mason looked over at his son. Too many young men were living their lives now with no respect for the still-recent mistakes of their fathers. Taking a moment before he continued, he blinked down at his whisky, sensing the walls closing in, as the ghosts of the past swarmed about, bringing back evil remembrances. Poking the glowing embers methodically further down into the grate, he anchored himself to his present surroundings as he let his mind travel back.

"The following I have on good authority from a former business associate... After two weeks stranded off the shore of Guinea on one particular voyage, with only a hair's breadth of wind behind them, the younger Hanley had become restless. The Captain, his father, had already taken his frustration with the elements out on his crew. The lack of movement behind them meant the supplies were getting low, and disease affected his slaves. At some juncture during this impasse, the Captain marked the passing of every hour without wind by tying a member of his crew to the mainmast and handing out twenty lashes. I can only assume he did not possess a sound mind. His son, who was no exception to the family rule, knew it was pointless to even consider challenging his father's authority. And therefore, to unleash his own misery, he employed his spare hours by beating each of the male negroes in turn.."

Joshua meandered over to the decanters, pausing with his hand on the stopper. He had heard stories before regarding the darker pockets of the trade, but never had he felt such disgust for those involved. Yet, Hanley had been no more than a boy at the time of his instruction in such practices; would he himself have disobeyed a parent in similar circumstances?

"Some years passed, the Abolition came, and Hanley's livelihood was outlawed at the age of sixteen. The news reached the crew as they anchored down at port in the West Indies. Young Victor reached out to a British plantation owner for work. He had built up a reputation for swift, implacable domination of his workforce, and was quickly offered a job on Lord Ealing's estate as an assistant to the foreman. He had been at the sugar plantation for over a year before his personal dealings with the slaves became apparent.

A local missionary worker became aware at this time of a distressed pregnant slave girl of fourteen, belonging to Lord Ealing. It quickly became clear that she feared for both her own life and that of her child. The mission worker begged the girl to confide in him frequently so that he might help her find some peace, and finally she confessed. She told him about how Victor Hanley regularly forced the Negro women to sleep with him in their own homes, whilst their husbands stood watch outside. There was talk of half-caste babies drowned in the nearby river, though no one could say for certain that he was responsible. She admitted Hanley had sought her out and raped her and begged the good Christian to help her save her unborn child.

The latter, out of abject pity, arranged a passage for her on a mission ship bound for England, and arranged to meet her at noon in the outskirts of the plantation. The girl never arrived. He searched the island for days, but found no trace of her, and without the law to back him in any regard, he felt there was nothing more he could do."

Joshua sat silently in his chair, his fingers picking at the seams in the leather. Fear and anger congealed together, and then an image of Miss Lightfoot at the May ball, standing alongside Hanley, floated into his mind; he had to warn her of the danger she was in.

Mr Mason drew his hand slowly over his clenched jaw, then rested his forehead on his palm, his fingers shielding his eyes from view.

"Over my time in Liverpool, I heard stories from seamen and businessmen of these horrors... People may call me a coward, but I was sorely relieved to receive a letter from my family summoning me back to run the business from home." His Father stood up, the low burning light casting a dark shadow across his face. He looked at his son with both kindness and pity in his eyes. "Not all men are good men, Joshua. There are many out there who take pleasure in the sufferings of others. You will learn in time who to trust, and who to shun - but for now, I am glad you came to me tonight."

Father and son moved towards the door together, and Mr Mason gave Joshua's shoulder a brief squeeze before leaving him at the foot of the staircase, restlessness for action, with the dark outline of an angry, embittered child haunting his thoughts.

Chapter 10

Bea clenched her fist tightly around the small weight of coins that remained from her hard-won guinea from Johnson's and plunged her hand deep into her pocket. She had decided to buy some extra-fine silk thread to produce a piece of lace, especially for Mrs Mason. A small gesture to show her genuine feelings, without raising suspicion from anyone in her family. A simple buds-of-May design, inspired by her walk that morning. She couldn't offer much, but she could offer that.

Market street was full of small children begging for coins, holding their grubby hands out for a single penny. She felt sorry for the little ones huddled in clothes that barely covered them and coughing so hard their chests shook. They looked like they hadn't eaten in weeks, and certainly they probably couldn't tell anyone when they had last taken a full meal. She had heard of men coming in wagons, scooping up the children that couldn't run fast enough, and shipping them across to the New World to work as white slaves in the burgeoning towns and docks. Her heart ached for them, but what could she do?

She kept her head down, avoided eye contact and walked up Market Street towards Kings Street. Carriages were racing past on important business for the gentile clients nestled within. Bea winced as young boys and girls risked getting dragged under their wheels as they raced alongside, shouting pitifully, with the hopes of a penny or two flying out. She watched one child, about eight, with two tiny siblings, run as fast as his legs could carry him close up against a grand black coach. He leaped into the air and landed on the side, half of his body sticking through the window and his feet struggling to grip on to the tiny ledge, clinging on like a slender monkey. Within seconds, the swipe and thud of a silver-headed cane had sent the boy flying back through the air onto the road. The little body landed in a heap and lay still. Bea lifted her skirt and sprinted the last few yards towards him. Her anger spilled out as people continued to walk past. "Don't move!" she told the boy as she knelt beside him.

He lay there dazed, trying his hardest to come around, to move on, hoping to grab another carriage. Months' worth of dirt clung to his skin, and his clothes looked like they had been made for him years ago, inches too short for his growing limbs, and thin with constant wear. His brother and sister were exactly the same. They cowered over him, terrified to lose their only carer. Bea carefully checked him over for broken bones, or an injury to the head. His ribs were sticking out, like the arches of a viaduct, and he hadn't eaten for a couple of days, judging by his desperation with the carriage.

"Can I be of assistance, Miss?" a man shouted as he ran over.

Without looking up.

"Please... Yes! I'm just checking him." She redirected her attention back to the boy, speaking softly to him. "What's your name?"

"David, Miss."

"Does anything hurt David?"

"Me arm and me neck, Miss... I'll be right."

"Please, - let me just look at you first?" The boy nodded his head.

"Shall I fetch a Doctor Miss Lightfoot?"

Surprised to hear her name, for a moment Bea looked away from the boy and up at Joshua Mason. He was standing over them, dressed in a dark suit and top hat.

"Oh."

"I will fetch my family doctor and I will be back as quick as I can, if you think he needs it?" He took his hat off and crouched down beside them, watching Bea as she carefully examined the child's head.

The boy shuffled away from the new gentleman, fear evident on his face, as his siblings clutched at one another.

"None of them lot, no docs, they'll send us back, we ain't goin' back!" He tried climbing to his feet.

"It's alright, be calm, lovey. I don't think yer need a doc." Her accent became more like her Da's in an unconscious attempt to soothe the boy. "You can move yer arm can't you, just bruised that's all and yer head took a knock. But ye'll need to rest for a day or sa." Bea reached into her pocket and felt for her pennies. "Here, take this. Buy yer selves some grub and stay hidden for a bit, alright?" She pressed them into his dirty fingers and smiled encouragingly.

Still terrified of the man, the child studied the woman; she looked more like him, spoke more like him, and she'd given him enough money to feed all three of them for over a week. Worried for their brother, the two younger children tugged him to his feet, as David clutched tightly on to the coins.

"Thank y'Miss…"

With a sibling under each arm, they quickly helped each other back towards Market Street and down one of the side alleys.

"Bea – Miss Lightfoot -"

Bea rose quickly to her feet and brushed off her knees.

"I must go. We'd better not act like we know each other had we – but thank you – you were the only one - the only one who would help." She quickly smiled at him and turned to go.

"But Beatrice, I must speak with you…"

She shook her head.

"Goodbye Mr Mason, I shan't keep you any longer." He started to protest, but stopped when he saw the pain on her face.

"Goodbye Miss Lightfoot, I hope to see you again."

Chapter 11

Bea's stomach swelled and churned as she watched the time ticking by all too slowly. Pacing back and forth with Rowan in her arms, she wished the ordeal would come quickly and be done with, sensing her Mam as tense as she was, in her usual spot by the fire, picking at her knitting.

"Beatrice, will you sit *down*; you are going to wear a hole in the floor with all that pacing. You're certain that note said three?"

"Aye, it did. Three o'clock," Bea replied.

"He said he wanted a word with you. What about?" Her Mam had been sharper than usual with her daughter ever since Bea had received the letter three days ago.

"He does not say - here, read it yourself, again." Bea held out the thick paper, exposing the four lines of elegant writing requesting a private audience with her.

"Don't you take that tone with me!"

"I've no idea what he could want with me."

"Then why are yer pacing? Y'cannot think he has any... *intentions*?" She spat out half a laugh, carrying a jealous undertone. "I would not want you to embarrass yourself in front of 'im."

"You have not asked as to my intentions!" Mrs Lightfoot snorted, and straightened her back, still picking savagely at her knitting.

"You'd be a fool not to consider him, if that's what he wants," her Mam snapped, snipping an offending piece of yarn vigorously from her lap. "Either way - sit down or go to yer room, you're makin' my headache." Bea moved toward the stairs. "Take your sisters too, there's a good girl," she added condescendingly.

A penetrative knock suddenly sent ripples through the house. Bea dropped Holly's hand and raced to the door. Both little ones ran to their spot behind the table for the second time that month.

As the door opened, the sun, riding high in a cloudless sky, was blinding compared to the shadow of the house. Standing like a statue with a green velvet jacket, green silk cravat and cream trousers, Hanley looked unusually handsome. A small smile played across his lips as he tipped his hat in a greeting.

"Good afternoon, Captain."

"Good Afternoon to you, Miss Lightfoot. I am so pleased you agreed to see me."

"Come in, please. What can I do for you?"

Hanley moved his hand towards her face, and using his thumb, gently brushed a smudge of flour from her cheek. A cold cough loudly echoed in the background. He quickly withdrew his hand on the realisation that they were not alone.

"Forgive me, you had - ", he offered, trying to mask his surprise.

"I was baking bread", she muttered, rubbing her cheek rapidly, making sure there was no evidence left. "Do you wish me to make your sister a second lot of lace?"

"Ah – no. No, I do not... - for the present, that is. I wondered whether you would do me the honour of coming for a ride into town," pointing to the gallant jig behind him on the path, "- as I mentioned in my note, there is something I would like to discuss with you in private - if your Mother would permit, of course?"

For that one moment, she lost her head completely, despite all her misgivings about the man in front of her, though she could never have known the impact it would have on the subsequent weeks, nor on her future. She thought only how much the thought it would vex her Mam, and how she would be free from the house, and the trapped feeling of the last few weeks; free from everyone and everything she was supposed to be. Free most especially of the new, sorrowful ache which sprang into her chest at every unwanted thought of Joshua Mason. She bounded over to the row of wooden pegs and collected her shawl and bonnet.

"Mam, Captain Hanley has offered to take me into town – I may accept, mayn't I?" She cast the words in a way so that if her Mam declined the offer, she would look rude.

"Well... I- I suppose... but would Captain Hanley not like to come in for tea first?" Her Mam rose, a little alarmed at the recklessness in her daughter's voice. Bea fastened her ribbon quickly.

"I'll be back in time to get the dinner," she added casually. The Captain interceded.

"Thank you, but I must decline, I only have a small window of time before I need to return to business. It was lovely to see you again Madam - I hope to take you up on your offer of tea soon." He presented her with a low bow as he drew to one side to allow Bea out of the doorway who was nursing a small fragment of joy at the idea of riding in a real jig.

Hanley created an impressive silhouette as he sat back on the velvet bench, nonchalantly flicking the reins, the sun bouncing off his tie pin. His eyes twinkled as they fixed on Bea, in whom another flash of guilt surfaced at the thought of Joshua Mason. A knot of regret tightened inside of her at her unthinking response to the Captain. She was confused by the two men, and what she meant to them both. Shaking off her rising doubt, she pushed the young merchant out of her mind and watched the horse's ears twitch in the war air as they trotted up the muddy track towards town.

THE FRESH LATE SPRING breeze brought a smell of luscious green grass and newly blossomed flowers to life. No conversation passed between them, instead there was a tight air of awkwardness. Hanley focused on the path in front, whilst Bea was in awe at the rapidly changing view. The jig turned off Lightburn Park and headed on to a shortcut on to Queen Street. She realised he was taking her the back way in to town, which meant one of two things: either he was ashamed to take her publicly through the streets, or knew she would rather cast her eyes on the beautiful views of nature, rather than the bustle of town. She hoped it was the latter of the two, but feared he did not know her so well.

The jig bounced lightly on the polished cobbles. The sound washed over them, as they grew closer to the tide of the town's daily bustling voices shouting their demands ever louder than the rest. As they neared the end of Queen Street, Bea shuffled, uncomfortable on her seat with the eyes of passers-by casting judgement on her. Any other young woman would sit proudly upright with her head held high, absorbing the interest with glee. But not Bea, who had been told all too often of her place in the world, and she almost cringed at the occasional looks which were confirming she was stepping out of it.

Recognising some of the faces, she saw several people she knew, and all were displaying a variant on her Mam's expression of disapproval.

As her eyes filtered through the waves of faces, one in particular came crashing into view. Standing motionless in the doorway of the Lancaster Bank, his piercing blue eyes locked onto hers, and adopted an expression of shock and confusion. Soundless words crawled from his white lips and tight-set jaw, as his eyes followed the direction of the jig.

She wanted to jump off, explain herself, and make him understand. Understand what she did not know herself: what she was doing, and why she was here. She wrenched her eyes away from Joshua to ask her driver to stop, but Hanley beheld an expression on his face she could neither fathom nor trust. His broad smile stretched from ear to ear with a stifled chuckle rustling in his throat. Without issuing a word, she snapped her head back towards the bank. Joshua still held tight on to her position, but his expression had changed to one of hurt and anger. She tried to mouth the word 'Sorry' to him, but recognition did not filter across his face, and every movement of the horse tore her further away from where she wanted to be. She could feel a warm hand being placed firmly on to the middle of her back as the distant figure of her friend turned away and walked in the other direction. Bea's vision began blurring in the corners. She drew a long-laboured breath and turned around slowly to see where they were heading.

The jig came to a pause at the crossing where Kings Street met with Fountain Street and Southgate. Starring at the old weather-worn medieval wolfstone, she remembered stories she had heard of how Ulverston had taken its name, in the olden days, from this stone. Gazing at the sun casting shadows and shapes over each etched curve, she wondered how much it had witnessed, and how much would it continue to see once they were all gone. Her heart ached as she tried to assess how to explain to Joshua what he had just witnessed; what reason she could give to restore his opinion of her. Would he even allow her the chance to explain, or was she now exiled from his life?

THE HORSE TURNED ON to a small tight dirt road, taking them high above the town. The track curved up through the muddy terrain and onto the long billowing tall grass as it glided up to the summit of the hill. As if they were creators looking down on their work, Bea and Hanley stood side by side on the empty summit. The sun shining through the newly forming clouds high above them created stark rays of light on the small pockets of earth, as a strong breeze carved through the landscape, bringing forth an abundance of smells and sounds.

Bea found herself wishing she could stand here all day watching the miniature town going about its daily business. Seeing the few ships waiting patiently as usual in the Furness estuary to enter the canal before the high tide ebbed away, a passage from her beloved Gulliver's Travels sprang to mind, out of nowhere.

'Of so little weight are the greatest services to princes, when put into balance with the refusal to gratify their passions'.

She felt Hanley all-too near beside her, and suddenly she felt on the brink, not only of the green summit, but on the edge of a line between one part of her life and another.

"Have you been here before?" Hanley broke her trance with his soft, mellow tone.

"My Father brought me a few times as a child, but I tend to venture into the woods or the old harbour now. How much has already changed since I was last here." There was a distance in her voice as her gaze scanned the expanded tableau.

"It is one of my favourite places for solitude... I thought you might enjoy it also." He shifted his posture to face her. "I brought you here so that I might speak with you alone without interruption . . . I have been contemplating this question for a while now, but no woman has ever come close to inspiring me into action, until you". Standing just a foot away, his tall muscular frame towered over her. The words took a minute to completely sink in.

Taking a step back: "Captain, I . . ."

He closed the gap.

"Captain, I do not know how to answer" she stuttered. "I am honoured by your... but I cannot . . ."

"You know, from the first moment I saw - or heard you - I felt you were a woman with whom I could spend the rest of my life," he interjected.

"I do not know you well enough for..." She couldn't even say the words.

"I have fallen in love with you," he uttered, the words dripping with charm, and a velvet softness. He had moved in slowly, and Bea, realising only just in time, jerked her head quickly to one side as his lips fell heavily onto her cheek. Loitering, he carefully drew away from her hot skin. Reeling from what had just taken place, Bea took another step away from him.

"I am sorry, but I do not care for you, sir, not enough for..." she replied clearly, honestly. Her heart ached and beat fiercely, but not for him.

"I was sure you were becoming fonder of me- accepting my gift, how we danced together, agreeing to meet me - I am sure in time you will come to love me and accept your feelings." He attempted to hide the incisive anger in his voice. He had not expected she would actually turn him down.

"But... I cannot make any such promise until I know for sure!" She felt uncomfortable in his presence. He was towering above her again, and not in a loving way.

"Be honest with me, Beatrice, is there anyone else standing in my way?"

"No one else has made me an offer, if that is what you mean." She could not say yes, nor could she say no; she did not know where she stood with any man at that moment in time.

"And do you promise you will not accept any other offer and in return I will give you time to consider?"

"I do not know."

He gently placed two fingers under her chin and raised her head up so that her eyes could lock into his – as Joshua had done not so long ago, she thought.

"Honesty...I am falling for you, Beatrice, and I believe in time you will fall for me - I am considered a good catch - I have a suitable position, money; I can give you a higher seat in society, take you away from here and make you comfortable. It is a match in which your family will rejoice."

"Sir . . . I have never sought your charity..."

His anger flared suddenly, with a potency that frightened her, and abruptly she was confronted with a glimpse of what her future might be if she did not hold strong in her convictions.

"It is not charity if I say I am in love with you!"

"Captain, I cannot accept your gracious offer". She placed a little more distance between them. This time he did not reciprocate, instead turning to look out down to the sea once more.

"I have been commissioned another vessel for America and will be gone for two months or so. I leave for Liverpool early on the morrow tide." He glanced at her. "You have until my return to think it over".

"I thank you, again, but my answer is, and ever will be, no," she replied softly.

"You have time to collect yourself; think it over, discuss it with your family, and I will consult you again upon my return." His patience was thin, but his determination to bend her will had strengthened. Bea nodded, feeling there was no point in discussing the matter further.

"I will send you word of my return. I have another engagement to attend to." He moved towards her again. "I will conduct you safely back to your home." All of Bea's instincts were now set against her putting one foot into the once-impressive jig, and she crossed her palms outward over her chest, shaking her head.

"I - I thank you, but I would prefer the walk... I would not wish to keep you; there must still be a great deal to prepare."

"If you are sure, my dear Beatrice". Hanley's anger had disappeared into his usual pleasantries as quickly as it had emerged, and this was to Bea somehow the worst aspect of him, of the whole interview. She now felt more uneasy than ever at his inconstant smile. He began walking over to his horse, which stood grazing happily in the long grass.

"I am - it is a lovely afternoon, and it would be a shame not to make use of it."

He took her by the hand and placed a long passionate kiss on her knuckles. Then in two steps, he was back in the jig.

"I will see you again soon, Miss Lightfoot." He tipped his hat towards her and commanded the horse to walk on, leaving Bea to the now-tainted view of the ships and her familiar harbour.

Chapter 12

A thunderous sound echoed through the valley as explosion after explosion left scars in the ever-declining landscape. Men ventured forth covered in a fine black powder as the soot filled clouds dissipated high above, and an endless humming from the new machinery issued from the pits. The demand for coal and slate was at an all-time high, due to the railroad and the accompanying housing that were being built as fast as resources became available. New pits and quarries were eating into the fells each year with countless men arriving on carts each day in the search for jobs.

Joshua stared at the blank page in front of him, feeling the weight of his responsibilities more now than ever before. Several discarded pieces of paper decorated with dark rings absorbed from hours' worth of dormant coffee cups lay scattered around the office. The usually comforting noise vibrating beneath his feet brought a skin-crawling restlessness. His head ached, and he could not muster the strength to fight it, paying heavily for the lack of sleep the night before. His mind tormented him with images of Bea and Hanley, side by side in the jig.

He asked himself whether he should see her again or resist the temptation and avoid her altogether. He gazed through the glass, studying the wind howling across the tops of the fells as large droplets drummed hard against the windowpanes. He closed his eyes and leant back in his father's worn green leather chair.

The hourly chime from the grandfather clock nestled in the corner of the room brought him back from a deep slumber. He must have been asleep for a good two hours, but he felt better for it. The rain flowed like a waterfall against the windows, absorbing the sounds from the outside world. His mind seemed clearer, no conclusion as yet on his ever-developing problem, but sound enough to make better use of the day. He needed to act.

BEA FELT LIKE A RABBIT in a trap. The rain was relentless, and the darkened sky hung heavily over the house. She could hear the waves battering against the rocks, carried by the raging storm-winds. Feeling exhausted, the past fortnight had been difficult enough, and then to top it all off Captain Hanley had proposed to her. She had walked for hours on a roundabout way home, putting off the inquisition from her Mam as long as possible. How could she possibly consider marrying the Captain? She did not know if she could trust him. No matter what pressure her Mam placed on her to marry for the advantage of the family, she wanted a fair stake at her own happiness. As soon as she had walked through the front door, she had feigned sickness, and took herself up to her sanctuary. She had waited up to confide in her sister, but when it came to it, she did not have the words. Instead, she closed her eyes and pretended to be asleep so that she wouldn't have to meet questions with answers that she did not have.

She curled up under her woollen blanket, attempting to shake off the tangled feeling in her stomach. With the sound of Rowan breathing deeply on their bed, Bea crawled out and laid her head against the cool, smooth windowpane. The repetitive drumming against the glass placed her into a trance-like sleep, allowing her subconscious to freely explore all her options, without the burden of responsibility or emotion.

BEA HAD WOKEN TO FIND someone had placed her on to the bed. She had slept the day away, and it would only be a few more hours until the sun would be up once more. At least the clouds had cleared away, and the stars were now visible, twinkling above. She felt awake and alert, and knew what she had to do. She slithered out from between her three sisters, already clothed, grabbed hold of the small, wrapped parcel for Mrs Mason, tiptoed down the stairs, and left.

The storm had left a sharp fragrance of salt, mixed with the fresh dew glistening on top of the vibrant green grass. The late May weather held a warm promise of the day ahead. The path was thick with mud, squelching under each step as she slid from one foot to the other. She held her lantern up high, attempting to see each obstacle which lay scattered across her path.

She sat for an hour, running over the words, the arguments, repeatedly out loud. She vacillated through altering moods as she imagined the countless outcomes that might take place, if they ever met face to face once again. Above all, she just wanted the opportunity to explain how naïve and thoughtless she had been. The churning sensation in her stomach matched that of the sea, and she watched the silver snakes of water channels slithering across the barren sands, only to be engulfed by the racing tide. The foam bubbled at the waves' edge as it clawed at the sand, dragging itself into land. In less than an hour the sun would be up, and the tide would be at its highest, bringing in the ships to dock.

Bea held tight to the small parcel in her hands, praying that this slight gesture might undo all the wrong deeds she had committed. It had taken her three nights to create the lace collar full of tiny buds of May and fledging leaves. She had placed a lot of love and care into the piece, and she hoped he would see it. Leaning back into the sodden earth, using the shawl as a pillow, she gazed upwards, wondering at the disappearing stars.

Bouncing vibrations from a horse's hooves stirred her from her light sleep. Apprehension breathed life into the cocooned butterflies. She waited to see if it was him or just an early rider passing into town. She did not move, did not breathe until she knew for certain. The hooves came to a halt; silence filled the static air. Bea tried to take long steady breaths at an attempt to calm her racing heart. The soft earth absorbed the sound of his footsteps as he walked over to her.

"Beatrice? Bea?" Bent over, he stared down at her. "Good Morning." He let out a chuckle, and any tension between them dissipated. "What are you doing down there? You will be wet through!"

"Passing time, I woke early." She noticed how warm his smile was and felt how deeply she had missed not seeing it.

Joshua Mason looked like he had been up for hours, even void of bed rest altogether. His shirt was missing his silk cravat, and hung unbuttoned at the neck, with a few mischievous strands of hair poking through. His matching waistcoat and trousers seemed dishevelled and lacked their normal crispness. He took his long black coat off and placed it on the ground.

She felt keenly in that instance once again the difference between them: she did not mind sitting in the grime, but he was clean, and put all the distance he could between it and his clothing. Doubt flooded in and filled her up. She tried to shrug it off, but it clung on tight.

The sunny bright atmosphere between them soon clouded over. A couple of minutes passed before either of them spoke.

Bea held the small parcel tighter in her clenched hands, wondering if or when she should give her token, which already seemed to have lost a little of its shine. Joshua's thoughts, on his part, fought with each other; he could happily have lain there and told her how much he had missed her, allowing his feeling to flow and grow with her. But for him to do so, he must first ask her what he had seen, what it had meant, and tell her what he himself had learnt. He knew that to completely fall in love with her, he must be honest, and permit the cards to fall where they may. He sat upright and gazed out at the shapes forming on the growing waves in the light of the dying moon.

"I have..."

"- There are..." Speaking as one.

"Sorry, I -" Joshua exclaimed.

"Please," insisted Bea.

"Thank you – there are matters I must speak to you about." Following his lead, she brought herself to a sitting position.

"Ask, I will answer honestly. There are things I need to speak of as well." The laughter had left her voice.

He turned his head away from the tide and studied her face. "How much involvement has there been between yourself and Captain Hanley?" The question landed heavy and flat.

"I have seen the Captain on five occasions, in total." He did not utter a word; instead he encouraged her silently to continue. "It began with him asking for a piece of lace through my Mam - I saw him for the first time when he came to pick it up. The second time was in Johnson's, when I was dropping more lace off to sell. The third time . . ." She took a deep breath, now realising how her unguarded actions might be seen by Joshua, and by others. "The third time he came to my home again whilst my Mam was there, and my sisters and gave me a gift of fabric, in - in return ... in return for the first two dances at the May ball."

"The result of which was the golden dress I saw you wearing, I presume?"

"Yes - that was the fourth time I saw him, but I promised nothing more than the dances. I do not know why I agreed... No, that's a lie, I do know... This might seem foolish to you, but for one night I wanted to feel like them, one of those ladies, - one of your class of ladies. They have the world at their feet. I wanted to know what that felt like. The other reason was to vex my Mam, she was acting a fool in front of him, so I agreed... I agreed to spite her". Her naivety shone through her voice. She watched him stand up and pace around her in small strides. "That is no excuse, I see it now. I see how it might look to you and I am sorry for that. But I did it for no other reason than to get the fabric."

"You sold yourself for cloth?" Joshua pivoted to look at her full in the face. She saw pain and anger in his eyes.

She sprang to her feet. "You do not know me well enough to say such things - I did not sell myself! Nothing... like *that* happened... Do you know how much work I would need to do, to make enough money to buy that amount of fabric? You might not need to think about money, but I do... My family does! It would cost me more than three months' earnings to buy that fabric, and that's without buying food for the table or a roof over our heads. I wanted... just once, to be better than myself. - Can you honestly say you would have noticed me that night if it was not for that dress?" Her anger flared equally to his. How dare he insult her. She choked down the tears which were threatening to fall. He had stopped pacing. She could feel him looking at her, as she didn't dare to turn around.

"What about when he exhibited you around town as though you were his?" There was still a trace of anger in his voice.

"That was the fifth time I saw him, the other day, when you were there - he asked to speak to me, alone, and took me out in the jig. He took me to the hill which overlooks the town, and... asked me to marry him..." The words floated in the air between them. "I said no, I turned him down, and it displeased him. He became angry, in fact."

"He did not hurt you?"

"No, he just left, as I wanted to walk home alone. He asked me to think it over, consider his offer, and tell him my thoughts on his return."

"Return from where?"

"He is captaining another vessel for two months, leaving Liverpool for America. I turned him down again, said I did not need time, but he would not listen, and he frightened me, so I did not argue further". There was a plea in her voice.

Joshua seemed lost in his thoughts, calmer but distant. She wanted to reach out to him.

"I do not feel affection for him, not like . . ." She was going to say, 'not like you', but thought better of it. "I am sorry," she said earnestly.

"You must see what he was doing? What it looks like to others? He has manipulated you at every turn."

She turned away, not wanting him to see the tears threatening to pour out. "And for that you will never know how sorry I am".

He crouched down behind her and placed his hand on her shoulders and guiding her round to face him. A tingling sensation rippled through her body as his hands glided down her arms until they were stroking the top of hers. The same breathless explosion she had felt the first time their hands had connected now returned. She felt foolish; how could she have been so careless, putting all this, whatever it might be, into jeopardy. Even if was only make believe, five minutes in Joshua's presence meant ten times more to her than a lifetime in Hanley's.

"I believe you, and I am sorry too, for your good reputation in the town, and for the presence of that *man;* he makes my skin crawl." He enclosed his hand around hers, entwining his fingers through hers.

"The mere thought of you and him together . . ." Joshua's mouth set in a line of hard animosity.

Bea instinctively placed her right hand lightly on to his cheek. She could feel his morning stubble, how hard it felt on his cool skin. As if suddenly aware of her position, she moved to take her hand away. His left shot upwards and clamped down on hers, embedding the stubble deeper into the palm of her hand. In a moment he had loosened the grip on her hand and slowly rotated his head to kiss the inside of her palm. The sensation sent shivers through her entire body and brought a flush to her cheeks. How much she desired to kiss him, to be held tight against him. Loosening his grip further, he glanced back towards her face and smiled at her reaction. Lowering her hand, he lay it between his, locking in the passion of the stolen moment.

"There is one more thing I must speak to you about." His tone became serious again.

"You do believe me about Captain Hanley? He means nothing to me, and I can see now the stupidity of my actions." The anxiousness flushed back into her tones.

"I believe you. I think you have been unguarded, but that shows more for your innocence than anything else". He shook his head affectionately. A tiny fragment of a smile crept into the corner of her lips.

"But you must promise me, you will have nothing more to do with that man." This time there was no mockery in the sternness of his voice.

"You have my word."

"I consider him to be dangerous". He hesitated for a moment whether or not to tell Bea all that he knew about Captain Hanley, but he saw that with the tangled web Hanley had already spun around Bea, the Captain would only try to ensnare her further if she were not told all of it.

Joshua began by telling Bea about his meeting with Hanley on the ship, and how his impressions from that encounter had led to him voicing concerns to his father. Bea listened silently, absorbing every word, their fingers still entwined. He continued to describe the Captain's upbringing on the slave ship; still she was silent, her hand squeezing tighter. He watched the rising sun reflecting off Bea's horrified face, as each word carved away another part of her innocence and left a darker understanding in its place.

The sun had risen over the sea when Bea exclaimed; "No more, I beg you. . . I cannot hear another word". Her voice shook with emotion.

She stared at him, wide-eyed and frozen, as though asking him to make everything right again, pleading. Without a word, he placed his right arm tightly around her, signalling that she was safe, and her head fell upon his shoulder. He held her tight and softly kissed the top of her head as her body relaxed into his firm hold. Her hair had an herbal, sweet smell, with a touch of smoke. He breathed her in deeply, absorbing her sorrow, and smiling to himself at her nearness.

"I am sorry," he whispered into her ear. The more he held her, the more she grew calm. Suddenly she pulled away from his hold and sat upright. Her eyes were calmer, but glistening.

"Do not waste tears on that man," he remarked tenderly.

"He has caused pain to so many, and yet I thought I was in no danger... He was kind to me, acted like a gentleman. How can he act one way then, and now another? It makes little sense... How can this ever be made right?"

At that moment Joshua felt a tremendous sensation of falling, relinquishing all bonds of control and conform. He looked at Bea, as though seeing her for the first time. He wanted nothing in the world but her, and he could no longer pretend that his interest in her was anything but love. He leant forward and slowly, gently, placed his lips on top of hers. She tasted salty, from the spray and the sea air, and with a small moan she gave way to his warm, insistent mouth. Bea thought the ground beneath her would give way as the tip of his tongue touched hers, teasing her lips open so that he could taste more of her. Joshua tugged at her hair and held her neck as he drew her to him tightly, and Bea clung to him, catching at his shirt, lost in an unfamiliar hunger. Abruptly, Joshua pulled away, out of breath. A smile spread across Bea's unusually pink face.

"I love you", he murmured quietly.

"...Truly?" Bea could hardly tell if she had imagined his words.

"Truly," he replied boldly, with a chuckle to his voice.

"I love you."

Joshua gave a small exclamation of relief and leant forward again. This time it was a slower, deeper kiss, both trying to tell the other something they had never found the words for before. Joshua broke apart from Bea reluctantly, feeling himself stirring below, and fearing what might happen if they prolonged their intimacy.

"You honestly mean it?"

"Yes - but I must speak to my father before we speak of this further". The warmth of his smile quietened any slight misgivings at this last statement. Bea allowed herself to smile radiantly back at him.

The cracking of twigs underfoot broke their blissful trance. The shadowy figure of a man pivoted and walked away in the opposite direction, as the couple broke apart nervously and the last shadows of the dawn gave way to a harsh morning sun.

Chapter 13

"Do you think he saw us?" Bea whispered as if someone might overhear her. She scanned the landscape, making sure no one else was about.

"We cannot be certain... I think he may have. I doubt, however, if he will be able to tell who we are from this distance." Joshua maintained a note of hope in his voice. He rose and began straightening his clothes.

"How much do you think he saw?" Bea could not hide the anxiety in her voice. Mirroring his movements, she shuffled around awkwardly. Gazing down at her dress, she noticed a large damp patch on her back and hip area. She felt unworthy of his attentions in her worn blue cotton. Afraid of the light, she became momentarily worried that if he studied her closely, he might forget his declaration of love for her and see who she truly was.

"I cannot tell, it depends how long he was standing there."

"Could you tell who he was? I cannot think why he would come this way unless he was heading to the shipyard... and then he might know me or my family."

"Do not worry yourself, I am sure it will amount to nothing," Joshua remarked in a quiet, soft voice as he leant down and gave her a light kiss on her forehead. She rested her head into the nook of his chest and placed her arms around him. For a single moment she felt safe, as if nothing in the world could touch her.

The cascading colours of the dawn gave way to a blanket of blue as Bea soon realised by the height of the sun that it was later than she thought. She glimpsed a ship on the horizon which had already passed them. If the man had seen nothing, there was still a distinct possibility that the seamen might have. She chastised herself for being reckless yet again, for there was no guarantee that once Joshua had spoken to his father, whatever that meant, he would stand by his word, and where would she be then?

She had to believe in his love for her, but the fragment of doubt she had encountered at the beginning of the morning returned to torment her. She suddenly remembered the small parcel balancing on the rock beside where they had been sitting.

"You will speak to your Father, will you not?" She glanced up at him with her head still on his chest.

"Yes, as soon as I am able, I will broach the subject with him, and I will send you word to meet".

She pulled away and lent down. "I have something, or should I say I made something for your mother." She held out the small gift in her hand. "You mentioned she liked my lace."

He slid the parcel from her hand and held it out in front of them both.

"I made her a piece, a collar, full of buds of May and leaves – I made it from fine silk thread so that it would have a softer, delicate look – worthy of her." She felt her cheeks blush and cast her eyes downwards.

"May I?" Joshua carefully opened the gift so that he could reseal it again and pulled out a long lustrous piece of lace. With the golden light shining through from the sea, he could appreciate the tiny buds, the delicate flowers, and the branches linking into the leaves. The perfect image of spring, and of their time together. He looked back at the shy, awkward woman in his arms, bashful of her talent and the thoughtfulness behind such a gesture. "You created this for my mother?"

Bea fiddled with a stray thread on her shawl, darting her eyes up and down, unable to hold his gaze. "Do you think she will like it? – Do you like it? - You can say that you bought it, that it's not from me directly."

"It will delight her; she will love it – I love it. I cannot believe that you made this yourself, just for her. I have never encountered your work this closely before; the fine way you have shaped the delicate petals and the texture of the buds. You have a gift, a talent." He looked up from the lace and found her standing in front of him, her gaze locked on her shuffling feet, unable to take the compliment. He wrapped the precious lace back into its protective velvet cover and gently placed it into his pocket.

"It is nothing really, I wanted to give you something, a gesture."

Joshua took a step forward, his body almost touching hers.

"Thank you, I cannot express how much it means to me." He cradled her head between his hands, lifting it up so she could see the sincerity on his face. In return, she gave him a bashful smile. He leaned in and kissed her, not wanting to stop and releasing her.

"I have to go. It is later than I thought, and they will be up and wonder where I am". She pulled herself from his arms, staring at him longingly. She wanted nothing more than to stay in the safety of his embrace, to create a world where only she and he existed.

"I promise you, I will send word to you soon". Bringing her in again, he was tempted to kiss her, but thought better of it. He glanced upwards swiftly, with a cheerful smile spread across his face, and took a step backwards.

"Goodbye then," she murmured, with a half-wave of her hand.

He walked over to his horse, which was grazing in the shade on a small piece of grass near the path. Bea started walking in the opposite direction, quickly at first, and then paused to look back. She watched Joshua with ease jumping into the saddle, sitting bold, straight, and elegant with his coat draped across his lap.

JOSHUA ALLOWED HIS mare to guide him home as he replayed the last few hours over again in his mind. His fingers traced along the outline of his lips with her taste still lingering in his mouth. In his youth he had stolen kisses before, but never with such urgent wanting. A light breeze floated past him, coming as a thankful relief to the heat beating off the now fully exposed sun. A small chorus of birds sang their farewell song to newly gained partners as they retired for the remainder of the day under a nearby canopy. His head ached with fatigue at the past week, longing for the first cup of strong coffee of the day, with a slice of ham and a plate of eggs. As he neared the top of the canal, a familiar stench of manure mixed with hot coal smoke filled his nostrils, with men shouting demands to one another over the hubbub of local trade. The almost orchestral sounds of metal clashing upon metal came to a crescendo with flaming sparks. These, along with the hallow thudding from solid wooden hammers pounding against a newly crafted hull, and the sight of fallen cloud-like sails with their contorted ropes dragging them downwards, filled his senses. Could he give all this up for her? He pondered the question as he surveyed the daily grime of the stark figures with their aching bodies, empty pockets, and fierce pride.

He swung past the Swan Inn, resisting an early pint of ale as last night's drunkards began their first sober moaning in the nearby gutters. He continued up Fountain Street, bidding good day to the early tradesmen and eager customers. With the countryside opening before them, the horse broke into a gallop through the vibrant green fields. The disgruntled sheep yelled out as they moved their young lambs out of harm's way, and the wild sunburst flowers filled the air as the horse raced higher and higher. Sweat glistened on her rich chestnut fur, and she snorted for breath as they stood staring down at the town below. He gave her a light kick and she sprung into a canter again as they raced through the last meadow towards home.

The loose gravel scattered under the weight of her hooves as she walked up the long drive to the house. The sandstone glowed under the early summer sun, and Joshua took a moment to appreciate the view. Standing tall and proud within six acres of vibrant gardens, framed by hand-pruned hedges, he remembered how his Grandfather had stood him in this exact spot when he was small, and told him that it would be his responsibility, one day, to ensure that the house and it's accompanying prosperity remained upright for generations to come.

If he could get his father on his side about starting a new life, then the rest would follow, he told himself desperately. The taste of her lips, the smell of her skin, came back to him again as he encouraged his horse to walk the last few yards to the front of the house, spotting his father leaving. A footman raced over to hold the reins as Joshua jumped down.

"Good Morning Master Mason."

"Morning Jones... Father, may I have a quick word?" Joshua stood beside the carriage, waiting for him to approach.

"Everything alright, my boy? You weren't at breakfast," Mr Mason replied casually, placing his documents in his briefcase.

"I could not sleep, so I went for an early ride," his son replied in a non-committal voice.

"Very good."

"Would I be able to speak to you on your return, sir?"

"Is it a pressing matter? I am to be away for a couple of days, on business." Mr Mason cast his eyes upward, studying Joshua's face.

"It can wait."

"Good - if that is all, I must be off". The brief moment of concern had evaporated, and the elder Mason was immersed in the day's affairs once more.

"Goodbye Father."

Without uttering another word, Mr Mason climbed inside the dark, polished carriage, tapped the roof with the hilt of his cane, and disappeared down the drive.

Joshua stood staring at the two sandstone pillars framing the vast oak door. It had always seemed natural to him that the door, and everything that stood beyond it, would belong to him and his own son one day. Ever since his grandfather had constructed the estate, the town and county knew that the Masons had arrived to stay. He tried to imagine himself in five years' time, with Bea, and their first son, running around the gardens, hiding from him in delight. The thought brought a smile to his face... but he knew they could never raise a family in Ulverston.

"Butterworth?" he called out.

Butterworth came striding out of the second parlour room, stood in front of him and bowed his head in a small tilt.

"Butterworth, would you be so good as to get the cook to make me some ham and eggs - oh and a large pot of coffee, and send it to my room? – Where is Mother?"

"I believe she is still in her room, having breakfast."

"Thank you, Butterworth." He made his way to the staircase.

"Very good, Master Mason".

At the top of the stairs, instead of Joshua turning left to his set of rooms, he turned right and headed down the corridor towards his Mother. He made sure the gift was still in his pocket before knocking on the door.

"Yes?"

"Mother, may I come in?"

"Of course." Joshua peered around the door to find his Mother sitting up in bed with a golden tray balancing on top of the covers. She held an elegant hand-painted teacup halfway to her mouth.

"Is everything alright, darling? Did you go out for a ride?"

"I couldn't sleep last night."

She took a sip of tea, gazing at him, the same look he had known as a child, almost, but not quite, as though she could read his mind.

How much he wanted to confess all to his mother, to tell her of the woman he had fallen in love with. If she could give Bea a chance, he knew his mother would love her too. But that wasn't the best step forward at this early stage, he knew; it was his father he needed to win over first.

"I have a small gift for you."

"Why, how lovely."

She gave him the same look again. He tried to ignore it. He brought his hand from behind his back and placed the folded lace on the bed next to her.

The look of suspicion soon turned to intrigue as she carefully unwrapped the tiny satin bow.

"Oh my, isn't that stunning!" She held it up so that the morning light would shine through it.

"It is from the young lace-maker you admire, commissioned – made - just for you." There were no lies in that.

"Are those tiny buds of May? I have a new day dress this collar would look lovely on. I will get Perkins to sew it on today. Thank you, lovely boy. I do not know what I have done to deserve such a gift, but I will treasure it." She smiled, studying the miniature details, pleased at the artist's style.

"I will leave you to your tea and take my breakfast; I am so glad you like it." Without another word, Joshua made his way out into the corridor and closed the door behind him.

Chapter 14

June 1831

It had been three days, and still Bea had not heard from Joshua. The tension played malicious tricks on her, prompting her to imagine various scenarios. Thus far, she had consoled herself with the fact that the young merchant might not have had the time to talk to his father, or the opportunity. However, she feared that if she did not receive word soon, she could no longer quiet herself with any similarly innocent excuse. She had been a little relieved by the fact that she had not heard rumours in the cottages, nor in the village, of her being seen by the strange man alone with Joshua, telling herself he could not have perceived who she was from such a distance.

She filled the time with her usual routine, but in private, she could not help herself remembering the kiss, the touch of his skin and the words he had uttered. How could he love her? He barely knew her and had encountered only a tiny piece of her life; if she brought him here, to her home, would he still love her? She saw herself as his equal, in the physical and the spiritual sense; he was a man, and just because he was born to money did not mean he was her better in heart or mind. But still she knew, in her fierce pride, his parents would never allow him to marry her; to allow a woman such as her to rise in society, and into their family. One question still presented itself repeatedly: what would Joshua Mason himself decide to do?

A little of the heat from the day's sun was still held by the grassy earth, giving way to an abnormally warm night. The cool salty breeze from the late evening high tide flowed through the open door and windows, bringing relief in waves.

Bea sat at the furthest end of the table, with a single candle throwing a warm yellow light towards her lace. Her two youngest sisters were fast asleep in their small cot, with their blanket kicked off at the bottom. Her two youngest brothers had fallen exhausted into bed, straight after a late supper.

The oldest, Matty, sat hunched over the kitchen table with his head resting on a pillow created from his arms, too tired to make the small journey up the stairs to join them. Her Mam sat opposite Bea, looking distracted by her knitting, but making small noises now and then, like a child hoping to gain attention.

"It is just gone ten o'clock; your father should be back by now. Matthew, go and fetch your Da - he might want company on his journey home." With no response from either child, she screeched the name again with a sharp offended bite: "Matthew!"

"Leave him be Mam, I will go instead and fetch Da back," Bea interjected.

"No, you will not, what wi' people think when you turn up at the Bay Horse collectin' your father? Matthew can go."

Realising what the argument was about, Matty stirred and move in his seat, ready to move once the winner had become clear. Knowing from experience not to get involved between the two of them once they had already begun, he savoured his last moments of rest.

"He is tired. I can go. Most of the men will remember nothing in the morning. I've done it before."

Bea gave her Mam back one of her stern looks. With a silent, grateful nod, her brother slowly stumbled his way up the stairs, whilst his sister walked over to the pegs and grabbed her green cotton jacket. Without another word between herself and her mother, she took the lantern in one hand, and closed the door shut with the other.

THE SALTY SEA BREEZE ruffled through the newly dressed trees, making them dance under the moonlight. The dry crumbling earth broke up under each skipping step as she rejoiced in the freedom of the unexpected night-time stroll.

"*Twas Friday morn when we set sail,*
  And we had not got far from land,
  When the Captain, he spied a lovely mermaid,

With a comb and glass bead in her hand,
Oh the ocean waves may roll,
And the stormy winds may blow,
While we poor sailors go skipping aloft,
And the land lubbers lay down below, below, below,
And the land lubbers lay down below."

Bea sang out without a care in the world as she meandered through the woods and down to the path towards the harbour. Walking past her normally comforting place, her mind became flooded with memories. The surroundings had now been both tainted and blessed the moment she saw Joshua. She turned her back on the scene and shook the bittersweet thoughts out of her head like a spider from a shoe.

As she drew closer to the Bay Horse, she heard male voices calling out and jeering. Heated words seemed to be aimed towards one person in particular, either agreeing with or refuting his opinions. She gradually drew up to the main door, which was bolted shut for the first time she could remember. She shuffled along the side until she found a gap through the one of the windows and peered in through an open pane of glass.

Anger was spilling forth from the men, seeping into every crevice of the room. A sweaty heat emitted from the pub, accompanied by the earthy odour of unwashed bodies. She could make out one man standing at the epicentre, high on a table at the far side, with all others present gathering around him, listening to every word of the speech he was enthusiastically calling out. He looked only a few years younger than her Da, with a sweat-soaked cream cotton shirt, a navy-blue waistcoat, and trousers in the same material. He had a trimmed dark brown beard, short curls which clung to his glistening forehead, and a slight tan from his work outdoors. She could make out a little of what he was saying: "We must resist... Now is the time... We are greater as one... " and lastly: "Riot!" The others threw up their arms and fists in agreement, shouting back in a mass of voices. She glanced around at several faces, trying to make out who they were. Some of the men looked familiar from the canal and shipbuilders' yards, but none of them were her Da. She wondered if he was still here, or if he had already headed home. She also wondered suddenly if he had come to the Bay purposely for this gathering, or if he had merely stumbled across it. After a couple more minutes, the speaker drew the meeting to a close, remarking about further similar proceedings the following week. The men stirred in their spots as Bea lent against the wall and waited in the shadows. They stumbled out the doorway, patting each other on the back, and headed off, each in their own direction.

Finally, after a couple of minutes, she spotted him.

"Da?"

Not hearing her, he kept on walking. She crept forward and shouted out again, but this time a little louder. Again, no response. She walked a little closer to him, making sure to stay close to the undergrowth.

"Robert Lightfoot!" Spotting her finally, he welcomed her with a strained smile and a questioning stare.

"Mam sent me, well she really tried to send Matty, but he was burnt out from the new orders and..." Her explanation tailed off as her gaze met the expression in his own. "Da... what was all that about?" She pointed back towards the pub.

"How much did you see?" He stared at her.

"I don't know, about ten minutes?"

"It was a meeting arranged by a man who is the Master at the Canal". He held out his arm to her.

"And the man who was standing on the table, the smaller one, shouting that it was time to act?" Her curiosity was stoked, and she wanted to know more.

"Him, aye - but you cannot tell anyone of it lass, it was a closed meeting." There was a warning note to his voice; not a threatening one, but it alarmed her.

"I promise, Da." She took a breath. "So - what was it about?"

"Workers ain't happy, so we are organising together to bring about change," her father replied briskly.

"Go on."

He took a couple of seconds to think but smiled back in response to hers; he had never been able to deny her smile.

"In the last thirty years, Ulverston's population has doubled, wi' men encouraged to come down off the fells, to stop workin' on the land and the farms with a promise for better wages in the factories and industrial sites. But the businessmen and Government ain't livin' up to their part of the deal. The work is there but the housing ain't, the wages are too low, and god knows little or no support if they're injured by the machines. For a long time now, we were promised a reform, a chance to have our say, to vote, but nothin's has been done about it. Even the Whig party said they'd back our cause, but that was a lie!"

"How, Da?"

"After King George died o'er a year since, they promised us reform, but it didn't come to pass; the people spoke out against it and Wellington left at the end of last year. To quieten us folk again, the Whig PM Lord Grey said they'd put a Bill forward for all men to have rights to a vote, and gain a seat in the commons for new industrial towns. Well, the Bill's been put forward, and now we've learned this very night that it got thrown out. Nothin' has changed, nothin' will ever change!"

"Do you really believe that?" concern filtering through her quiet voice.

"They stand on the backs of us workers but are scared to give us a voice. If they're too cowardly to give us our say, we'll never get the vote. That I know to be true." His voice became louder, more embittered.

"So, what yeh goin' to do about it?" Bea felt a sense of dread, but also of pride in her Da. This man was far-removed from the put-upon, world-weary husband she knew from home.

"We're goin' to make sure they stand up and listen to us," he said.

"But how? They have the power, the money, the voice - why would they listen?"

"If they don't listen, we will speak out all the louder. - We are an industrial town - if we stop, they stop."

"Strike? I heard that man mention a riot. Is that how you are going to make them change their minds?"

"Not at first, not if we can help it - but if a man kicks us down, then sometimes we must kick back harder, so that he won't take us for dogs again", he growled boldly, with the last dregs of courage from his evening beer.

"Da, you need to be careful, look at what happened to the French - I don't know for certain if they are much better off."

"The French had the right idea; they just went about it the wrong way. Change is a-coming, 'tis just a matter of time". He sauntered ahead of her whilst she contemplated his words.

"Promise me you will be careful with talk like that, Da? It can be dangerous".

"I will, lass, I know that well enough."

"What's the next step then?"

"We will meet again to discuss how to carry our action forward."

They stopped outside the cottage garden. She was about to open the gate when her Da placed his hand on top, stopping her.

"Promise me you will not speak of this to anyone?" He held her gaze.

"I said it before and I mean it, I promise no one will hear of it from me."

"Especially your Mam."

"I'm not going to share it with her Da, but you're not either – so why did you tell me?" In that moment, she felt valued to him, and proud to be a member of her own class, for one of the few times in her life.

"You're old enough and quick minded enough to understand what's happening, my girl, and it will affect your future one day. If I told your Mam she'd not understand, and think the worst o' me, and o' my politics. You can imagine, lass. "

"- And tell everyone."

"Aye . . . And if anyone found out before time, I could lose the business". A cold harsh reality descended on them both, and both smiles faded.

"What are you going to say when we get inside?"

"I'll think of something." He placed a smile on his face, the same mask he always wore when entering home.

"You're a grand lass." He gave her a pat on the back as they took the last few steps to the front door. As if rehearsed, they both took a deep breath as Bea turned the handle.

"And where have you two been?" Her Mam shrieked as she slammed her knitting down. "I've been half worried something had happened to you both!"

"Sorry love, I was talking business, poor lass was waitin' outside, and I didn't know..."

Bea slipped upstairs and sat in her window seat, staring out at the milky opaque night sky, her mind brimming with recent information, and an ever-present sadness for the love she knew could never come to pass.

Chapter 15

During the early hours, a foolish thought had entered Joshua's mind, possibly due to the effects of three glasses of single malt and refused to let go. At the outset of afternoon business hours, the following day, he would speak to Mr Lightfoot, on the pretence of putting in an emergency order of rope. Would he be open to the concept of a union between himself and Bea? Half of the plan was real; ropes on two of his father's ships needed to be replaced, and the Mason company had already done business with the Lightfoot's - but no Mason had ever visited the Ropewalk. He would be quick; in and out before Bea would know he was there. He had hoped that the first time he met Mr Lightfoot in person would be to ask for Bea's hand in marriage, but now he wanted a dress rehearsal; to gauge her father's attitude towards his person and his lineage, and towards his own daughter. It intrigued him as to what kind of man he would meet - a reflection of Bea, a stern figure, or a doting parent.

He selected his best suit to make a sound impression: smart, business-minded, hard-working – everything Mr Lightfoot would want in a future son-in-law. He left the office after lunch and readied his horse, planning all the while what he wanted to say, rehearsing the speech so that his nerves wouldn't get the better of him. He went via the canal and harbour, in case Bea was there, and he could give her a few private words of encouragement, but she wasn't. She would be at the house, of course, he concluded, looking after the family. He would pass by that way, instead.

Joshua jumped off his horse and guided it quietly toward the Lightfoot's garden. Suddenly he felt foolish. What was he doing? Why had this seemed a prudent idea?

He saw an older, middle-aged woman standing next to some washing billowing on a makeshift clothesline, connecting one tree to another.

"HOLLY; ROWAN - COME HERE." the woman screamed. Two little girls raced to her side, their heads low and fearful.

"Look – LOOK!" Their gaze, with Joshua's, followed the direction in which the woman was pointing. "Mud, MUD on my clean washing... do you know how much time it takes to scrub your filthy sheets? You ungrateful *brats*."

The older woman swung her arm into the air as the children braced themselves. But before her hand came into contact, an older girl ran between them and received the full impact of the slap across her arm.

Joshua watched Bea as she hid the girls behind her, protecting them against what he guessed was their mother.

"It's my fault, Mam; I should have been watching them, they were only playing."

Her mother leant forwards. "How will they learn if you keep protectin' them? All you're teachin' them is that they can misbehave and suffer nothing. I'm their mother, not you - I'll be decidin' their punishment."

Bea stood firm, refusing to back down, her arms reaching behind her back, nestling the girls further into her dress.

"All you're teaching them is to how to fear you - I'll wash the sheet again and have a word with the girls."

"I am their mother..."

"And a fine job you've made of it." Bea regretted the words as soon as they left her mouth.

Slap. Joshua watched Bea's head snap back as the hand came down against her cheek with full force.

Instantly it looked red and angry. In that second, Joshua wanted to charge out from his hiding spot in protest but felt a force holding him back. He watched Bea carefully, who neither reacted, nor was shocked by the action, and he suddenly realised that this wasn't the first time she had born such blows. The Bea he knew stood in conflict against this image, full of light, carefree and curious. The girl he saw now was cast in a shadow of pain and deprivation, with the weight of the world on her shoulders. Now he understood why she had wanted to vex her mother in regard to the fabric and Hanley's request for a dance.

"That's enough," said Bea quietly.

She turned her back on her mother and whispered something to her sisters, who ran off silently. Then she grabbed hold of the dirty sheet and carried it to what Joshua suspected was some sort of washhouse. Their mother strutted back to the house in anger.

Shocked by the bitterness seeping from Mrs Lightfoot, Joshua wondered with a bitter twinge whether it was this life of drudgery, childbearing and loneliness that had made the mother and daughter so different. He sent out a silent prayer for his father to at least agree with their marriage, so that he could take her away from this cold, grinding surrogate motherhood. He now understood her protective character, why she had helped David that day; how she knew to look for certain injuries. Joshua guided his horse back the way he had come. What he had hoped to achieve was an insight into Mr Lightfoot and his attitudes, but what he had in fact received was a deeper insight into Bea, and the loveless world she came from. He had intruded on a private moment, a part of her life she might not have wanted to share, but it had given him much to consider.

Once he was clear of the house, he climbed back on his horse and made his way to the Bay Horse, in need of a drink. The heathery golden ale refreshed his senses as it trickled down his throat, and he tapped out a cigarette. As a second pint absorbed into his bloodstream, Joshua thought of the courage Bea possessed: despite the cards they had dealt her, she was stronger than he himself, he could see that clearly enough, and he loved her more each day for it.

At a nearby table, he overheard a few men talking. One in particular was becoming a little too loud for his friends.

"But the meetings aren't making any difference, we need change now!"

"Lower your voice Tam, you don't know who's listenin'," a deep voice grumbled.

Without turning round, Joshua could hear a shuffling and noises of protest behind him.

"We need to show 'em we mean action – why are we waitin' to get permission from the Lancaster group? This is our town and we need to take it back."

"We're more powerful as one." a new voice interjected.

"Charlie says we need to wait, so we'll wait!"

"Aye." Two secondary voices mumbling together.

"But if we stop, if we all stop now, what would they do? Nowt – nothin' they *could* do, is there." The man had a slight chuckle to his voice at the prospect.

Joshua thought of what he had overheard Mr Marshall discuss with his father and listened more closely to the party.

"We can't do anything if we're in jail. - Now hush your voice Tam, we're leaving."

"Fight, that's what we'll do. Fight the lot of them -starting with that one!"

Instantly Joshua spun round and saw the three men dragging their friend from his seat.

"Get him out of here, John," the barman called over.

"We're going." Holding a hand up to the figure behind the bar, the gaze of the man restraining their companion landed on Joshua.

"Forgive my friend Sir, doesn't know what he's saying."

Baffled, Joshua nodded his head in response and turned back round to his empty vessel. He was clearly outnumbered, and this was not his fight. Not yet.

"On the house, sir." The bar man placed a fresh tankard down with a worried glance. The two men locked eyes in an instant of understanding, and the alehouse returned to its usual afternoon murmur.

AS HIS MARE CLIMBED the last small hill on the path back to the house, Joshua's gut churned, bringing forth a wave of nausea mixed with the taste of the ale. He told himself angrily to have some courage. The view of Bea's defiant face came into his thoughts, bringing him a spark of hope and peace, and he felt the muscles under his legs contract as his mare kicked into a gallop. *I won't lose her*, he thought determinedly.

"Butterworth, is my Father home?"

"Yes, Master Mason, waiting for you in the study." Butterworth answered.

"Waiting for me?" Joshua headed down the corridor without waiting for a response and knocked on the door.

"Enter," came the brash response.

By the tone of his father's voice, the young man knew something was wrong. He decided in that moment to keep hold of his daunting request regarding Bea, and to wait until his mood had improved.

The large Georgian window let a low golden light into the dark room. The usual warm glow from the candles and fire was absent, and instead shadows loomed in the corners of the room. His father was waiting behind the desk, with his deep-set eyes staring at him over the top of his reading spectacles. His right hand reached down and pulled a gold watch out of his waistcoat pocket. With the ease of an hourly habit, he flipped the gold engraved casing back and studied the face.

"What time do you call this?" he enquired in a cold, tense voice, taking Joshua by surprise.

"Did we have a meeting arranged?" Joshua replied in a hesitant voice, confused by how he might have given offence to his father.

"No, we did not have a meeting in the books, you should know this."

"Then please inform me, how should I be late?"

"I expected you back an hour ago."

"Forgive me... I stopped off for a drink on the way home to clear my head after a day at the books..." Joshua moved to sit down on the chair opposite the desk; if the questions were going to continue as they started, he might be here a while.

"You were not with her?" Joshua froze, his hands halfway to the arms of the chair.

"Explain *this*." His father threw the letter he had been holding in his left hand towards his son, who straightened out the crumpled edges mechanically, and read the four spidery lines with a sinking heart.

"*Dear Sir,*

Forgive me for writing this letter, but I thought it my duty to inform you.

Your son has been meeting with a young woman of low birth, alone, in the early hours at the old harbour.

A concerned citizen."

"Well?" Like a savage dog, the fury spat out of his mouth as he leant over the desk, ready to do battle with his son.

Joshua clenched his fists, sweating. That unknown figure had indeed seen them and had known exactly who they were. Feeling like a fly struggling in a spider's web, the more he moved, the more he became entangled in his own emotion.

"Father - I was going to inform you . . ."

"So, this is true then?" he flung his arm out in an enraged gesture towards the letter which lay, weighted, between them.

The argument Joshua had in his head to win his father over on Bea's behalf had just evaporated, along with any hope he had had of gaining even a small measure of ground.

"Say something!" His father slammed his fist onto the desk, making everything on it jump into the air slightly. "I did not spend all that money sending you to Cambridge for you to waste your time and my reputation on a cottage girl, and in public. - If you are in need of a woman, son, I am sure there is somewhere else you could go. Somewhere... more discreet."

His father's words sparked life back inside of him. "Beatrice is NOT a woman who... She is a lace maker. We have never been... intimate."

"I am therefore meant to believe that you rise regularly at dawn so that you can... *talk* to her?" He let out a distorted laugh.

The sound brought shivers down Joshua's spine. He had never witnessed this side of his father, and for the first time in his life, he did not like what he saw.

"Yes," he replied quietly. "That's all we do, is talk."

"What could she possibly have to say that would be of interest or worth to you? Women of that class are only good for one thing - you may pay them, if you think they have earned it, whatever the service - and leave."

"How dare you talk about Beatrice like that." Joshua exclaimed, fighting with every part of him not to hit his own father. He was met with an exasperated snarl.

"Do not dare me, my boy. What could she possibly be to you?"

Attempting to control his behaviour, Joshua took a few steps backwards.

"Her name is Beatrice Lightfoot and I . . ." He hesitated, and some of his feelings for her as he said her name, were made unintentionally plain.

"The rope-maker's daughter?" There was both shock and disgust in Mr Mason's voice.

"Yes, she –"

"She is a peasant! The lowest person you could... *associate* with." The shame at his son's behaviour was expressed clearly in every word.

"Her father is a business owner who owns his own company – much like you - and she is a clever, bright and beautiful young woman. She was made for a better life." Focusing on his shallow breathing at an attempt to dissipate the threat of more anger busting forth, Joshua tried to remember his planned line of reasoning.

"Do not liken that shed of labourers, that the Lightfoot's run to our enterprise. The father barely makes the means to support his own family."

Joshua moved over to the fireplace and leant against it as he pulled out his cigarette case.

"All I am trying to assert is that he is a business-minded man, just like you and I, sir. And do I not have enough money for us both?"

Mr Mason was incredulous. "You cannot possibly mean to say... You cannot in your right mind... You are my eldest son; you must marry for money and position. It is your duty to raise this family up, not to associate with the classes that serve us!"

"I will marry whom I wish . . ." Joshua remarked calmly as he flicked the cigarette butt into the empty grate. His father barked out a disdainful laugh.

"You will marry Lady Dawn Richmond; we have arranged it."

"But I do not love Lady Dawn, I do not even like her; we have nothing in common."

"And you have things in common with this . . . ?"

"Beatrice. - Yes, I do. She is not like the other women... she is articulate, honest, courageous, and – yes - I can speak with her; she has a wonderful understanding of the world."

"It will pass with her – this feeling you indulge in - and where will you be then? Put her out of your mind and move on to the woman you were born to wed."

"It will not pass father, I - I love her."

"I forbid it - unless you want to be cut off from your family and my money, you WILL desist. If you do not, I will disown you, cast you and your little whore further into poverty, and I will destroy your reputation. How will you live then? You cannot gain further employment; I will see to that. Your life will be like hers is now, living from hand to mouth. Is that the future you want for her? Is that what she wants? Or does she see you as her ticket out of her little lace-making hovel?"

Joshua felt numb. "You ... would do that?"

"If you choose her, you will no longer be my son. And what of your mother? Would you inflict that pain on to the woman who has loved you and raised you to know she must never see you again? I will cut you off right here and now and you can tell your mother that she has just lost her only son to shame and disgrace." The sheer determination in his voice bit into Joshua deeply.

"Will you not even meet with Beatrice? See what I see?"

"Enough damage has already been done by your actions; I will not add to the rumours by allowing this girl any more of my time."

Joshua was torn again for the first time in his life. An image of what he had witnessed yesterday at the Lightfoot cottage flashed into his thoughts. Could he act in any way that would condemn Bea to that life, after promising his love, promising to hold her to him? But where would they go now? What would he do if his father disowned him even in their business circles? Not knowing where the money would come from to feed his family, full of the anger not being able to provide for her and their eventual children, what could he offer? Would they both become cruel like her mother? He couldn't risk her happiness; he wanted to protect her. And there was his own mother, the kindest, warmest woman he knew. He owed her just as much as his father; she had always been present, graceful, and trusting...

"I ... will obey you, sir ... for my mother's sake," he whispered furiously.

"Then we will say no more on the matter. You know what you must do. Good evening."

Slamming the door behind him, Joshua took the stairs two at a time and flung open his bedroom door. The once-safe haven felt enclosing and claustrophobic to him now. He strode his way over to the half-empty decanter on the sideboard and poured himself a double measure. Shakily, he grabbed his silver case and placed a cigarette in his mouth, allowing his lungs to fill with smoke as he sank into his leather chair. He downed the whiskey in one and dragged heavily on the cigarette, before making his way back to the decanter for another.

In one mouthful he cleared the second glass, barely giving it time to touch the sides. All he wanted to do was to drown away the shame and despair, numbing himself, and erasing the last ten minutes. Standing, staring at the decanter, lost in mid-action, his mind suddenly conjured up a vivid image of Bea's face. The image abruptly transformed, her love turning to sorrow and disappointment. He had let her down; he had not fought hard enough for her.

Hatred for himself, and for his father, boiled up inside him. It had been an impossible choice, and he should have known it.

In one furious movement he flung the crystal tumbler against the opposite wall and blinked dazedly as the tiny hazardous shards scattered to the ground. The cold glow of the candlelight shimmered off the glittering debris and melted through the distorted liquid as it dripped down the wall. He fell into his leather seat once more and lit another cigarette, letting the smell of whisky hover in the angry air.

Chapter 16

The abnormally unrelenting June heat caused Bea's cream skin to bronze. The air was fragrant with wild roses, honeysuckle and newly birthed sweet peas. Rowan and Holly giggled as they played catch in the long grass, picking at the wildflowers. Even the ginger cat enjoyed the weather, determined to hunt every insect she came across, stalking her prey silently, camouflaged in the tall grass.

Bea pegged out the dripping weathered clothes on the line and watched them fill and sway as like the limbs of dancing puppets. Her mind kept flickering back on to the events of the past week, and the information her Da had confided in her. She had felt guilty then, even more so now: if he found out she had been meeting with a gentleman, or worse still, fallen in love with one, how would he react? Would he treat her like she too was on the opposing side? If she and Joshua were to marry, would his interests not become her interests too? She was in turmoil, without an answer to quieten her misgivings. It was almost two weeks since she had last seen him, and she couldn't help but let her concern over his silence grow.

The dry parched earth rumbled beneath her feet as the sound of hooves galloped down the lane. Her Mam was in town running errands and anyone needing her Da would know to go to the Walk instead of the cottage, and it was unusual for anyone from the town to take the path to Outcast. The rider wore a long black over coat and a broad-brimmed black hat. He pulled hard up on the reins, bringing the horse to a skidding halt in front of her.

"A Miss Beatrice Lightfoot?"

"Yes?" Bea replied, wary of the man sitting high above her, his face masked in shadow.

"This is for you" he leant down and held out a small envelope. She took it and examined the thick ivory paper. A single patch of ruby wax, with some sort of image pounded into it, sealed it shut. She pulled a penny from her apron pocket and dropped it into the man's hand. Nodding his head silently, he pulled up on the reins, and kicked his horse back into action, heading back up the lane at the same speed he had come down it.

Bea watched the man disappear. She turned the envelope around and saw her name etched across elegantly in midnight black ink. She rotated it around again, attempting to work out the image encrusted in the shining ruby seal.

"Bea? Bea? Who was that Bea?" She heard Holly's little voice blaring across the swaying golden sea. Bea quickly shoved the valuable item into her dress pocket.

"Bea!" She first saw the strands of grain part, and then a small head popped out, face beaming with excitement. Rowan's tiny legs, too small to take the larger steps of Holly's, had kept her behind a little, and she tumbled into her sister with a cry of surprise.

"Bea, who was that? What he want?" Holly giggled as they fell breathlessly into a heap at their sister's feet.

"The man on the horse? He was just a messenger."

"But what he want?" Holly demanded, not so easily fooled.

"He was lost. He wanted directions to Sandside, to the Saltcote shipyard". Bea tried to sound as convincing as possible.

"Oh." They both sighed together, realising the stranger was not as exciting as they had first thought.

"Look at your two red faces, I think it is time for your nap." Bea touched the side of their roasting red cheeks.

"A little longer?" Holly pleaded, Rowan pulling her sad face.

"No."

"Sing us a song?" Bea folded under the pressure and broke into a laughing smile.

"One song."

AFTER TWO VERSES IN the cool shaded room upstairs, the girls fell into a deep slumber. Bea relaxed back against the wall and quietly pulled out the crumpled envelope. She took a moment to steady her nerves and picked at the wax seal. Silently, she peeled back the corners, trying not to make a sound. Four beautifully written lines in the middle of the page read.

"Dear Miss Beatrice Lightfoot,
Would you do me the honour of meeting with me on Breconrigg Common? Tomorrow afternoon at two.
Yours, Joshua Mason"

Bea repeatedly read the few lines, hoping to unveil their intention. There weren't any romantic undertones, and it was void of any notion of a potential outcome. She hid the letter behind a cushion on the window seat before joining her sisters on the bed, wishing fervently that the next twenty-four hours would pass quickly.

BEA HAD CONVINCED HER Da the night before that their old mare needed more exercise than she was getting, and that she should take her out on a long ride. The mare was almost the same age as Matty and had been in the family since she was a folly, reared for one job alone, to deliver rope to the shipyards. But whenever she was not needed, though this was seldom the case, Bea took the chance to escape with her over the dunes and through the woods nearby.

Bea spent the morning grooming the mud and dust off the mare with damp hay so that her white pelage seemed brighter and more presentable for Joshua. Receiving suspicious glances and comments from her Mam about how she didn't normally bother grooming before a ride. Bea shrugged them off and used the time as a distraction; her stomach churning up more of a stormy sea than the still pond it usually carried.

The stout white mare trotted merrily down the coastal path as the floral breeze fluttered around her. Riding bareback, with her dress hanging over the animal's flanks, Bea felt the seasoned sturdy muscles contract between her legs as she galloped at full speed across the open fields. Bea clung on tight with her thighs, and held the bridle with one hand, reaching for the sky with the other in unshackled delight. The trees were covered in a blanket of leaves now, providing a little shade and some privacy. The butter-yellow flowers on the gorse bushes lined the opening to the woods and filled the nearby air with a sweet smell of almonds.

Bea leant back, staring at the sun sparkling through the vibrant emerald leaves, feeling the trust of her mare underneath her. The morning nerves slowly ebbing away.

"Beatrice? Bea?" A voice carried through her trance and brought her back to the present.

She sat up straight and glanced in the voice's direction. Standing beside a tree, shielded by the undergrowth, a handsome youthful figure, ruffled from the ride and with a glow in his face, stared back at her, grinning at what he had just witnessed.

"Oh - Hello." She had not realised how much she had missed him until this moment.

"I thought that had to be you. I looked for you on the top, and when I could not see you, I thought you might be here."

The view of her sitting bare back with her feet hanging loosely on her horse like a woodland elf brought forth a laughter inside of him, a happiness he had not felt in weeks. He compared her to others with who he had been riding; like the inescapable Lady Dawn, who would come dressed in her fineries, daintily shod, and showing off her best stallion. The difference was stark, and it captivated him.

His intense stare made her feel naked, as though there were nothing she could hide from him.

"Will you walk with me?"

"All right." She looked around carefully, making sure there were no extra eyes upon them this time. Joshua helped her dismount. He placed his hand gently around her waist, pulling her tight against his body as she slid off the mare. The strong contact sent shivers down her spine, and left her breathless, but he quickly let her go.

They walked side by side; Joshua tied off his tackled horse to a nearby branch as Bea allowed hers to graze freely nearby, knowing her mare would never wander off alone. Awkwardness fell between them, their hands close but not touching. Joshua glimpsed Bea's face; her bright hazel eyes seemed even greener in the woods, against her tanned skin. The temptation posed by her full crimson lips was almost unbearable. The carpeting moss tickled her bare toes, wild blueberries occasionally bursting underfoot. Bea lifted her skirt off the ground, allowing the tall ferns to stroke her legs as she passed by.

A cluster of foxgloves with their cascading cones of tubular fuchsia bells draped themselves, one on top of the other, seductively as they waited for a passing bee to taste their sweet nectar. Cowslip and tall buttercups decorated their thin aisle on either side. Her idle hands snatched at the nearest flowers, as she nervously wondered if he was waiting for her to speak.

"How... are you?" the words stumbled out of his mouth.

"Oh - Err... enjoying the sunshine with my youngest sisters. And you, sir-Josh... um?" she replied in a confused manner, thrown by the topic of conversation.

"Oh, busy enough, busy enough. Family all well?"

"Yes... all healthy. Yours?"

"All in good health too."

His voice trailed off, attempting to think of something else, delaying as long as possible the real reason they had to meet. Bea felt her skin yearn for him, an invisible string coming from her chest connecting to him somehow. She had to stop herself from reaching out and touching him, to become entwined with him, and utter words of love. She feared his odd distance with her, the small anxious voice bubbling up from her gut growing louder. She stared down at the decimated petals at her feet.

"When I had not heard from you, I thought . . .," she said slowly, carefully, choosing her words correctly.

"I am sorry, I know I said I would come to you sooner . . ."

"But...?"

"But it – everything - became a lot more complicated," he mumbled.

"How so?" Casting his eyes down, he took a single step back away from her. "Please Joshua - Do you still love me? Or have you changed your mind? If you have, you must tell me."

Realisation stepped in and panic over came her as she turned her back on him.

"I still love you", he whispered in her ear. He spun her around so that she could see his earnestness. The glistening pools in her eyes shone back at him, showing him the pain he was about to cause. Wanting to steal one last moment with her, he stroked a hair away from the side of her face and placed it behind her ear. He gazed at her beautiful, frightened eyes. His hand continued downwards, lightly brushing down the side of her neck, gripping quickly behind her head, pulling her forward. His mouth met hers again, his tongue tugging at her lips, as both lovers felt the heat of their wanting spread like an aching nettle sting outward and down. A single thought emerged amidst his desire:

"This is not fair on her".

With all the willpower he could muster, he released her.

"No," he muttered breathlessly and plunged on. "That man – that person saw us - when I went to speak to my father, he had already received a letter about what they had seen. He . . . he has forbidden me. He has forbidden us." She stared at him in pain and longing. Then a cold clarity spread across her face.

"I see... you kiss me, and then tell me I am not good enough. . . I take it... your father knows who...*what* I am?"

"The letter said you were... low born. But I told him your name; that you are the Ropemaker's daughter." His voice was full of shame.

"I am not good enough for your family... I had known that already... but there was a small part of me that hoped you might fight for me on your own terms." A harsh voice belied the sadness in her eyes.

"I fought for you!"

"Not hard enough, then."

"If I went against my father's wishes, he would cut me off – he would have done so that night. And what would we live off then?" he exclaimed, suddenly annoyed at her lack of understanding.

"I am not one of your society ladies, I already live from hand to mouth. The reasons you give me, they do not scare me - but they scare you - I can see it." She picked at the flowers once more, attempting to stay calm, but snatching viciously at the petals, and clutching them in her fists.

"Of course, I fear it, I would be a fool not too. Your family does not choose to live from hand to mouth - why would we?" The frustration boiled up inside him; why didn't she see that if he truly had a choice, it would be for her?

"To be together." Her voice crumbled under the words. He reached out to her, but she shrugged him off. "And no, my family did not choose their lot, but we all work hard for the little money we have - unlike some." Regretting the last words as soon as she said them, even though she believed it, she took a step back and looked at her feet.

"You mean me? That I do not work hard?"

"I mean the gentile class."

"My grandfather built this business up to what it is now, and it is my responsibility to carry it forward."

Standing a foot away from each other, with anger and betrayal brewing between them, each stood their ground.

"And what background did your Grandfather come from? Working? Middle? Or Gentile?"

"Why does it matter where he started?"

"Because it matters - if the funds came from the family in the first place, then they never had to begin with nothing to build up to something. Your class grows upon the back of mine. It is you who determines how much we get for our hard work; you pass the pennies down the line and expect us to be grateful for the crumbs we get! When it is *you* who don't know what it is like to work hard, from dawn to dusk, with every part of your body aching, and *still* not having enough to feed your family!" She heard her Da's words in her own reproaches.

"You are right; I do not know what that is like, nor do I want to find out. Why would I purposely place myself in that position?"

"It is not I who has made clear our difference. Maybe it is for the best that this does not go any further." Suddenly the gap between their two backgrounds seemed too big to bridge.

"You do not mean that...? But surely you can see, I cannot turn my back on my mother, on our business?" He moved silently in front of her and slowly placed his two hands delicately on her shoulders.

"I... I understand - I cannot compete with your family, and I do not wish to. It's... not fair, Joshua. Why did you make me hope?"

Her strength shattered under his touch, his comfort. The true extent of never seeing him again suddenly became unbearable. Like a cleansing waterfall, soundless tears overflowed the edge of the dam. He leaned his forehead against her, melding their thoughts together.

"Because I love you, Bea".

"I... love you too - but we must - bid farewell." He wrapped his arms around her, making them one person. He leaned in for one last kiss, tasting her salty lips, unwilling for it to end.

As he pulled away, a dark thought entered his mind: how would he be able to protect her against Hanley. The Captain would return soon and want to claim her.

"Promise me you will protect yourself against that wolf, Hanley?"

"I am not yours to protect any longer . . .," pulling away from him.

"But I promise you, I will try." A sadness echoed through her voice. Her mind had cast Hanley out, and instead been filled with Joshua, but now her gut churned with what she must face in his stead. She ambled towards her patiently waiting mare.

"Please do not speak as though... as though he might..." A bitterness blossomed inside of him; toward his father, toward Hanley, but mostly at himself; for not fighting hard enough, for being scared.

"It is true," she pushed away his grabbing hand. "I am duty bound as you are. If my parents urge it, I am not in a position to disobey. For that, I suppose we are alike". Her voice was calm and numb with fatigue.

"But he is a monster!" Joshua shouted, furious at the thought Hanley might get his way after all, and that it would cost Bea her freedom.

Anger boiled inside her, every inch of her life was being dictated by men.

"He might well be, but what can I do - tell me? What do you want me to do? You stand there and tell me we have no future together – am I to live my life alone, and childless, out of respect for what you couldn't give?"

She had to leave, enough was enough, and if she stayed, her pain would only grow. Soon the anger would give way to grief, and she needed to be far away from him, and from his touch. The mare waited patiently as Bea used a nearby stump to leaver herself up once more.

"Bea, we cannot part like this -"

"We should have never started - Too poor to marry the man I love; too poor to refuse the man I hate."

Her voice was calm, but her words broke Joshua's resolve, and he sprang towards her. She kicked her horse into a gallop, as his cries rang out behind her.

"BEATRICE!"

Chapter 17

July 1831

"Bea, what's wrong? Has something bad happened this past week?" Beth tugged at Bea's sleeve to walk beside her.

It had been five days since she had bid farewell to Joshua, and part of Bea was still fuming. That same part of her nevertheless was unsurprised; why would a gentleman have risked everything for her?

"You know you can talk to me, you can tell me anything, and it won't go any further?" said Beth gently.

"I know I can and thank you – I don't know how to put it into words yet, that's all."

They watched their parents trudge ahead of the group, showing the way to the parish church. The Lightfoot's didn't attend on a regular basis, Mr Lightfoot blamed it on the amount of work at the Walk, and Mrs Lightfoot couldn't be bothered, though she told people her absence was on account of her fainting sickness. But occasionally, they needed to show face and reassure the community they were a good Christian family. At the same time Mr Lightfoot was fortunate enough to collect a few extra orders after the service, and Mrs Lightfoot fuelled up on enough town gossip to last her a month.

Beth paused in her step, allowing more distance between the two of them and the rest of the family.

"We can hold back a little, let them go in first."

Bea nodded. She needed to tell someone before it consumed her.

"At the May Day dance... I met someone."

Beth looked surprised. "Who?"

"Mr Joshua Mason."

"The gentleman you danced with - Now you need to tell me everything." Beth couldn't help smiling.

Bea started from the beginning and gave her a brief outline of all her encounters with Joshua, and all that she both knew and suspected of Captain Hanley.

"No wonder you are out of spirits. Why didn't you tell me any of this?"

Bea gazed at the church. They were the only parishioners left in the graveyard, and the sounds of the small choir inside attempting a hymn drifted through the worn oak doors.

"We had better go in." Bea walked forwards, but Beth took a firm grip on her dress.

"Bea?"

"I was ashamed. I was a fool. It felt like a dream being with him – that he would choose me. But in the end, he didn't... and now I am lost more than ever. I need to leave, escape."

"And do what? Where would you go?"

"I don't know." Bea wiped away the tears forming with the back of her hand. "We need to enter, Beth, otherwise Ma will come looking."

Her sister relaxed her hold and nodded her head.

"Talk after? We will come up with a plan."

"When do you need to head back?"

"Not until two; will have plenty of time."

"Thank you." Bea pulled her sister in for a hug before opening the dark oak doors.

Their parish church was quite large for the area, bringing in all the hamlets and villages together. At the front of the church sat Lord and Lady Richmond, including their three children and accompanying families.

Bea and Beth hurried down the central aisle, giving a brief nod to the vicar and a curtsey to the Richmond's, before slipping into the family pew.

"Where have you two been?" Said Mrs Lightfoot through gritted teeth.

"My shoe – a stone - Bea helped me balance."

Another hymn broke out as the congregation stood up together. Bea felt a little tug on her dress and saw Rowan looking up at her, motioning to be held. Her little arms wrapped around Bea's neck and gave her sibling some much-needed affection. *How could I possibly leave you?* thought Bea.

She scanned the crowd and saw the familiar faces of families she had been brought up with. Farmers, canal workers and labours. Her gaze fell on

Lady Dawn, two years younger than herself, with beauty, wealth and social standing - everything she knew she would never possess.

Next to her, Bea expected to see her brother, but with an unpleasant lurch in her throat, she saw Joshua. Bea felt anger rising again. She watched him, singing along with his lady; how right and perfect they looked next to one another. She watched his lips move. She had kissed those lips; they had touched hers. She wanted to do it again.

Why would he stand beside her in my church? When only days before - suddenly, his gaze met her own, and an expression of pain flashed across his countenance. As if reading her thoughts, he looked sideways at Lady Dawn, and then back at Bea.

Rowan started pulling at Bea's cheeks, demanding attention, pulling funny faces in an attempt to make her laugh. After the song had finished, they all took their seats once more. Joshua focused his attention back on the vicar.

"He's here."

"Who?" whispered Beth. Bea nodded towards the young couple at the front, and Beth's eyes widened. She squeezed her sister's hand and didn't let it go until the end of the sermon.

ONCE THE SERVICE WAS over, the vicar led the congregation out of the church, beginning with the Richmond's, followed by the front pews, moving towards the back of the church. Joshua kept his sight on the door as he walked past them. Bea gave Rowan to Beth and wove in and out of the crowd, ducking past the vicar, shaking hands with the wealthier attendees, and made her way around the back of the church and through the graveyard. She wanted to hide, to scream.

"Bea, wait."

"Leave me alone Joshua, go back to her." Bea could hear his footsteps getting closer.

"I need to speak to you, to explain..." She felt his hand tap her shoulder to turn around.

"Explain what? That she is the one you are to be with, I know already!" She wanted to kiss him passionately, to feel his body against hers. He stepped closer. His hands were aching to touch her.

"She is my family's choice, not mine..."

"Why, when you two are clearly perfect for each other... Please leave me alone. This doesn't do either of us any good."

"I cannot." He was standing close enough to feel her breath on his cheeks.

"She will be looking for you."

"Let her look – I've missed you – I still love you and I didn't want us to part the way we did." He reached out to her, but she shrugged him away and took a step back.

"*Stop* – Can you not see? - What much good is love anyhow?"

"Do not say words you'd..."

"I'm not sorry for what I said - it is all true, then and now. – *Please* leave."

"Bea?" Beth was standing at the top of the mount behind them, looking anxiously down at her sister.

"We need to talk." He tried to take her hand in his – how much she wanted to hold his.

"No, we don't. Leave, go back to her, before someone else sees...*Please*."

"Bea -" Beth made her way towards them. "Sir, I think you had better leave before my family come."

"Yes, I - you are right."

"Goodbye Joshua."

Without waiting for a reply, Bea took off down the hill towards the fields. She stopped amongst the tall grass and wildflowers and made sure she was alone before placing her face in her shawl and screamed. The last weeks, months spilled out of her until she was empty.

"Bea – it's me. I told Da you were ill and headed back early."

"Why, Beth?"

"They asked where you'd run off to."

"No – why did he have to be there? Why do I feel so lost? Why do I love him so much when I know I can't be with him?"

Beth took a few steps forward, wary of her angry sister. She had never seen her like this before.

"Because you fell in love - and by the looks of it, so did he."

"Sometimes Ulverston is too small – now especially, for us both to make our homes here. I wish I could leave."

"You need to give yourself some time, Bea, and work out your next step – do not rush into anything. You know I'm right. Come - we had better get you home before they catch us up, or there will be more unhappy questions to answer."

Chapter 18

Two weeks had passed since Joshua had seen Bea at church, and she had refused to speak to him. He had spent the days distracted at work, and the evenings in an amber haze surrounded by smoke. There was nothing he could do to shake off the void he felt at knowing he could never hold her again; that her absence was a prescribed necessity. Yet without her, everything tasted like bitter ashes.

"Joshua?"

"Yes, father?"

"Were you listening to a word I was saying? – you need to get a grip on yourself son, you look awful. Are you ill? Do you need the doctor?"

"No, thank you, I do not need the doctor."

"I hear you come back to the house at all hours. Spending your nights at the club is not good for you."

"I know this father."

"What would people think if they saw you like this? They would question our reputation and take their business elsewhere."

"I am sorry father; I will try to do better."

"Don't try - do."

"Yes, father."

"I need you to finish these accounts and write a report on where we might make some transportation cuts."

"Cuts, sir?"

"Yes, cuts. There are rumours abound of strikes; possibly marches. I want to be prepared, whatever the outcome – to cut out the rot before it taints everything else. You will have to face challenges such as these once you take over, it will be good practice for you."

"Yes sir, I will get these back to you as soon as I am able."

"Today, Joshua."

"Yes, sir."

Mr Mason slammed the door behind him as his son slumped back into his chair. He picked up the sheets left on his desk and stared at the numbers, names and stock. How could he make cuts to the running of the business without putting more good men out of work? He had indeed been a first-hand witness to the rumblings of a strike, and yet had been so consumed with his longing for Bea, that he had failed to realise the magnitude of the impact it would have on his family, and on their livelihood. Naively he had presumed that, being out of town, it would not affect the quarry and their mines.

Nevertheless, if another round of men lost their jobs, surely it would cause more upset, and fuel the fire of their leaders? He understood all too well that times were hard for the workers, but striking wouldn't resolve anything. Many were already struggling to feed their children, and weeks without wages wouldn't help to fill the already empty bellies.

The angry words Bea had spat at him on that fateful day rang clear inside his head; *"Your class grows upon the back of mine. It is you who determines how much we get for our hard work; you pass the pennies down the line and expect us to be grateful for the crumbs we get."*

She was right - but what could he do? To protect his own, he had to sacrifice hers. Joshua clenched his teeth and sighed, dipping his pen wearily in the stained inkwell embedded in the corner of the desk. Lately he seemed to do nothing but bringing troubles to the doors of others.

AFTER HOURS OF DEBATING with himself, and calculating the value of each man, donkey and sack of slate, the report was done, and so was he. He dropped the papers off with his father's clerk and used the excuse of running an errand to obtain some fresh air. Outside the street was alive with the usual burgeoning bustle, carriages cutting down anything in their path, and townspeople gathered in clusters gossiping outside shop doors. Businessmen tilted their hats at Joshua as they strutted past, recognising him as one of their own.

Joshua placed his hand inside his pocket and gave a pair of grimy children holding their hands up in supplication a bright shilling. His father would have disapproved at the amount, and the thought gave him even more satisfaction in bestowing it.

"I wouldn't do that if I were you, my good fellow - they will seek you out and come back for more. Just like stray dogs."

Joshua turned round to see Mr William Bell standing behind him, tapping his cane jovially on the cobbles.

"William - good to see you. What are you up to this day?"

"Got a meeting with some shareholders; must try to calm their nerves with everything that's going on, the mutterings, you know, the mutterings. Now - do you fancy partaking at the club with me later this evening? Dear Max, will be there."

"Why not, it has been a dreadfully long day." His father's words popped into his head, but he told himself that he would certainly make a fresh start the following morning.

"Splendid - I had better run along - but I will see you later." William called out his farewells behind him as he strode back up the street, swinging his cane briskly.

Joshua made his way down market street, ambling past the shops, with no particular interest in what lay inside.

"Mr Joshua Mason, what a pleasant surprise." *Would he get no peace today?*

"Good afternoon - Lady Dawn Richmond, Miss Charlotte Ashby, how are you ladies today?" Joshua tilted his hat adroitly to each lady as they stood outside Johnson's. Both looked elegant in their light summer dresses under the afternoon sun.

"What good fortune to meet you here - why, we were just about to take a ride up to your house and deliver an invitation." Charlotte gestured to their carriage a few feet away.

"Indeed? Another charity event with my mother?"

"No - this time it is for yourself in fact. We have decided to hold a small gathering tomorrow at the house." Lady Dawn reached her hand out to Charlotte, who produced a perfectly gilded envelop with his name on the front in neat maroon handwriting.

"Thank you for such a gracious offer. But unfortunately, I have a prior engagement." The lie came all too easily.

"What could be more important than a party with your dearest friends?" asked Charlotte, pouting, and looking between Joshua and her companion.

"If you happen to become free once again, then the invite is there. It would be so lovely to see you. Besides, I know Lord Richmond in particular would enjoy a discussion on the latest movements in the local industries with you." Joshua thought it strange that Lady Dawn would refer to her own father as Lord Richmond; an attempt to impress him; he guessed.

"Thank you, I will keep that in mind." He smiled and tilted his head in acknowledgement.

"Well, we must go. Pressing matters to attend to." Exclaimed Charlotte, turning towards the window of fabrics once more.

"I have no doubt. A very good day to you, Lady Dawn and Miss Charlotte."

Chapter 19

"Snap out of it, man!" Max commanded.

He and Joshua sat in the immaculate red leather armchairs which populated the corner of the wood panelled room, the finest crystal glasses filled with smooth single highland malt balancing in their hands. Muffled voices from nearby conversations floated over, followed by intermittent ecstatic cheers from winners at the card tables. The flickering saffron light from beeswax candles bounced off the dark lacquered wood, creating a languid, comforting atmosphere.

The heat of the room, blended with the whisky, made Joshua's head swim with abstract thought.

"There is nothing to snap out of - I am fine!" Joshua lied through erratic draughts on his cigarette.

"To hell with that - I have known you long enough to know when something is bothering you," Max slurred through his words.

"Leave it be, Max." The constant badgering was making his patience run thin.

"What you need is a distraction -"

"I do not need a distraction, I need left . . ."

"Lady Dawn has arranged a garden party at Conishead tomorrow afternoon - what say you?" he exclaimed, already half celebrating his cunning plan.

"I know this already, and the last thing I need is a garden party."

"What you need is some attention from an excellent woman!" The sentence stung Joshua's heart, and he ached for Bea once more. How little his friend truly knew what was going on.

"Max, I am warning you, leave it," he blurted out, slamming his glass on the small, varnished table between them. He reached for his silver case once more and tapped another cigarette on the top.

"Lady Dawn has requested you to attend, what say you? I must not take no for an answer."

Realising he would have to agree to gain anything resembling a peaceful night, Joshua groaned.

"I'll come for two hours," he replied, defeated.

"Good, good! Now what about a game of cards? I feel lucky." Max staggered to his feet and stumbled to the opposite side of the room, failing to realise that Joshua had not moved an inch, and was still staring at his empty glass, a hazy self-disgust written all over his face.

THE MIDDAY SUNLIGHT stung his raw eyes and thudded against his skull. His sluggish mind could not recall how or when he had sauntered home, only his pounding temples informing him how much alcohol he had consumed. Unfortunately, he recalled agreeing to attend a certain wretched garden party in a few hours' time. He checked his watch. Two hours to make himself feel human again. Slowly, carefully, he pulled himself out of bed, sipped at a lukewarm coffee, and sank into his large copper bath. With the feeling of last night finally washing away, he readied himself mentally for the ordeal to come.

The town was alive with the bustle of Market day, making him regret his choice to leave the house before he had even reached his destination. Farmers bustled pass, herding their goods into small pens, their cries mingling with the raucous noise issuing from stallholders and sailors. The streets, lined with mud created from the recent downfall, clogged up under hooves and feet alike. Manure, ammonia, coffee, fish, fermenting summer berries and pungent spices all swam together to form the signposts of market day. With relief, his horse soon turned on to The Ellers, and past the thumping, trudging grind of the mills.

Instead of continuing on to Dragley Beck, Joshua turned the animal on to Watery Lane. He saw the top end of the Ropewalk, and the earthy scent of hemp filled his nostrils. Images of Bea, the smell of her earthy skin and the longing for her returned. He paused for a moment, hoping for a spilt second to catch a glimpse of her, willing her to walk around the corner so that he could steal one more moment. Then, sighing, he pulled his mare's head to the right and encouraged her down West End Lane toward the back passageway to the Priory.

He was relived to reach the cool protective shade of the trees, and with a handkerchief he mopped his glistening brow. After a half hour of slowly trekking through the woods, happy with the stillness and the fresh woodland smells, he came to the clearing beside the house.

"There you are, we had quite given up all hope of you. Max said you were coming," a high-pitched voice called out over the lawn. Taken by surprise, Joshua spun round to be greeted by Lady Dawn coming towards him. She was dressed in a dust-pink silk dress, corseted around the chest and high waist, flowing out in a full skirt to the ground. The neckline was low and suggestive, cutting across the shoulders with a hint of her bosom at the top. Her hair was pinned up with curls and pearls, exposing her neck and the top of her spine. She held a lace trimmed parasol over one shoulder to keep her porcelain skin staying white. Lady Dawn Richmond was an attractive and accomplished young lady, and at the ripe age of nineteen, any man would be a fool not to snap her up.

Joshua knew he should be falling at her feet, paying her every attention to make sure she was his for the taking, but he felt nothing but loss, and loathing, and his hangover.

"Forgive me my Lady, I took the scenic route and lost track of time." Joshua bowed his head in a slight nod as she approached.

"You are quite forgiven - now, let my manservant look after your mare and come with me for a glass of wine, you must be parched." She clicked her fingers, and a servant came running out of the nearby undergrowth in the direction of the stables.

"There, now come with me," she giggled in a flirtatious manner, linking arms with him and guiding him down to the front lawn.

"Has the rest of the party arrived?" Joshua polity enquired.

"Ah yes, we are a small gathering this afternoon. The others are on the bottom lawn."

The rest of the conversation inched away in awkwardness as they sauntered over.

"Ah Joshua my boy, we had thought you had stood us up, had we not Lady Dawn? But you are here now - here wash this down," he said, planting a large glass of red wine in Joshua's hands.

"Thank you, Max", he took a large gulp of wine before continuing. "Time has not been on my side today, I do apologise."

In the centre of the lawn lay a table covered with a stunning lace tablecloth piled high with bowls of freshly picked strawberries from the walled garden, and pyramids of delicately scented cakes. A large decanter lay empty except for a small red pool at the base, with a second standing next to it, three-quarters' full.

The backdrop to this tableau of summer luxury, Conishead Hall was a grand, ornate house which stood elegantly surrounded by immaculate gardens, fused seamlessly into the exotic woodlands. The warm sandstone, worn by generations of gales surging from the sea, stood bold and imposing, gilded by a deep golden reflection shining blankly off regal Tudor windows.

Joshua gazed at his five friends as they conversed with ease; to them this was home, the world where they belonged. Three months previously he had been one of them; certain where his happiness lay, and what the future held in store. Now he felt estranged, a willing traitor. Could he ever fully step back into his old life, or feel at ease again with them?

"What do you think, Joshua?" William Bell asked languidly.

"Pardon?" Snapping back from his thoughts, Joshua found himself caught off balance in the flow of conversation.

"William was asking you for your thoughts regarding the rumours?" Charlotte Ashby clarified in a mildly judgemental tone.

"Which rumours?" Joshua replied calmly, attempting to hide the slight panic he felt at the thought they could have heard about Bea.

"The rumours about the workers - a potential strike – what we spoke about yesterday, my fellow" William asked with a quizzical expression.

"Oh, those rumours - yes, well, I would always think it wise to prepare, and certainly there is chance something might happen, the workers are not happy. But we should wait until we have more information before giving real credit to any such mutterings." Joshua let out a long breath and tapped another cigarette with relief.

"What other rumours did you think I was talking about?" William asked with smiling curiosity.

"Oh, no others, forgive me - something distracted me."

"What is wrong?" Max whispered to him under his breath.

"Sore head, nothing more - Lady Dawn, will you take a stroll with me?"

"Yes, what a marvellous idea, shall we all then?" rejoiced Max enthusiastically. He gave Joshua a questioning look as he poured himself another glass of wine. Lady Dawn held out her arm gracefully for Joshua to take, as they strolled down the sloping steps towards the shrubbery. The two ladies, Charlotte Ashby and Eleanor Braithwaite, followed behind, giggling and whispering like two mischievous girls behind their governess. Joshua glanced around at the wide variety of shrubs and trees surrounding them, not common to the area, and found himself genuinely interested in their heritage. He asked Lady Dawn to enlighten him as to their origin and upkeep.

"I truly cannot tell you. I do not care for plants – of course I enjoy looking at them; but the rest I leave to the gardeners. That is what they are here for after all." She threw him a dazzling smile.

"What does interest you?" he asked quietly, almost to himself.

"I enjoy a delightful dance, but it must be full of interesting people, not like the May ball - was that not awful? But amusing to watch the townsfolk attempting to dance, I grant you! How Papa keeps telling me we must show face for the town and all that; I suppose it makes these ridiculous events a little more interesting for them." She let out a little chuckle at her own amusing comments, encouraged by her friends joining in.

Joshua took a deep breath. He was becoming annoyed at her shallowness, and his hangover was doing little to soothe things. Was this how his father had decided he would commune with his future wife? His mind flickered back to the dance where he had encountered Bea in her simple golden dress, and the delight he had felt at finding her once more. He would not give Dawn the pleasure of tainting that memory for him.

"Really, I rather enjoyed it."

"Well, we are having a proper ball here at the end of August, you will attend, will you not?" She squeezed his forearm. Joshua, not wanting to commit himself to anything further, said nothing and looked away from her.

"A ball, how lovely!" Charlotte interrupted the conversation gleefully as she approached the couple, with Eleanor in tow.

Joshua took the interruption as a welcome cue to make his escape, slipped his arm out from his companion's grasp and re-joined the men.

"Yes - in four weeks - Mother has allowed me to arrange it all, as I may be giving my own balls soon enough, she says." Lady Dawn gave a little cough, and smiled pointedly at her two female companions, who giggled back conspiratorially, and stared at Joshua.

"What will the decorations be like?" Eleanor enquired. "You are always so good with themes."

"I have not decided as yet, I am still waiting for inspiration," Lady Dawn declared modestly. "But I wanted ivory and pink for the drapes, with -"

"Who are those wretches?" Charlotte suddenly cried, pointing down to the private cove that lay thirty feet below them, beyond the garden boundary.

"Where?" Said Lady Dawn.

"Down there, on your little beach." Charlotte pointed, her condemning finger showing three small figures playing by the high tide.

"How dare they - That is a private beach, the townsfolk know that. They must leave!" Lady Dawn cried.

Joshua peered at the people, seeing a young lady and two children. They looked blissfully happy as they ran around in circles, chasing the waves and catching at each other's skirts. The thought of disturbing them and asking them to leave felt wrong, but at least if he did it himself, he knew it would be achieved with a degree of politeness.

"I will go down and ask them to leave on your behalf if you would permit me?" Joshua interjected.

"Thank you, how noble of you," Lady Dawn responded somewhat theatrically.

Joshua left the company with a curt nod. Masked in shadow by the last stretch of trees, he noticed the young female face as she spun round – Beatrice. The sight of her stopped him in his tracks. He watched her as she ran and laughed, attempting to catch the two little girls playing tag. He had never seen her so free and mischievous, finding himself falling in love with her all over again. He pondered for a moment if this was the opportunity he had been looking for? He felt the crowd behind him, along with the gut-wrenching realisation that Bea would leave his sight for the second time.

"Bea?" There was no answer, so he edged closer. "Bea?" he called out slightly louder. He knew he must speak to her in such a way that his friends would not suspect any prior acquaintance. "Beatrice!" he called out again.

One of the little girls stopped and tapped Bea on the arm. Facing the high tide, Bea bent down to hear her. Holly pointed in the direction of the woods, and Bea spun round, and froze as Joshua came into focus. The bright sunlight stung his eyes for a moment as he stepped out of the shade.

"Beatrice, I -", he walked a little closer.

"Joshua, what are you doing here?" she interrupted him, fearful of what he might say in front of the girls.

"I must speak with you," he said hesitantly.

"There is nothing more to say between us," she asserted quietly, turning around to face the girls again. Her thunderous heart was banging in her chest, trying to get out.

"There is plenty more to say, can I not have a few minutes?"

"Hello." Holly and Rowan said together, broadly grinning.

"Hello." Joshua replied, with a half-wave and a smile. Bea gave her sisters an annoyed look before turning back round.

"These are Holly and Rowan."

Joshua bent down to the same height as the girls.

"Hello Holly and Rowan, I am Joshua - a friend of your sister. May I speak to her for a few minutes?" Smiling, he could make out some likeness of Beatrice in each of their faces. The two girls nodded their heads then looked up to Bea with a grin. Bea let out a sigh.

"You two play here – right here - while I talk to this gentleman". Bea spoke clearly, pointing to the spot where she would be standing a couple of feet away.

"I told you to leave me alone at the church," she whispered to him, as the girls hurtled off towards the waves. She had not thought she would see him again so soon. Her heart climbed into her throat. She was immeasurably grateful that her sisters were there, so that she wasn't tempted to reach out to him.

"Sorry," was the only word he managed get out of his dry mouth. She merely looked at him; still hurt, still wanting him, still proud, strong and beautiful. "It has been tearing me up inside, not seeing you. Speaking to you..." He longed to take her hand but resisted.

"If nothing has changed, then what else can I say? The cards have been dealt, and you hold them all."

"You know I have no choice."

"That is a lie!" she replied forcefully. The two girls stop playing and look on with concern. She continued, lowering her voice, "You had a choice, and you made it. This discomfort is simply because *you just can't live with it.*" He reached out for her, but she snatched herself back. "Do you think I have no heart? That seeing you will not break it all over again?" Tears filled her eyes.

"I think more of you than of any woman alive. Do you not see how much I love you?" His fingers brushed the palms of her hands, the fiery spark igniting again.

"Not enough, it would seem. I would do anything to be with you - do you think my family would rejoice at our connection? I would defy them for you, for us. You speak of love, but this is not love. You had a choice, and you chose other than me. I now must live with that; that I was not enough for you. So, don't speak to me about love." The truth and the pain were clear in her face.

Her words remind him he was not alone, and his group would wonder at his absence.

"You have to leave the beach," he muttered, ashamed again.

"What?"

"They sent me down to ask you to leave... Lady Dawn". Bea blinked. Then she closed her eyes, as though in pain.

"Is not that fitting... Your wife has asked me to leave..."

"She is not my wife, and never will be!"

"Please, good sir, do tell my Lady Dawn that she has won; I shan't trespass on her lands – your lands - any longer."

Collecting the girls' small hands, she marched them back down the beach, Joshua staring after her until only the traces of their games were left in the sand.

Chapter 20

Curled up in the centre of the discarded ropes, Bea lay silently weeping for the life she could not live. The sweet earthy smell of hemp mixed with the salt of her tears filled her nose and mouth. The reassuring texture of the coarse fibres on her skin brought her back to a safe place, rooted in childhood memories. She traced her fingers over the creamy caramel material, following the strands twisting around each other; seeing for the first time how intricately the smaller fibres came together to form the larger, stronger rope. Bending it in her hands, forming it into a loop, the cracking hemp generated a rhythmic, melodic sensation. Amongst the familiar tangled snakes, she drifted away into a dark, depressed doze.

"Lass? What you doin' down here?"

"Hello, Da."

"What's wrong, lass?"

"Nothing, Da." She tried to shake off the feelings from the last few hours. Her Da sat down next to her as she nervously picked at the threads, avoiding his eyes. He could always tell when she was lying.

"You haven't curled up down here since you were a lamb," he remarked in a soft voice.

"Da, I can't tell you now," she turned her head towards him and attempted a half-smile.

"You can tell me anything lass." He stroked the top of her head.

"I know Da, just... not right now."

"Well, when you're ready." He leant down and gave her a light kiss on her forehead.

"Are you still heading to the meeting tonight?" She wanted a change of subject to distract her from persistent thoughts. After her last conversation with her Da, she had realised the impact the reformers were about to have on the town area and even her home. She was a working-class woman, and now more than ever she wanted to re-connect with her life and act. The meeting tonight might be a good place to start.

"Aye, why?" he asked, with a questioning look.

"Can I come along?"

"You know the rules - no lasses allowed." He turned to get up.

"I know, but could I stay outside and listen in – it's a dry night?"

"Why d'you want to come?"

"I want to know more about it; like what you said before, it will be my fight one day." He looked at her carefully for a moment, with a strange, heavy hesitancy, and then sighed.

"Fine, but you've to stay out of sight - and no word to anyone."

Bea smiled at him and followed him out into the daylight.

MEN'S VOICES FILTERED through the open windows of the Bay Horse, as Bea crept up through the edge of the trees, making sure no other person was around to witness her clandestine participation.

She made her way around the back end of the pub towards the sea wall. The golden light streamed through the window and blended with the late evening sun. Someone had propped a few of the square wooden panes open to allow the sea breeze to enter. Bea edged forward and peeked through a bottom pane. She recognised the speaker from last time, addressing a tight-knit circle of men as the latecomers gathered in around them. A ringing noise came from the barman's bell, carrying over the men's voices as a sign to begin.

The head man pulled away from the central hub of people and walked over to the table, leaning against the back wall. Illicit word had spread through the town of the meeting, and they packed the pub, with men from many trades and dwellings. Bea slid her head back down and crouched on the damp earth. She leant against the cracked plaster wall and settled herself ready for the next hour. The sea breeze was stronger than usual, bringing with it a fresh scent, and she took a long gulp of it. The sun gave way to the crescent moon high above, casting a rainbow of colours on the exposed sand, and the pools of water left behind in the narrow channels.

The suffocating sensation from before crept back out from the hole inside her where she had buried it. What world could she create, that would allow her choices? None. She felt frustrated: just because she had been born a woman; she had to sneak about in the dirt so that she could hear about the plans and decisions which would affect her future. Bea knew the answer to the burning unrest she felt, but did not want to admit it to herself, not in so many words. She was not content? - Not at all – and for the first time, she had an urge to act on her frustrations. She tried to breathe deeper again, telling herself there was no point in rushing in headlong without a proper knowledge of the facts; no one would let her do anything unless they trusted her appraisal of their struggles. She was startled out of her reverie by a clear cry from the leader of the assembly.

"Men: we have less than a month to plan our strike and to create the march across town. It is our time to show that their companies, their fortunes, cannot survive without us!"

The men shouted back in approval and banged their pewter tankards on the wooden tables.

"For too long they have stood on our backs and made promises, only to break 'em. They have told us: better wages, better 'ouses, a right to be heard as shareholders in their doings – have we seen any 'o these things?" His passionate, educated voice rang out across welcoming ears.

"NO!" the men shouted as one.

"They have pulled men from our farms, and those farms now stand rotting, to the ground because there is no one to work them. Our women and children stand in the streets and beg for scraps because the labour they were promised is not there!"

An unknown voice ascended over the crowd. "But what change will it make? I've heard all this before - Me and my kin hail from Manchester; we were working there eleven years ago. I stood in St Peter's Field and heard these same words. That Hunt fella told us to stand up for our rights, to take down the government. But instead they took *us* down, in that field. Me brother was stabbed that day, standing next to me. His blood weren't the only one mixed in wi'th' mud!"

"I hear you my friend – I myself was there alongside others in this room but that is why we must rise up, no matter the cost, to change the way o' things, so your sons never have to stand like thee, in the fields, and fight 'til the death for their bread and their hearths."

"My neighbour watched as his child, no mo' than four years, died in his mother's arms starvin', because the mill owners have cut our wages again."

"We went on strike last year for seven weeks; I lost count of how many people died, and when the Yeomanry beat us, cut us down, forced us back to work, what did we have to show for it? Nothing, apart from new graves in the ground."

A cane banged against the floor, calling for its owner to be heard: "If Magistrate Forester should find us 'ere, an' discover our meetings, he could arrest us under 'The Seditious Act' and the 'Sixth Act'; we are riskin' our necks tonight, just bein' here. They have hung men for lesser crimes!"

"Aye, we are riskin' our necks being here and so did the people around Manchester as they rose up. They petitioned the king, wrote to parliament, like we have done, and look what happened to them." The head man pulled the men back with his reply.

"That day, there were tens of thousands of us standing in St Peter's field. We were peaceful, no weapons. All we wanted was a voice, to be heard, to stop the corrupt government from taxing our grain, and cutting our wages. And yes, they slaughtered us. Six-pound guns fired into the children. I reckon hundreds died that day, either in the field, or after, when their masters cast 'em out and blacklisted 'em. Men and women watched their families starve, just like we do today. Fear is what they use to frighten us back into our place. And so, they will always be the victors – *until we refuse to run*. I look at each man here, and I see clearly that the mill-owners, the landowners, the quarry-owners who control parliament: they have had their time. It is finally our moment, to reform this retched country, and give the power back to her people – so that *no more* children die in the arms of their mothers. Let them know we are in no doubt - we mean to take back our livelihoods. We the north, are the forgotten land – well I say *no more!*"

The crowd exploded as one voice, and almost everyone was in support of his words. Bea was stunned, and full of a cold, nervous fire. Could those stories be true? The ordeals other families faced made her uncharacteristically grateful for a small part of her own. What was more, if they had let the women join before, then why not again? She suddenly felt like she was betraying both sides; like Judas, one side loving the Romans with their bright silver, the other belonging forever to Jesus - but who was who, she could no longer tell.

"On the third Friday in August we will strike - we will march through *our* town and show the money-men we will stand by like sheep *no longer*!"

"AYE!" The men's anger created ripples across the pub.

"Let the north rise again! For the men, women, and children in St Peter's Field! Are you with me?" he called out with triumph.

"*Aye!*"

Chapter 21

The wretched stench of death surrounded him as he stood at the helm of the ship. The grimy tricolour tied high above fluttered in the breeze as the men removed the last of the iron shackles and bloodstains from the deck before setting a course home to France. The mile-long row of merchant vessels lined the fraying hem of the vast dock like pearls sewn on the collar of a dress, and the narrow side-walk was full of the bustling merchant classes, barging pass one another as they relayed messages, and sailors bidding farewell to their loved ones, some with sorrow, others with no little measure of relief. The gulls cried out over the activity below, and the condensed wall of noise cascaded through every crevasse of Liverpool docks, spilling over the harbour wall. The timber crates cracked under the weight of their cargo as the sailors dragged them from the ships. Ropes slithered across the deck as the seamen still on board pulled in the vast masts, the wood sighing gently as it relaxed back into place once more.

"Gregson?" Hanley bellowed, standing at the starboard side of the ship, overseeing his men with his usual keen eye.

"Aye, Captain?" Gregson came running out from between two lean sailors.

"You oversee the removal of the cargo. Make sure that man Stanley signs off on it."

"Aye Sir - and where will you be if we need you?" asked the first mate nervously.

"Not that it is any business of yours, but I have an appointment with a lady, and a hot bath. You will not need me, will you, Gregson." It was not a question.

"Ah - no Captain, no."

"Oh, and get this messaged over will you, it is of the utmost importance that it is done quickly." Hanley pulled out a letter from his breast pocket and shoved it into Gregson's callused hand.

"Aye, Captain." The first mate placed it directly into his pocket, knowing better than to look at the address.

"I will come for you tomorrow before we head back to Ulverston. Make sure my ship is ready to leave." Hanley cast his gaze one last time over his men and cargo before heading down the ramp.

Gregson dipped his head in acknowledgement, and bawled across the ship, to Hanley's satisfaction: "Right - you heard the Captain! Get to work, or you'll have no rations, th'night."

Hanley flung his nap sack over one shoulder and strode through the alleyways winding towards the centre of the city with authority. A passing thought of the translucently soft skin belonging to his favourite Liverpool lady held steady in his mind; a nice contrast to the women who had been sharing his bed as of late, he thought bluntly. But needs must, wherever he found himself.

TUCKED NEATLY AWAY down a narrow street, a Georgian town house that had seen better days, opened its smudged red door to Hanley before he had raised a hand to knock.

"My Captain. It has been a long while. You are just back?" Her gin-scented breath wafted in front of his face.

Betsy leant invitingly against the door frame, stroking Hanley's new beard, and winking at the men walking past behind him. Her tight-corseted plum-silk dress left little to the imagination as it shimmered in the early morning light.

"Morning Betsy - is she engaged?" he asked disinterestedly, stroking the girl's left cheek, letting his fingers slide down her neck and between her full breasts. Without waiting for a reply, he entered past her into the dimly lit hallway, and she closed the door behind him in answer. The flickering flames fought to stay lit on the wax stubs left over from the night before, and the peeling paint on the tall walls created shapes and shadows in its smoky light.

"You tease Hanley... got any other presents for me?" she whispered, guiding her hand over the front of his trousers. "Mary, tell Elle that Hanley is here". She gave the front bulge of his trousers a light squeeze before letting her hand drop.

"If there is enough of me left, after Elle". Hanley drew out a slim wind of sunset-pink silk from his sack and placed it into Betsy's delighted arms.

Hanley lay in a large copper bath filled with hot steamy water, a musky fragrance hanging in the air. Elle knelt beside him, stroking his hair, washing out the weeks' worth of muck. It was a tradition he had to wash himself clean again after one of those voyages, he liked to think it cleaned out the soul a little.

"You seem distant, you alright Victor? Was it a tough one, this voyage?" Hanley liked Elle, he confided to her about most things, including his name.

"You could say that... we hit a storm off Africa, the ship became sodden, rotten... we lost twenty bodies on the way to the West Indies." He began rapidly to scrub his own with a rough bar of soap. Elle placed her hand on top of his; he stopped and leant his head against her naked chest for a moment. "It is not that, which distracts my thoughts."

He plunged his body under the water, submerging his head. In the soapy depths, his ears full of water, and the room out of sight, he found himself not in the murky bathtub, but back out at sea, when he was a lad, twelve or thirteen years of age. Frantically kicking his legs, trying to stay afloat in an all-encompassing darkness, accept from the lanterns swinging off the hooks along the tall ship in the distance. He gasped triumphantly, almost at the side of the longboat bobbing next to him, only to feel his father's enormous, claw-like hand forcing his head back under from over the side. Just before the fountain of bubbles ebbed, he felt the hand relax again. He met the air, spluttering and choking.

"Do you think I wouldn't notice the ones you used to your liking? You reduced his price by at least a third. Your actions are costing me, boy. How is it I ended up with a son like you?"

His father gripped a tight fistful of his hair and slammed him back under. This time Hanley had swallowed some water and struggled to hold his breath. He began hitting his father's hand at an attempt to break his grip, feeling his hair almost tearing from his head. His father pushed down deep in the water like a kitten in a sack before finally letting go. Hanley kicked hard to break the surface, water spilling from his mouth like vomit.

"Maybe one day I'll finish the job and replace you with another son. Pull him out." Hanley felt a pair of arms yank him from the sea, and deposit him writhing and choking on the bottom of the longboat.

Elle tried to pull the thrashing Hanley back up to a sitting position, avoiding his arms and legs as he kicked about. He coughed up a mouthful of bathwater as Elle grabbed a clean towel. He leant back against the warm copper, spitting. She gently dabbed at his white face.

"You were back there again, eh?"

Hanley didn't speak; he didn't need to. Over the years, he had forgotten certain aspects of his past, particularly his childhood. But now and again, the same recurring images fought their way through, especially when he returned from one of those all-too-familiar jobs. He knew his soul was black; dammed and unredeemable. And yet, sometimes, he wanted to be other than himself. To wake up a different man, with no weight, and no pain; to feel an abhorrence at any notion of cruelty, instead of the usual inexorable, natural pull towards it. He snorted inwardly; miracles like that were a fool's fancy. But all the same... perhaps that was what he had found in Beatrice? Some sort of light? Like her name? Maybe it would be different with her, maybe she could change him. If she would come to him as his wife; a willing, loving woman... Was he even capable of that kind of life...? He couldn't remember the last time he had bedded a woman without force or who hadn't given herself to him under the bounds of a transaction. Hanley clenched his fists, pushing the anxiety away. Nervous about seeing a woman? But then, what if she rejected him again tomorrow? He didn't know what he would do. He needed her; he had to have her.

"There, is that better?" Elle's voice drew him back into the room. He studied her face calmly as she continued to wipe away the cold beads around his temples. She was a kind woman; she had never judged him. Her youth was gone, her breath smelled like gin, she had been in the game too long. He laughed inwardly. They were more alike than she knew, old Elle and him. Corrupt in body and mind; they made a good match. He closed his eyes and let his limbs relax once more, and his mind emptied as his body responded to her touch, her hand warm and firm as she slipped it under the water. His neck arched a little in pleasure as he pictured Beatrice.

CAPTAIN HANLEY CAREFULLY directed his ship into the mouth of the canal on the early afternoon high tide. Small rippling waves spread out from the large wooden keys, as he stared out across the glossy blue behind him, the high sun reflecting on each small wave. The trees formed a towering aisle directing the sailors' sight to the encumbering Fell, which stood silently watching over the town. His thoughts jumped back to the morning two months ago when he had stood on that Fell with Beatrice and asked her to marry him. The only time he had ever allowed emotion to lead him. What a success that had been.

Anger surged at the memory of those wide, fierce eyes; her hair moving gently in the breeze as she stepped away from him. If she dared to decline him again, she would know what his anger could achieve. He threw out the heavy thick rope to one of the canal workers, who threaded it through the eye in the saddle of the heavy Clydesdale horse, which dragged his ship into the side of the canal. The man tied off the end around a solid iron anchor as Hanley felt the ship moan one last time before she settled into place.

"Look after the ship Gregson, we dock for a week. The men need a rest before we head back west, to home." He glanced over at Ryan and Pierce; their raw hands stiff over the rough ropes as they tied off the rigging.

"Very good sir, shall I book rooms at The Sun?" Gregson replied quickly.

"Fine." Giving a brief nod, Hanley scanned the crew of men, his mind distracted with the task ahead. The sun hid behind newly formed clouds, and a cool breeze whipped through the narrow space.

Ensconced in the back-parlour of The Sun for the third time that year, he took a mouthful of tepid ale, and remembered how much he had missed the homely brew since he had been away. He stared down at the creamy white top in his pewter tankard, watching as the miniscule bubbles burst reluctantly, his mind reliving last night's events. A sneer spreads across his lips as he licked away the creamy yeast on the tip of his finger. What would she taste like, he wondered? Sweet, that was for sure. His eyes glazed over as his mind slowly gave way to the alcohol and desire. He swayed to his feet abruptly and made his way to the door as another man came in, resulting in a tussle.

"Watch it."

"What – did - you say to me?" Hanley slurred a little.

Realising who he was dealing with, the man backed down as quickly as he could, but it was too late. Hanley sent a flying right hook into his face, and before the stranger could raise his hands to protect himself, he kicked him furiously in the stomach. He no longer saw a canal-worker writhing on the floor, instead he was looking down at himself as a twelve-year-old boy, crumpled on the deck of the ship. He kicked the man again twice in the head before anyone dared intervene and drag him away. Hanley growled at the distressed onlookers, staggered across the courtyard and ambled up the lane, and barely thinking about what he was doing, made his way up to the Outcast cottages, unseen.

She was picking the wild red berries growing amongst the hedgerow, a little way down from the path up to the small line of squat dwellings. He watched, studying her movement. The sun was shining on her glowing skin, her neck newly exposed with her hair braided to one side. He yearned for her more than ever, his body awakened after last night and craved to be satisfied once again as he became transfixed on her slight curves. As he stepped around the tree for a better view, a stick loudly cracked under his weight.

"Hello?" She spun round, alarmed.

Hanley slunk out from under the tree line and smiled. "It is only I, do not fear. Good afternoon, Beatrice. You receive my message?"

She surveyed him as he stood in front of her. His appearance differed from before. His skin was a dark honey-brown, gleaming, and smooth, tarrying well with his dishevelled clothing; grease and oil smudged across his camel trousers. His jacket hung open, exposing his creased waistcoat and shirt. His hair, a little lighter from travel, sat loosely atop his shoulders. She noticed a leaf caught between two strands, and suddenly an icy wave of panic rose in her chest. Her heart drummed against her rib cage, pushing out any breath she tried to hold on to. Why was he in the trees and not on the path? Why had he been watching her in silence?

"Yes, I - I did, thank you," she replied in a measured tone. "You are a little early, are you not?"

He ignored her question. "You look well, Beatrice." His piercing eyes made her uncomfortable, almost naked. She looked down at the berries gathered in her apron, melting from the midday heat, the juice soaking into the fabric, unable to raise her face to his.

"Have you thought any more about my question, Beatrice?" He moved directly in front of her, his hand brushing her shoulder in a familiar manner. She could smell the warm ale on his breath. Trying to regain some distance, she took a step backwards.

"I – I have thought about your proposal and, though you are most generous to have made it, my feelings remain as they were before." Her fingers picked at the berries in her skirts, squashing a couple in her anxiety. The smile vanished from his eyes; something lifeless had taken its place.

"I would have thought you might have come to realise what it is I am offering you. You do not belong here - I can offer you the entire world." He stepped forward again, cornering her amidst the bushes. He stroked her cheek lightly as she turned her head away from him. "I can give you things that no one else can. No other sailor can offer you what I can... why then do you refuse me?"

"I refuse because I do not feel I will be happy, away from here, away from my family." She was lying, and they both knew it. Her heart leapt into her throat as his hand slithered over her neck, his body casting her in shadow.

"And yet a part of you wants me, Beatrice, I know that much." His face was a hairs breadth away from her own.

"Sir, Captain -" she choked out, "I do not feel any..." She shuddered under his touch.

"Did you not come to the dance with me? Did you not happily accept my gift to you? You cannot tell me you did not fully understand the meaning behind those gestures?"

"I am sorry... I can honestly say I did not. I accepted the gifts without thinking – I thought you merely pitied me..." She was pleading now; if she could not free herself soon, she was afraid what might happen next.

"You are young, yes, but you are not as naïve as you may wish me to believe," he played with her, his lips hovering above her ear.

"I am deeply sorry for misleading you, Captain, if that is what you feel I have done, but I cannot agree to marry you." Her words were sharp and firm as she shifted her body back further into the thorns. He looked at her for a second, then smiled wryly.

"But I must have you."

He closed the distance between them, forcing his body against hers. Anger, alcohol, and passion blended together.

"No woman who has refused me; left me unsatisfied." He gripped both her shoulders and pushed his groin against her, letting her feel his size and strength.

"Sir *no*! Please that is the ale talking, let me *go!*"

He leaned in and kissed her hard on the lips, quieting her voice. It was rapid and full of hunger, and his scent and heat filled her nose as he pushed his tongue inside her lips. His touch was nothing like that which she had experienced with Joshua, full of tender desire and a gentle insistence. For a split second at the thought of Joshua, her lips gave into Hanley's motions, which only fuelled his hunger more.

This is not Joshua, you are in danger, free yourself.

"I knew you wanted me. I felt you pressing against me." His lips hovered above hers, his hand reached up to her breasts and rubbed hard against her stained muslin.

"Not like this – Captain - *please stop -!*"

"Tell me yes, and I will stop."

She tried to shift under him, but it was no good, he was too strong. Fear spread through her body like fire, causing her eyes to fill with tears. She could feel an evil pleasure building up inside him. His jaw was set, his eyes were dark and empty, and his unresponsiveness was more terrifying than anything else. The thorns in the undergrowth were like tiny knifes, cutting into her back.

"I – can't -!"

He lifted her skirt with his other hand and stroked her inner leg, waking her up to the helpless reality of what he intended to show her.

"No - NO." She tried pushing him away, but his hand clamped over wrists. It forced the juices of the ripe red berries against her, staining them both as she tried to wrench her hands free in terror.

"You are a tease!" he panted in her ear. "You must feel how much I want you." He pulled her closer to him, his body alive with lust.

"No! *No*! Let me go, *please* do not touch me there." She shook, her body twisting around, her skin burning under his grip. He forced his lips against hers, thrusting his tongue deep into her mouth, causing her to gag.

"I will have you; you have already sold yourself to me."

Footsteps echoed down the path. As though a cold bucket of water had been thrown across his face, Hanley dropped her and sprang back. She slumped to the ground like a rag doll, gasping, and scurried backwards across the ground like a frightened animal. Hanley looked back through the trees to the path, anger and adrenalin pulsing through his muscles. He glared at her in a moment of visceral hatred, and within seconds had vanished back into the woods in the direction he had come.

Chapter 22

Bea quickly pulled herself up.

"Was that Captain Hanley I saw?" Her Mam met her as she turned the corner to the house.

"What?"

"And what's that rotten mess?"

Her eyes glanced down at the front of her dress, red, sticky and damp. Her skin crawled at the thought of his angry, hating touch.

"Was that Captain Hanley I just saw? I swear it was." Her Mam repeated. "I thought I saw him leaving as I was coming down the lane." Frustration tinged the edges of her voice.

"Aye, it was" replied Bea shakily.

"What did he want? Did you offer him refreshment?" Her Mam gestured with her hand, wanting Bea to come closer, peering behind her to see if she could spot the Captain on the path.

"He did not... he wanted nothing."

"He must have wanted something - Look at the state of you, no wonder he left."

"Mam, leave it will you?" she pleaded softly.

"Did he...?" She took a shrewd look at Bea's face and demeanour. "Did he... proposition you?" She gripped the fence post tightly.

"He..." Bea did not have to speak for her mother to understand her answer.

"And?"

"I refused him, twice. I cannot marry him, Mam." Her mother gasped and drew one hand to her bosom in shock.

"He... he proposed *marriage*?" Bea looked at her, confused and ashamed.

"Aye."

"You turned him *down*? You accept gifts and rides in jigs, but you refuse marriage? Why would you do such a selfish thing? Do you have so little regard for this family that you refuse to lighten our burden and enlarge our prospects just to satisfy your own pleasing?"

"No, he is.... He frightens me. He has a violent temper." Bea's voice rang out clearly.

"As do many men, that is often the way. Happiness will come in time; you will learn how to please him and soften his moods. He is offering you prospects, money, and a better position than you'll ever have here. Those are the real things on which to build a marriage." For once in her life, she attempted to soften her approach, though her words were laced with a hint of bitterness.

"I want to marry for love, marry someone who I can look up to. Someone good, like Da."

"Do not be a fool, you are not in a position to marry for love. You are twenty-one now, your youth will soon disappear." Bea fought back, longing to be alone. "It is time you unburden this family and start making your own."

"Burden? I bring money into this home, good money I might add. I look after the little ones, and I cook for you and the boys."

"You do your fair share, that is all. It is time you listened to me, for once in your life. I am still your Mam, and you are still my child!" Bea took one agonising, desperate look at her, and walked blindly off towards the fields. "Where are you going? I am not finished talking to you!" Her Mam screamed. "Beatrice, come *back*!"

Bea walked unsteadily down the track away from her house. Once she was out of sight, she picked up her skirt and ran. She felt free as the cool breeze washed over her heated face. Tears finally flowed freely, and she let them fall as she ran, until her feet could no longer carry her. She collapsed under an ancient oak tree, the roots springing up through the ground to form a toughened nest. Laying under the tree, she stared up at the net of leaves above her, closing her eyes and praying that the ground would swallow her up forever.

BEA WOKE AFTER A DEEP sleep; the sun was no longer above her, shining through the leaves. Instead, it was tilted to the right of her, casting long shadows through the shrubs. She must have slept for a good few hours, she thought. She lay there, listening to the cascading noise of nature blending with a trickle of sound from the canal. She needed to speak to someone who would understand and listen. Reluctantly, she moved from her newly formed nest. She needed Alice.

THE OFF-KEY CHIMING welcomed her like a church bell, signalling a place of sanctuary and calm. The familiar smell of the old shop brought comfort to her. She looked over the latest bizarre artefacts lining the walls. A bright, colourful taxidermic bird stood motionless in a glass case. She had seen nothing like it before, the vivid hues of the impossibly long feathers demanding attention. She spotted another creature, a small animal she had only seen in a couple of books her Da had given her. A monkey she believed it to be, with its patchy white and black fur spread across the tiny slender limbs. She had once hoped to see these animals one day, on some far-fetched adventure, but not like this. There should be life in their eyes and movement in their limbs as they flew across the treetops, but they were now rigid statues of what they had once been.

"Alice?" She called out, pulling the velvet curtain to one side.

"Hello?"

"It's Bea, may I come through?" She edged her head further through the gap.

"Yes, come through, I'm so happy to see you." Her light, warm voice blew gently on the dying embers inside of Bea. At the sight of Alice's kind smile and outstretched hands, she broke down, sobbing.

"Oh Bea, what is it?" Alice dropped the minor items in her hand and in two steps she was cradling Bea like a baby. Bea let the last day, the last few months, flow out of her. Salty tears leaked their way into her mouth and dripped onto Alice's shoulder.

Alice stroked the top of her head as Bea let out a long-laboured breath.

"Come, love – you shall have tea and cake, before I ask anything – and then, only if you are ready to tell."

Bea felt lighter, somehow unburdened after she told Alice all about Joshua Mason and Captain Hanley. But kept out the truth of the earlier ordeal, under-playing what really happened, too ashamed to admit what had almost occurred. Just the act of beginning able to confide in someone, to say the words out loud, allowed Bea to see her situation in a new light. Alice encouraged Bea to stay for supper and gently advised her to tell her Da the complete story. But Bea knew she could never let him see the mistakes she had made, and the risks she had taken. She felt stronger, however; not alone or speechless. She looked up at Alice and clasped her hands, smiling at her, before turning back to the buttered cake, staring tremulously at the coloured bird through the gap in the curtains as she quietly ate her supper.

Chapter 23

August 1831

Bea had neglected the old harbour since she had bid farewell to Joshua, unable to cope with the memories. But now, she longed for them; a small reminder of happiness and love, instead of the fear and dread now filling every inch of her. She lowered herself down on to the wall and wrapped her consoling shawl around her shoulders as the cool wind burrowed through her. She became lost in watching the carriages embarking on the journey to Lancaster. They would race across the sands during the lowest tide, arriving just in time to avoid becoming engulfed by the rapidly rising waves, eating their way back up the sands. She had grown up hearing the stories of people and horses being swallowed alive by the hungry quicksand, a game of chance if they left a couple minutes outside the allotted time. As a child Bea had imagined that the poorer town-folk were somehow an offering, a sacrifice to the monstrous sea and sand, preying it didn't demand one of her own.

She watched the people leave on their journeys and felt envious. They had a plan; a destination when she did not. After Hanley had paid her his dreadful visit, a part of her knew she would never be free of him if she stayed. But if she could not remain at home, what could she do? Move to Lancaster on her own, work in a shop, in a mill, and live in a grimy bedsit, unable to pay the rent or the food in her belly with half the pay of the men, itself not enough to live off. Or she could follow in her sister's footsteps and work in a grand house, serving people like Joshua's family, knowing her place. Those prospects seemed almost more suffocating than remaining here. What did she want? Perhaps she could get involved with the Reformers, appealing to her Da. She wanted to help the fight, to throw herself in to the cause and find her own path.

"Beatrice?"

Bea stared round and then turned back towards the sands.

"What are you doing here?" her hoarse throat croaked out.

"What happened? Why have you ignored my messages? Refused to meet me?"

"I - it does not concern you anymore, Joshua - please leave." Her voice was calm and low.

"I want to know." His voice was stern and clear. He could see something was wrong. Her face was sullen, and she had lost her colour, and her spark.

"I do not wish to discuss it, please leave me alone." *If he leaves soon, I can hold on;* she told herself.

He lowered himself down on to the harbour wall, easing back into the familiar spot.

"Beatrice, I still care for you, we can forge this alternative path together. But first - please tell me what -" she winced and jumped at his soft touch on her shoulder.

"Why do you keep giving me cause for pain, sir? You have washed your hands of me, you do not want to be a part of my life."

"That is not true. I - " He stopped; her hunched distress startled him. "Beatrice, look at me - please look at me." She turned her head gently, focusing in on his eyes. "I have been looking for you – I have been coming to this spot each morning, hoping to find you. I wanted to tell you I still love you, and I *cannot* walk away from you." He delicately placed his hand to the side of her face, but she flinched at his touch, blinking with mistrust at his statement.

"Are you in earnest? You have chosen me over your family?"

"You doubt me? I thought it was my family I could not leave behind, but in fact it was you - you are a part of me."

"You say this now, but you will change your mind when you know."

"Trust me, tell me."

"I cannot..." She dropped her head as her courage failed her.

"Bea, you are frightening me, what has happened?"

"He is back... I turned him down - Captain Hanley - but he said I already belonged to him... he... tried... he tried to -" she began falteringly, the words catching in her throat.

"When did this happen?" he asked, straining to remain calm.

"A week past."

"What did he do, exactly?"

"He - he had just returned and requested that I see him. He came almost to the house, through the woods... and I refused him again. He didn't believe me; said I was his. He attempted to - force himself... I tried to fight him off... Then my Mam turned up, and he left."

"He cannot be allowed to get away with this!" Joshua's eyes had become dark and hard, and for a moment Bea was terrified of what he might be capable of.

"No, please..." she begged him, unable to catch her breath.

"I must - what action is your father taking?"

"None."

"That cannot be!" he exclaimed.

"I didn't tell him."

"Why?" His voice became softer again as he sensed conflict in her.

As she contemplated how to answer the question, her restless fingers twisted the fabric of her dress. "The shame."

"Bea, you have nothing to be ashamed about."

"I do" she nodded her head slowly.

"In what way?"

"I encouraged him when I should not have - he said it was my fault, and he is right."

Joshua gently laid one hand over her fretting fingers.

"Listen to me carefully this is NOT your fault. You welcomed his original attentions, but you did not encourage his subsequent behaviour. You have made your position quite clear to him, have you not?"

"Yes," she muttered.

"He blames you because it is his character to do so. None of the shame belongs on your shoulders." He eased his hand to the side of her face. "You are the most beautiful, loving woman I have ever known. We must not allow him to get away with this. I shall see that he does not."

Already tormented with the idea that she might have hampered his prospects with his family, Bea shrunk away from him. She could not bear pulling him down further.

"I cannot ask this of you. Please, leave me and this. . . ordeal behind you and walk away."

"I would do anything for you - I love you, do you not see it?"

"I love you too, but I cannot ask you to leave your family and all that you know behind anymore. If it got out, we could not remain here, your father would see to that, they would shun us from society. So where would we go, what should we do? It is too much to ask, I am not worthy of that, I see it clearly now."

"My dearest Bea, yes you are." He stroked the side of her face and wiped away the silent tear with his thumb. "If society cannot accept us being together, then we will leave this town and not look back. We can start afresh in Liverpool or Bristol. If you will do me the honour of marrying me, of course?" His last few words lingered between them. As the reality sank in, it brought forth a sense of happiness she did not dare acknowledge.

"Do you honestly... do you honestly mean that?"

"Yes, I do." He leant forward, delicately holding on to her, and brushed his lips softly to hers. In that moment he felt whole again, and he knew without a trace of doubt or discomfort that he had the will to make his promises come to pass.

"Tell me; what changed? I thought you could not leave your family?" The temptation of a kiss was breaking her resolve, and she tried to continue a rational trajectory before she gave in to him, as she knew she would.

"I had thought I could not; fear made me doubt both myself and our love. Fear of losing the comfort I have, of breaking with my family's expectations, but it turned out that the biggest fear I laboured under was the thought of losing you. - You have changed me, I do not look at things in the same way, I cannot go back. I love you, Bea, and I cannot lie to myself or to anyone else any longer." His hopeful smile brought a little light to her face.

"I love you too – but...," she gestured towards herself and what her position implied. "This has changed nothing for you?" Joshua looked at her, and his face spoke of peaceful resolve.

"You spoke once of building a new life: we will do it together. We will escape and make our own adventures."

"And we will do it together? Love and support each other, no matter what?"

"I promise you that in a month, you will be Mrs Mason, and we shall start a new life together far from here." He leant forward to kiss Bea again, and this time, she did not pull away.

Chapter 24

"Hanley!"

A light spittle of rain fell on to the various men spilling forth in groups of mill workers, shop labourers and seamen. Gathering in small conferences like gossiping wives, they compared stories of misgivings, animated and gesticulating. A few of the seamen attempted to sober up against the dirty wall, their eyes confused by the multiple figures passing by. Two sailors stood in the lengthening shadows cast by a sleepy sun, as they changed money into goods.

"Hanley - Get out here!" Joshua bellowed louder, from the very depth of his lungs.

A stillness swept over the men, their attention now falling on him with hopes of a fight. They were eager to be entertained, not ready for the night's revelries to be over, particularly given the sport Hanley would have with this gentleman.

"What d'you suppose you want with my Captain?" one seaman slurred.

"That is between himself and I", Joshua replied curtly.

"If you come here and start wi'th'Captain, then it ain't between you and him, it's between all of us." An eager groan of agreement stemmed from a pocket of men. They crowded around Joshua in a horseshoe.

"Hanley - show yourself or do you let your lackeys fight all your battles?"

"What you want, Mason?" Hanley stepped out of the doorway, in the process of redressing himself.

Joshua recalled Bea's words; what Hanley had attempted to do. His temper rose and felt his blood pulse in his ears. He waited until Hanley was clear enough away from his men, then with no warning, he leant forward quickly and smashed his fist into the right side of Hanley's jaw. Hanley staggered and toppled backwards into his crew with his jaw in the air. After a couple of moments, he doggedly regained his balance and turned to face the younger man. A broad grin spread across his lips. Fat rain droplets fell with regularity upon Joshua's head.

Ignoring this threat from above, he shook off the pain in his knuckles. The shoal of seamen closed around them both; acting as one, they edged closer. Hanley pushed them away, arms outstretched, indicating his decision. With the back of his hand, he removed a speckle of blood pooling in the crest of his lips.

"I take it you have been to see that whore of yours. I had heard rumours of you and a girl - it seems like we both like to play in the dirt."

Joshua could smell alcohol, sweat, and the smell of an unwashed female body. An onslaught of adrenaline swept over him as he closed his fist again, ready for the next round.

"Watch -"

Suddenly the air was jolted from Joshua's body as a sharp pain contracted internally, making his stomach convulse. He doubled over, attempting to regain some breath back in his lungs, as his mouth watered, and the back of his throat filled with sick.

Hanley leant over next to Joshua's ear.

"Tell her she is a teasing whore – how dare she betray me, I have already paid for her and I will collect from her what is mine in time."

"If you go anywhere near her again -"

"You will do what?" A disturbing smile stretched across Hanley's face.

"I know what you... It is clear what I should do with vermin like you." Joshua spat out the pooling sick inside his mouth, trying to control the urge to retch.

"You know nothing about me, and you will do nothing."

Suddenly aware of his audience again, Hanley's tactic changed.

"I know she desires a man to show her what to do, not a boy. You could never satisfy her like I can."

Hanley laughed as he made a rocking sexual gesture to the men. They cheered him on lustily as they copied his moves in Joshua's direction. Abruptly Joshua roared and threw himself towards Hanley, hooking him under the chin with all the force he could muster. Hanley almost fell, and when he had shaken the ringing from his ears and massaged his face a little, the smile had disappeared from his lips. He was done with merely playing; it was now time for the kill. He pushed his chest out and rolled his shoulders back. A daring hand landed on his right shoulder.

"Cap: eyes watching," one of the more sober men whispered loudly in Hanley's ear.

"We need to finish this." Hanley hissed at Joshua.

"Agreed."

"Tomorrow at dawn," Hanley demanded.

"Where?"

"At the edge of the woods, past Dragley Beck."

"Fine." Joshua turned his back on Hanley, pushing his arms out against the weight of the gathering men. He heard a tide of laughter reaching out at his back. He recognised some familiar faces on the street opposite, shaking their heads in disapproval as they fostered tomorrow's gossip. He bowed his head, avoiding all eye contact as his mind formed a plan for the next seven hours. He headed toward Ford House to find Max.

"...TELL ME AGAIN WHY YOU are fighting Captain Hanley over this girl? Are you quite certain she is worth the risk? He is a damn excellent shot, Mason. You could have the pick of any lady in the County – you have Dawn ready to make love to you at the smallest excuse, and you pick a cottage girl over your future - and your family?"

Max had been attempting to find a reason for Joshua's actions with which he would be satisfied for almost an hour at the club, in a haze of whiskey and smoke, as his friend attempted to give him an adequately detailed picture of the last few months. At first Max had thought it was some sort of wild joke. But as Joshua continued to explain, a sobering resistance forced its way into his objections.

For the sake of his long-established friendship, he was unwilling to support what could be Joshua's ultimate destruction, and remained defiant until the last, finally unable to watch Joshua walk alone out of the doorway with his swollen fist and set lips. Like a boy beginning dragged by his governess on a walk in the rain, he meandered behind Joshua as the first rays of dawn broke over the hills. Thrashing his cane on to the helpless plants in his path, they crumpled helplessly under his anger and frustration. Joshua purposely walked by the animal tracks, avoiding detection on the way to the woods. Trailing misty rays of glowing air, the sun stirred behind them. Blackbirds and wrens warmed up their vocal cords, ready for the daily performance ahead.

"Are you with me or not? I must know for certain." Joshua came to a halt without warning and turned to face Max.

"I am with you because I do not want to see you hurt... but not for one moment do I condone or understand why you are pursuing that girl - to the death."

"Her name is Beatrice," remarked Joshua thinly.

"I do not care what her name is, you still have not explained -"

"Trust me, can't you, Max?"

"That is your business then, I suppose. But why are you chancing your family's entire prospects on her? Your father will probably have no other sons; you are placing his future in jeopardy as well."

"Should I choose my family over future happiness? She is unlike any other woman I have ever known". Joshua looked steadily at his friend, willing him to see that what he felt for Bea was greater than either of them, or the lives they had once planned.

"That is because until now you have only allowed yourself to know well-bred, society-trained, accomplished young women. There are many other kinds."

"Max -"

"Is there no chance at all for you with Lady Dawn? You are well suited, and with her title you could make a name for yourself - I thought that was what you wanted? To be independent, to forge your own path?"

"But I will... do you not see? We will forge our own path together, move away and start a new life, make it my own. My father will always be the master, and I, marching to the beat of his drum, if I remain and marry the person he deems right. Why should we always conform? How can we call ourselves free men if we bind ourselves and our offspring to a narrative of rules we do not even fully understand? She has made me see I can be more, do more - with her beside me. "

"Because of Beatrice?"

"Because of Beatrice."

Max took the extra few strides and fell in behind Joshua.

"Is she happy that you should give everything up for her?"

Max's unrelenting attitude grated on Joshua's nerves.

"It is not my choice to leave my family behind, nor my business prospects. My father made that decision for us."

"You cannot honestly believe that any family of note would entertain her as a daughter? I am with your father on this one - if you chose to marry her, you choose to close the door upon all that came before. You would become tainted by association."

"Including yourself?" Joshua spun round, infuriated, clenching his fists.

"Naturally," Max replied coolly. "Let's win the battle first, before we win the war, shall we?" he replied gently at the look on his friend's face.

They reached the edge of the clearing. The early morning mist had barely absorbed into the earth as the golden red sky began its advance on the fading night. Like a lion at the back of the pride, Hanley lurked patiently on the outer edge of the trees for his prey, perched on a stump and barely visible amongst the ferns. His hair was slicked back into a ponytail, and the young growth of a red beard shimmered against the dark copper tan of his jaw. He might have been mistaken for an outlander or pirate with his worn leather jacket, stained shirt, and dirty boots. A disturbing clarity shone in his face as he cleaned out the barrel of his pistol. Next to him, a small broad man leant against a silver birch, staring at them as they approached. He wore a mucky ill-fitting jacket and leant down to whisper into Hanley's ear as the others approached. Joshua took a moment to steady his nerves. He grabbed his silver case from his inside-pocket. Only a single cigarette remained. Praying it was not an omen, he tapped it lightly on the lid and placed it in his mouth. As the first wisp of smoke fluttered from his lips, he felt his focus sharpen and his intent clear.

Another man weaved himself through the trees on the far side; Mr Armstrong, also from the gentlemen's club, who had stepped in on occasions like this before without hesitation, and without asking questions.

"Are you sure, my friend?" Max placed his hand on Joshua's shoulder.

"Gentlemen, please approach to the centre of the clearing" Mr Armstrong commanded.

"Joshua, are -"

"Yes." Joshua flung the cigarette stub into the undergrowth as he turned round and gave his friend a strained smile. He could feel his heart beating twice for every footstep he took, rubbing his clammy hands against his trouser legs. Mr Armstrong carefully carried a large rectangle mahogany box, and crouched calm and collective as he opened it, indicated his approval at the treasure inside. Hanley positioned himself casually two feet away from Joshua, with clarity in his eyes and an agitated grin on his taught face.

"Nervous?" he sneered.

"No" Joshua replied, his voice a pitch higher than he would have liked. He coughed and cleared his throat.

Hanley laughed loudly from deep within his chest.

"Well, this isn't going to take long, I see."

"Gentlemen, once you are ready, I would like to go over the rules of the duel..."

Mr Armstrong reciting the formalities and turned the delicately engraved box in his hand toward the two men, displaying the pair of Wogdon & Barton Flintstock duelling pistols. With their softly gleaming walnut handles and engraved silverwork, they seemed harmless, couched silently in their bed of crushed velvet.

Mr Armstrong pulled out a guinea. "Please call, heads or tails?"

"Heads" Joshua quickly called out.

Mr Armstrong tossed the coin high.

"Heads; Mr Mason, would you like to choose your pistol first?"

Mr Armstrong held the box directly in front of Joshua. Like a child hesitating over an array of crafted chocolates, his hand hovered. He gently picked up the pistol nearest to him as he cradled the weight in his palm. Hanley took his without a second glance.

"Gentlemen, on my first command you will turn away from each other. On my second command you will walk ten paces forward, and on my third command you will turn and face each other. You will not shoot until I have given the order to do so. The first person who draws blood, wins the duel. All proceedings will be over. Do I make myself clear?"

"Yes".

"Are we ready? Then, first command gentlemen please." The two men rotated on the spot until their backs were facing each other.

"Second command gentlemen please."

"...Eight, nine..." The numbers rolled on as his throat tightened, dry and hollow. *"Ten!"* His feet froze to the spot as he took a long, steady breath.

"Third command gentlemen, please."

Joshua slowly turned his feet back towards the inner circle. His eyes fixed on Hanley. He wondered how many times he had done this before. Unheralded, thoughts of his life five years ago sprang to mind; strolling around Cambridge, he would never have thought he would be standing in this moment ready to shoot another human being.

"Pistols." He felt the icy smooth silver under his thumb as he cocked back the barrel.

"Aim."

He straightened his arm out in front on him, tunnelling his sight on Hanley alone. *Merely a dog,* he thought emptily.

"Fire!"

Joshua's index finger tightened around the small, cold trigger. With a forceful kick, the pistol jarred back in his hand. A lifetime passed before his eyes. Clinging on to the last breath inside his inflated lungs, he heard a deafening noise in his ears, as though far off in the distance. A cry echoed out around him. His gun toppled from his hand and landed with a thud before his feet. His heart stopped for a single moment in pure fear, and then, when no pain came, his breath exploded out of his chest. No wound. He checked himself again, making sure he was not mistaken. Still, the continuous ringing noise stood out against the muffled background. Life came back to his shocked body. Stunned, his eyes fixed upon Hanley, who was bent double, a few steps back from his original position.

"Did I... actually ... hit him?"

A wet red patch was forming on the right side underneath the Captain's armpit. From Joshua's position it did not a look like a mortal wound. He could feel a hand patting him on the back and Max's voice reaching through the abyss.

"You did it, you bloody well did it! How fast you were off the draw and hitting him like that in the ribs, disrupting his aim. You would have been a dead man if you had not pulled it off; the shot missed your head by an inch - You all right, there, Mason?"

"Yes, yes I am ..." Joshua glimpsed Hanley's face as he pulled himself upright. The fury in his stare was palpable.

Mr Armstrong declared calmly to no one in particular: "Mr Mason wins, drawing blood from Captain Hanley."

"I am not satisfied; it is barely a scratch!"

"I will only allow one attempt."

"This is not over Mason – come, Gregson!" Hanley winced as he tried to stand once more. Joshua let out a long, deep breath of relief as they moved away into the woodland thicket. Max chivvied him on, taking him by the shoulder as they walked.

"We had better leave in case your shots were heard. Come on, man."

"I could do with a drink."

Joshua smiled weakly, and followed without protest, attempting to ignore the rising dread in his gut. He could not help but think that instead of putting the bear down, he had only angered it further.

Chapter 25

"*What kind of weak, pathetic creature would allow a girl such as her to make a mockery of him; no son of mine would suffer a woman to bring him to his knees... You're a bastard, a disgrace - yes, you always were a weak one, boy. You own her: she is yours, make her realise it ... To send that pitiful excuse of a man to fight you! He saw you bleed from his shot, and in return you allowed him to walk free?*"

"BE SILENT."

"*You do not deserve my name or my blood... Peoples across the oceans fear our family, but not one person in this small town of peasant-folk fears you - I should have drowned you like a pup the minute your mother brought you into this world.*"

His father's face stared back at him from the glass, cold, furious, and full of death.

With a cry like an animal in pain, Hanley's clenched fist smashed into the mirror. With a start, he broke from his reverie and stared stupidly at the dark liquid welling up in the small cuts in his knuckles. Slowly, he picked out a piece of glass from his flesh, gazing at its point, watching as a wine-dark droplet threatened to fall onto the wooden boards.

"Captain?" Gregson stepped into the room. He had seen this behaviour from Hanley before. He knew better than most that his employer was tormented in more ways than one. Still in a state of violent stupor, Hanley swung round, pinned Gregson to the wall and held up his bloody fist in the man's face.

"I AM HANLEY," he bellowed, no recognition in his eyes.

"It's Gregson, sir..."

Hanley hesitated for a moment, and then dropping his first mate, he strode over to the dresser, picked up a half-clean glass, tipping out a few shards of broken mirror, and filled it with rum. He gulped down the medicine and poured himself a second. Once the colour had returned to his face, Gregson began a careful approach.

"I'm here to dress you, sir…?"

"Aye, aye. Do what you must." Hanley sat down on the edge of the bed as Gregson knelt beside him and peeled the blood-stained shirt away from the wound in his side.

"Have a care, man."

"Sir."

Joshua's bullet had grazed him, nothing to what he had survived before. Gregson dipped the clean cloth into the washstand bowl and patted away the crusted blood. He poured a small amount of rum onto the wound, wiped it away, and prepared to sew up the two-inch of torn flesh.

"I am going to take away everything she loves." The comment came from nowhere, and Gregson knew it needed no reply. He knew it might require him to assist further soon, and he hoped it would be to his advantage, in some small way. He listened carefully, trying not to break the spell. Hanley spoke again, as though to someone behind the sailor.

"There has been no one like her… I wanted her… her light, you see… She was so sweet, and clean… she could have saved me. But instead she mocked me, made me look like a fool. I will make her understand me, how she should have understood in the first place… and when I am done with her, she will regret her foolishness."

AFTER A NIGHT OF THUNDER and lightning refusing the town sleep, the heat finally relented. The dry parched earth drank in the rain, transforming the landscape into a wash of green once more. The weary Ulverston inhabitants awoke to a forceful sea breeze, shaking the foundations of their stone cottages, and rattling their chimneys. Bea could hear slates being flicked off from their roof, smashing to the ground as though in excitement. She stared out the window, watching the loose hay, leaves and petals throw themselves against the thrashing trees.

Holly and Rowan were still curled up together by the fire after a restless night. Bea had been wondering over the past couple of days if she would ever see her family again. She would be leaving in a week or so, to make a new life with Joshua, and still could not find the words to tell them. She nestled herself opposite the girls, occasionally stirring the pot of stew. In a strange way, she felt as if these two were her own children. She had been more of a mother to them than their own; teaching them what kindness and love really looked like. Her heart ached at the thought of never knowing the women they would someday become. She suddenly realised, if their young minds would remember her and all that they did together, or would she end up being some forgot dream? Standing up, she gently swept back a curl of hair away from Holly's face, grabbed the pail by the door and made her way outside.

The wind blew away the stagnant thoughts in her head as it tore through her own hair. Her dress clung to her legs and body as she attempted to fight through the compact air to the water pump.

"How dare you!"

Bea faintly heard her Mam's shrill voice battling through the elements behind her. Bea continued to pump the water, her face set, ready for one of their usual confrontations.

"Are you listening to me?"

Her Mam's fingernails bit into Bea's flesh as her hand prised her daughter's hand from around the pump handle like a hawk clawing into its prey.

Bea spun round. "That hurts, get off me, Mam."

"Good!" Her Mam's eyes were wide and round, filled with rage.

"What are you doing?"

"What am I doing? What have *you* been doin' with yourself more like?"

"What do you mean?" A cold lump rose in Bea's chest.

"It is all over town, Mrs Dent says." Her Mam's lips were quivering.

"What is? Get off my hand, it's hurting!"

Bea dropped the pale and used her spare hand to try to prize free from the painful hold, adept at the movement after years of practice. The persistent wind stole mouthful of words from their lips. Rubbing her hand, her mother spat her reply venomously.

"That you - a harlot - are... *meeting* regular with men. I used to jest about it, to warn you - but it seems it was true all along!"

"It's not true - it's not like that."

"It's either not true, or it's certainly like that?"
"I am not a harlot!"
"So, you haven't been meeting up with men in secret?"
"I can explain, I - "
Bea failed to spot her Mam's hand coming as it smacked hard against her cheek. The throbbing pain followed by a wave of heat engulfed her face. Seizing a moment to steady herself, she glimpsed her mother's livid face. The disgust was clear in her dark eyes and her twisted snarl.
"You -"
The words spluttered out in shock. Bea couldn't count the number of times her Mam had slapped her, but this time it felt different.
"I should do a sight more than that. You never cared proper for this family."
Her mother's dramatic temper escalated, and her arm swung towards Bea again, but this time she was ready.
The lack of warmth and understanding made it a challenge for Bea to stop her own temper from rising. She gasped and tried again.
"I can explain!"
"Your Da will be home any minute now, you can explain to him before he gives you the strap and the door."
"You would cast me out? You've not even *listened* to me!"
"Nothing you have to say will save your father's good name."
"The truth might - if you would only hear it."
"HA - they have already condemned you."
In that moment Bea could swear her mother sounded almost happy. Happy to be in the heat of such a drama.
"By whom? Mrs Dent, by any chance?"
"Yes!"
"You trust Mrs Dent more than your own child?"
"I've a good reason to."
"Boys - into the house - explain this." Her Da's deep steady voice broke through their argument. Bea felt his arm warm and firm on her shoulder.
"I went to see Mrs Dent, as is my usual... And she told me - it is all over town - *that Beatrice is a harlot and been meeting up with men alone at all hours at the harbour and in the woods.*"

"Bea's a good lass, she'd n'er be doin' the likes o'that – would you love?" Her Da squeezed her shoulder reassuringly.

"She just *confessed!*" her Mam hissed.

"I did not confess to anything!" Bea took a deep breath, pushing down her quickening temper.

"You told me you have been meeting up with men."

"No, I did not say that. I said I could explain, and then you hit me!" Bea clenched her fists in an attempt to control herself.

Mr Lightfoot turned his daughter to face him.

"Beatrice, have you been meeting up with men? Or ...?"

"I have never lain with a man."

"But you have..." Her mother pointed at her, ready for a second onslaught.

"Martha! Let me." Giving her a warning look, he looked at Bea anxiously. "Have you met with a man at night, in secret? The truth, lass."

Bea took a long steady calming breath.

"One man, the best man I know save you Da, and...", she took a gulp of cold air, "we are in love AND we're going to marry, a week from now."

"What's his name?"

Something had broken in her Da's voice; it wasn't anger, Bea could tell that, but a deep wrenching of the heart, unfamiliar in her stoic, trudging parent.

"Joshua Mason."

"Not Captain Hanley?" her Mam gasped in surprise.

"No!"

"Mr Mason's son, who owns the quarries, mines and ships?" asked Mr Lightfoot slowly.

"Yes."

"He will never marry you! You turned down Captain Hanley for this boy...? His father will never let you marry!" her mother interjected hysterically.

"I turned down Captain Hanley because he is a vile man - he tried to... I... cannot be with him."

Mr Lightfoot stepped between wife and daughter.

"How long has this been going on?"

"I met Joshua at the May Day dance."

"You've been meetin' with 'im in private?"

"Yes, in the early hours - but it's been proper Da, we've done nothing wrong."

"You think it's proper to meet a man alone, away from home, at night?" Her Mam spoke each word slowly so that their import would sink deep into her husband's thoughts.

"We only talked; nowt more happened. But we were spotted one time - that must be where the rumour came from."

"You might as well be a whore - at least this way you would have got some money out of it! He will never marry you, foolish girl, and now you have ruined yours and your family's prospects - The only hope you have now is to take up Captain Hanley's offer."

The words filtered through Beatrice's wall of strength, cracking it, and bringing it crashing down. She tried to fight back the tears, knowing they would only add fuel to her Mam's ever-abundant fire. Mr Lightfoot paced on the spot, the cool wind making his angry face even whiter.

"How long have you -?"

"A few months. His father found out and refused . . ."

"Ah-ha - What did I tell you!" her Mam choked.

"So, we tried, but we cannot be apart, so we are going to be married without his blessing." Bea could feel the tears falling, even as she said the words that gave her hope of a new happiness.

"And what, live off fresh air?" her mother chortled.

"No - he is an educated gentleman; he will find work." Bea was tired of the onslaught of insults, tired of the never-ending fighting; fighting to be heard, to be alive. She turned to her father.

"Da? I am sorry - Say something?" Bea tried reaching for him, to force him to make eye contact.

He froze to the ground, thoughts overtaking motion. Then he snapped.

"You've been plottin' and schemin' this length o' time behind my back? I thought we had no secrets 'tween us, lass - I thought you understood how I felt about that class o' people. But now you're sidin' wi' one o' them - Leavin' this home for him!"

The pained betrayal was evident in his voice. Bea had never seen her Da like this before. He was scaring her for the first time in her entire life.

"I am sorry Da, that I did not tell you – I mean, I was going to tell you - I thought - I knew you would be against it."

She reached out again for his once-comforting safety. Instead, he grabbed her wrists and thrust them to one side. He took a step back and cried out in a hoarse voice she had never heard before.

"*When did you get so devious?*"

"Sorry, Da," she breathed.

"No... I don't want to look at you..." He turned his back on her and kept walking.

"Da, please -!" she cried after him.

Her Mam stepped in front of her as she invaded her space, stopping Bea's chances to plead further.

"How could you be so selfish?"

"I need to speak to Da," Bea attempted to push past. Her Mam's fingers gripped her upper arm, nipping flesh and fabric as one. Bea was limp as a doll, still watching her father's back.

"What about me? What will people think of me in all this? Did you think about that whilst you were acting as you have?"

"I do not care what people think, only for Da, and for those who care for me."

"You should: this will follow you around for the rest of your life."

"Let me pass - I need to explain to Da."

"He does not want to see you, you hurt him with your lies and deceit." The bitter truth hung heavy in the air between them.

"I want to try - leave me be - you are hurting me."

"Maybe you should have thought about that before now!"

"GET OFF OF ME." Bea bawled into her Mam's face. She wrenched her arm free, looked about her desperately like a frightened doe, and, not seeing her father, she gave a heaving sob, and dashed into the cottage.

Chapter 26

Later that afternoon, a man on a black horse pulled up quietly where little Holly Lightfoot was playing, a place she shouldn't be, under the grimy eaves of the shed, and told her to give a smartly sealed letter to her eldest sister without her parents noticing. Holly, hoping it would cheer Bea up enough to get her to come and play, snook upstairs and slid it under the bedroom door. With a quick thankful kiss on the top of Holly's head, Bea wrapped her shawl tightly around her shoulders, and ran silently out the back door to meet with Joshua.

Bea stopped walking and turned to face the dark lane, stretching emptily behind her. Twenty minutes of solitude in the night air had cooled her excitement a little and brought forth an unfamiliar nervousness. She squinted and thought she saw a figure standing behind her on the road, but nothing moved. Perhaps it was a shadow or a branch stretching out awkwardly across the path, she told herself, ignoring her gut that was telling something was wrong.

She continued walking again, but more slowly, trying to tread softly. Then the back of her neck and her chest went tight and cold as she heard, without mistaking it this time - footsteps behind her. Without another thought she ran down the lane towards the harbour, to where Joshua would be waiting. The following footsteps took chase, as the drumming sound of the pursuer's feet echoed in her chest. With her palms clammy, she tried holding her skirt higher, so she had more room to move, but she knew with a quickening terror that the footsteps were growing closer, no matter how hard she ran. Only a little further and she would see Joshua, she thought. She pushed harder, and then -

A churning feeling stirred in her stomach as she flew through the air. With a crack, her hands hit the rough gravel, and her elbow gave way as the side of her face slammed into the sodden earth. A bright, sharp pain radiated around her left eye and temple. Losing focus, she attempted to pull herself up. She slumped down again as her head spun in circles, whilst hot liquid trickled down her cheek. The footsteps had stopped. She strained her mind to focus on the shadowy figure now above her.

"I loved you," a familiar voice said calmly. Bea used all her strength to heave herself up with her good arm. "You made me love you. You made me hope for change." He bent down low next to her.

"Captain? ...I am sorry..." she gasped, trying to rise again.

"You sent your little boy to fight me, to frighten me off. You have played us both like fools."

"What? Who do you . . ." she tried to get the words out between her shallow breath's. Her heart was climbing its way out of her chest and into her throat. Everything felt wrong. She needed to get away, to call out for help. Where was Joshua?

"*Whore*."

He gripped her tighter on to her shoulder, and with one movement flung her on to her back. She cried out in pain as the back of her head bounced off the ground; her head cloudily, unable to stitch one thought to another. His icy hands squeezed hold of her calves and with one forceful action, he spilt her legs apart. Realising what he meant to do, she failed her arms about, screaming. Ducking from her reach, he crept in between her thighs, pulling up her skirt. One of her hands caught him on the arm, and with no hesitation he punched her brutally full in the face. Blood filled her mouth and stopped her screams as she tried to spit it out. He clamped down on her wrists, shifting them together as one in a swift, practised motion above her head.

"This is all your fault - Look what you've made me do, Beatrice... You gave yourself to him, so now you can give yourself to me . . .".

He grasped at her jaw with his free hand. He slowly leaned down, staring hard into her eyes, and kissed her. Bea shifted around, trying somehow to break free.

"I like it when you struggle, it pleases me." Hanley groaned into her ear. "No one can disturb us this time... I knew you would come if your little boy asked." His hand was yanking her skirt higher around her thighs.

"NO." She cried thinly, her voice sounding low and coarse, as though not her own.

"Stop fighting, I know you want me; I have more of a right than he does..."

His face hovered above hers, and his free hand moved down to the front of his trousers.

"NO. NO. *NO!*" She howled as loudly as she could, feeling him shifting his trousers out of the way. His sweaty hand clamped over her mouth. Her mind, protecting her for what was about to come, became numb. The growing pressure on her nose and mouth made it difficult to breathe as she fixed her gaze on the dark sky above. With one hand he pulled her under garments free. First came the damp, sickening pressure, followed by pain. It was sharp like her Da's gutting knife, tearing upwards in her pelvis. With every thrust the pain became stronger, ripping at her insides. Her body rocked back and forth on the spot, making a shallow indent in the ground. He groaned in her ear with pleasure, still clamping down on her mouth. His movement became faster as he began making a strange noise. She felt his body become tense and then release as he howled into her neck. He pulled out of her slowly, as though drunk, leaving her legs hanging open.

"A maid after all."

She remained ridged, unable to acknowledge what he had just done. He realised his hands off her and yet she still could not move. She was indented into the ground, she was dirt, this was now where she belonged.

Her gaze travelled down; she felt the fabric of his trousers rub against her legs; he was still kneeling between her ankles. The breeze changed direction, bringing with it a sudden onslaught of foul smells, but not that of Hanley. She strained her eyes further to get a clearer picture, but it was too dark. It made little sense; the silhouette had suddenly become shorter and rounder than before. Panic engulfed her at the idea of reliving the same encounter with a fresh assailant.

NO, her thoughts called out, *No, not again!*

A force inside of her filled her with determination and the strength to fight as rage brought sensation back to her limbs. *This* was not where she belonged.

This time he was not pinning her down unlike Hanley, she was able to move. She had to be smart. If she acted too fast and tried to run, they would only beat her down. But she could try to fight her way out; she had to. With her hands above her head, she grasped for a stone in the dirt. Finding one, she gripped it with bloody fingers, and heaved her arm up with all the strength she could muster. The rock came smashing into the side of the second assailant's head. A crimson trickle flowed out from his hair, the shine visible in the moonlight.

It threw the new figure backwards, but the force was not strong enough to knock him out. She quickly pulled her arm back for another strike.

"Oh no you don't, you bitch!" Snarled the other man as a hand came from behind and grabbed the hand holding the stone. She rolled her head backwards and glimpsed Hanley bent over her. His fingers restricting her blood flow as the strength of his hand crushed the muscles against bone, causing the stone to tumble out of her grip and thud to the ground.

"*Get off me*!" Bea screamed.

With her other hand, she quickly grabbed a handful of dirt and dried leaves and flung them at the man in front. Hanley behind her laughed as he reached out for the other hand.

"Fucking bitch!" the other cried out. His knuckles slammed into her jaw as she felt her neck crack backward under the force. Her head swirled around in a raging current, as the voice inside her head cried out; "Please, no; don't!"

A disgusting moaning noise emerged from his throat. Like a horse's long tongue curling up to consume a piece of apple, she felt his hot mouth slide from her chest up to her neck. She waited until his head was closer to hers and tried to bite him, but missed as he moved backwards in time. An amused chuckle rippled out of Hanley's mouth.

"I told you she would be feisty".

She gazed downward at the other man and kicked her legs out. If she could hurt him enough, he might let her go.

"Fight all you like, whore. But you won't be getting out alive. This time you've gone too far, he won't let you live – you'll have no further use to him now. I'll be killing you either way, you little slut..."

Before she realised what was happening, Hanley's right arm struck the front of Gregson's chest twice. Jolting forwards, a shocked, questioning expression spread over his face whilst his open mouth made no sound. Bea could make out a small glint of silver, coated with a thick ruby liquid in Hanley's right hand, as he pulled his arm back. Gregson looked down at the red liquid bubbling gently from his lower waistcoat. Bea found her voice once more and let out an ear-shattering scream. She could feel the warmth of the blood as it dripped and pooled into her dress. The first mate pressed his hand against his chest, not taking his sight off Hanley and gave out a gut churning moan. Then his body slumped down directly on top of Bea with a dull thud.

"Help me out?" For a moment she thought he'd done it to save her until Hanley bent down towards Bea's ear and whispered.

"Did you really think I would let you get away with what you did?" his chilling, bitter voice echoing in her thoughts. "That I would be happy with just a fuck?" His bloody hand stroked the side of her face as if comforting a child, smearing a red stain from cheek to hair. "Do you think I would not find out about you and the Mason boy running off together? - That was meant to be *us*. You and I... You cannot humiliate me and go unpunished... the entire town knows you are a whore... well, now you are a murdering whore, spread-eagled for everyone to see. And I will watch as your life crumbles around you, everyone you have loved will pay the price for your choices, and if I cannot have you, then no one else will!" Hanley gripped her throat and kissed her again in a final goodbye. "You caused this."

As he pulled back, she found it difficult to recognise him. She noticed anger and fatigue etched into his face where there used to be a handsome warmth. That was now gone, leaving behind a stranger.

Her stomach felt warm and wet with Gregson's blood. His body had become limp and heavy, squashing the breath out of her lungs, and she could not build up enough strength to lift him up and slide herself out from beneath.

Hanley dropped the knife beside her hand and took a step backwards. She noticed something familiar about that knife... something about the jagged edge, how it was missing a tooth. She saw, half-conscious now, marks etched into the wooden handle, but the dark blood obscured any chance at reading them. She tried to reach out for it feebly, but Hanley had left it an inch too far.

"Please - help me... Please do not... -" She thought, she saw something pass over his face that had never been there before: pain. But then he walked away, calling out over his shoulder:

"I will see you again soon, Beatrice."

Bea gasped for help one last time before the world became black.

Chapter 27

"I didn't do it. You can't put me in here - I'm *innocent*." The men clasped tight on either side of her, ignoring her cries, and hauled her into the dark, dank room. Bea stumbled backwards, slipping on the slimy straw underneath her feet.

"I need to speak with the magistrate! I have to -". The heavy lacquered door slammed shut as the bolt shunted through, sealing her in. Bea pounded her fists against the door "*PLEASE*." Clinging tight to the small iron bars, she stared through the square hole in the door. Already departing, one shouted in a rehearsed manner:

"He'll see you when *he* is ready!"

Without another word, the men wandered back down the corridor they had just dragged her up, taking the only source of light with them. Bea leant back against the door. There was a sharp pain on her temple and smeared crusted blood down her face. Her left eye was swollen shut, with a dull ache and a stinging sensation each time she tried to blink; her right eye bloodshot and itched. And yet worst of all was the pain inside, a constant physical reminder with each cramping sensation in her pelvis. A sharp stinging sensation called out angrily with each step, and the evidence was smeared across her thighs; he had taken her maidenhood. She felt disgusting, filthy; as if she would never be clean again. Unwilling to confront what had happened fully in her mind, she trembled, focussing instead on the physical aspect of her new condition, feeling about for a dry patch of straw with which to wipe herself, to wipe away *him*. She could feel the large, stiff bloodstain over her stomach area, and suddenly a vivid image of the dead man lying on top of her came back to her, filling the moment. She gasped involuntarily, and in the silence of the dark room, she finally allowed her tears to fall as she crumpled to the floor. Pulling her legs up to her chest in an attempt to make herself disappear entirely, she rocked back and forth, trying to shut everything out; trying to die inside her head.

SHE HAD AWOKEN TO SOMEONE slapping her face. As her swollen eyes had peeled slightly open, she had made out an older man and woman standing over her, staring at her in fear. She remembered the stench of the dead man hanging limply, pinning her down. The unmistakable scent of death had filled her senses; the powerful taste of metal had hung in the air. She remembered trying to plead with the man and women to help her, trying to tell them she had been attacked, but her voice had died in her throat every time she tried to push the words out. They had stood there, whispering to one another, the woman throwing her a disapproving glare as she hugged her ragged knitted shawl around her as though to protect herself. She remembered the sound of little footsteps running down the path towards her. How the squelching mud had become louder, stirring the older woman's interest. She could remember hearing the panting breath issue from the small boy as he said something to the woman. The woman had nodded her head and patted the boy on his shoulders. Then Bea had passed out once more, their three strained faces hovering as though disembodied above her.

BEA INCHED AROUND THE pitch-black room, her cramping legs cried out for movement. Following the lines in the walls, her fingers explored the rough bricks as her feet shuffled in the filthy straw. As she carefully crept about, a disgusting odour met her nostrils. She stumbled closer to the dreadful smell, keeping one hand skimming over the wall whilst the other tightly pinched her nose to stop her gagging. Her foot encountered an empty metal bucket, her toilet for the duration of her stay. The idea of being in the dark long enough to resort to use it even once terrified her. Every second she was here, suspected of murder, gave Captain Hanley more time to escape. Her Da, and her brothers and sisters suddenly sprang to mind; all the accusations her mother had screeched at her were as good as true now. Anger and grief swelled up inside her; she roared at the top of her lungs and slapped her hands against the wall, heartbroken at her own stupidity. The wall absorbed her distraught frustration.

So close to a life of happiness with Joshua; what would he think now? Her physical trauma and her anguish gave way to fatigue. Her throbbing red hands, covered in a mossy slime, grasped on to the forgiving bricks. Catching her breath, she leant against the enclosing wall. Something inside her fought the overwhelming desire to surrender, but she pushed it away, taking a deep breath, and then almost retched at the stench as her left foot shuffled the newly discovered toilet out the way. She fell back against the wall once more, curling up in the dirt and cried herself to sleep.

SHE WOKE TO A HAMMERING sound as the vibrations travelled through the door. A click, followed by a thud, resonated behind her.

"Hello?"

Bea scrambled to her feet, peering through the bars once more. The taller of the two men stood outside the door this time. Bea cautiously took a few steps back, allowing space for the door to open. Within a single stride, the man entered, bearing a lantern. For the first time, Bea could see an accurate picture of where she had been placed. Mucky straw lined the ground like a sty, with blackened green moss growing on the damp old bricks, permeated by streaks of orange, where years of trickling water had left their mark. He gripped her hard, nipping her skin through her dress. She didn't fight or resist; if she seemed demur and humble, the magistrate might be more inclined to listen to what she had to say.

They both squeezed down the long corridor over the smooth slabs of stone. Her feet skipped in step as he hauled her over the stones. Bea noticed another similar cell door further down the corridor, with a familiar face peering out between the bars. A man she had seen before... but where, she could not remember.

A small room opened before her, with a tired wooden table, and four chairs scattered around. In the middle of the room stood Magistrate Forester, and a smaller man, who she just about recognised as one of her jailers. Fixed around the room were a handful of candles, drooping to the side in their tarnished stands, half burnt through, and in the middle of the far wall lay a modest Inglenook fireplace. Vacant of a warm welcoming fire, the empty grate gaped, dark and unsettling. Bea realised she must have been in the cell most of the night. She wondered if her parents had noticed she wasn't home; whether they were out looking for her or had already disowned her. Part of her understood now; though she knew her mother had misjudged her motives, she felt a tearing regret that she had not been tied more closely to her apron strings; just a year or two longer of innocence, and she might have been safe.

With his hand still clasped around her arm, the larger man dragged Bea into the centre of the room directly in front of Mr Forester. The magistrate was a tall, thin man, a foot higher than Bea, and dressed in a dark brown coat which had seen a few years of wear, by the look of its shape and style. With a powdered wig which had seen better days, and a face devoid of expression, he made a redoubtable figure. Bea took a deep breath, readying her nerves for the onslaught ahead.

"Beatrice Lightfoot?".

"Yes."

"Take a seat I have a few questions to ask." He gestured to the nearest chair.

The smaller man also sat. Mr Forester examined her, studying every inch of her.

Bea blurted out abruptly, "I know how it looks, sir, but I must explain . . ."

"Please, allow me the courtesy of asking the questions here." Mr Forester held up his hand in a sign of silence. Bea heed the warning with a single nod. "First, I must ask you what reason you had for being alone on that road at that time of the evening."

"I was to meet someone, urgently."

"Who was that? The man found dead on top of you?" Mr Forester asked gravely.

"No, it was... another man," Bea mumbled, aware of how that too seemed incriminating.

"You were to meet another man? Then who was he?"

Bea knew she could not bring Joshua's name into her testimony. It was too late for her family, but not for his.

"The man I'm intending to marry."

"And he is not the dead fellow?"

"No." Mr Forester made a motion, showing she should elaborate.

"I received a letter from my sweetheart, saying he needed to meet urgently at the harbour - I thought...Whilst I was walking, I heard someone following me, just beyond the path, so I ran, but they attacked me from behind. . ."

"By the dead man?"

"Maybe, I don't know, it could have been at first, then it was – it was Captain Hanley attacking me, threatening me and . . . he...", she felt sick, almost unable to speak the word "he forced himself into me." A memory flashed back into her mind, the pain between her legs as Hanley groaned into her neck. She turned white.

"Captain Hanley attacked and raped you? That is a grave accusation."

"He. . .he – I know. . . But it is true." The pain at least was evident in her voice.

"I see. Then what happened? How does this other man come into it?"

"After – after – the... He... he took the Captain's place, the other man; he... Hanley stood behind me. . . they acted like it was just a game...." She wrapped her arms around her chest, protecting herself, staring ahead into nothingness.

"So, you attacked this man? You stabbed him to get free?"

"No. I didn't stab him, I hit him with a rock, a pebble really, to free myself, but then suddenly Captain Hanley was the one who stabbed him."

"Why would Captain Hanley stab this man? try to help me understand you... first you say Captain Hanley attacked you - perhaps raped you - and Captain Hanley killed him without warning? . . . Even though, as you say, they seemed to be engaged in a game together, against your person. You must admit that it makes little sense. Why would he, Captain Hanley, molest you, but kill one of his own sailors for doing the same?"

"I don't know why he acted the way he did... why he killed that man and left him dead on top of me. I think... revenge - I think in his eyes I betrayed him. I encouraged his attention at one time - before I knew my sweetheart - and he felt I had made him a mockery of."

"He killed another man, because... you hurt his feelings?"

"No... Yes! I don't understand it myself, all I know is that he wanted to cause me dire hurt. And he has," she finished quietly. The magistrate took a laboured breath.

"Should I tell you what I think happened? I think that man saw you, and yes, attacked you as you have communicated - and in response you killed him for fear of your life. How you had a knife, I do not know. I discovered you covered with the body, covered in his blood, and with the murder weapon lying next to your hand. You have embellished your story somewhat, in an effort to protect yourself and your lover no doubt, although why you bring Captain Hanley into the circumstance is beyond me, for the present. Or perhaps the rumours about you around town are correct?" His voice was collected and civil, but his body language was agitated.

"No! They are lies! They planned it, I am sure they planned it - by the Captain."

"Why? – explain to me why."

"*I don't know.* Ask him! Ask him why he did it, put him in that cell and question him. Where he was tonight?"

The magistrate looked at her sternly, like a disappointed tutor.

"Take her back to the cell". Before the last word could sink in, the two men grabbed an arm each, hauling her up to her feet.

"No... *No!* You must believe me." The thought of returning to the cell, to the dark hole filled her with panic. The magistrate stood over her, raising his dominating hand to quieten her.

"I am under no obligation to do anything of the kind. We will see in time how innocent you are. For the moment you are to remain here."

"Please, can you at least tell my Da that I am here? He is the Master rope-maker down at Outcast."

Mr Forester nodded. As Bea disappeared down the corridor, he turned to the small man still seated at the table.

"Go down to the rope-maker and tell him we have his daughter. Do *not* give him details. We will see if he has any light to shed on the matter."

MR LIGHTFOOT STUDIED the knife once more. His mind was already shaken, and the after-effects of a night at the Bay Horse weren't helping matters. He couldn't deny that the knife was missing a tooth in the right place, and though the handle was caked in blood, there were his initials etched into. He looked up at Mr Forester, grey-faced.

"The knife is mine, aye. I couldn't find it yesterday," he offered morosely.

"Are you saying it was stolen or misplaced?"

"Someone had stolen it", Mr Lightfoot suggested.

"But you cannot be certain?" Mr Forester felt the fish tug at the end of his line.

"Well, no, but what sense would there be in young Beatrice takin' it? She'd know I'd miss it."

"You tell me."

Mr Lightfoot clenched his fists around his cap but made no reply.

He had known Nate Forester since they were both lads, he had tried to rule over him and his brothers even then. So, after school, they'd come up with a plan and pull a trick on him. But now as men he had the badge and power to teach them a lesson.

"One more question, and then you may see your daughter, briefly. What do you know about a certain Captain Hanley?"

It threw Mr Lightfoot off guard; he had not expected to be asked about the Captain.

"Not much, to be fair sir; I know he showed some interest in my daughter at one time, or so says my wife – but that's all."

"Very good," Mr Forester nodded his head in a non-committal way.

"What will happen next, sir?"

"There is to be an inquest tomorrow to deem whether your daughter acted in self-defence, or whether a murder has been committed".

Mr Lightfoot's felt his heart shrink several sizes in his chest; the room became smaller.

"May I see her now, then?"

Chapter 28

"Beatrice Lightfoot. Your father is here to see you." Mr Forester barked through the iron bars.

The dark red crust which had formed over the top of her long brown eyelashes, cracked and peeled away as she strained to see.

"Da? *DA?*"

"I'm here lass, I'm here lovey." Mr Lightfoot reassured her.

"You have a quarter hour."

Mr Lightfoot held the lantern out in front of him and cried out at what he saw. In the corner of the gloomy, stinking cell was his daughter, in an almost unrecognisable condition. The front of her dress was covered in blood, now almost black. Her hair was also dark with dried blood, as was the right side of her face. Her eyes were swollen and purple, and her hands and feet were scraped and caked in dirt. Worse was the way she held herself. The girl Mr Lightfoot knew was open to life, holding her head high, with a light step, a strong smile, and a hand always reaching out to someone who needed it. The person in front of him looked like she struggled to stand, too weak to be seen.

"Da, I'm... I'm sorry – Da...". When she was small, and she had done something foolish or cheeky, he would tell her off, full of bluster, and send her away out of his sight to 'think about it'. After an hour, she would come and sit on his lap, tell him how sorry she was and seal the forgiveness with a hug. In truth, he could never really be angry with her; he always knew she would feel truly sorry, and what was more, there was nothing she could have done to stop his love for her; his lovely little Bumble Bea. Looking at her now, he knew a simple embrace would not solve her problems. He wasn't sure anything could. He longed for her to be that little lass once more, so he could protect her in the only way he knew how, to warn her of the dangers to come.

"Da?" He heard the grief in her voice as he placed the lantern on to the ground at their feet.

"Oh Lass, what are we going to do with you?" he enveloped her in his arms, feeling her tense body finally give way and relax into him. She shook gently as her silent tears soaked through his shirt.

"Da - I did not do it - I p-promise." Her voice caught in her parched throat.

"I know, lass, I know."

She pulled out of his grasp and stared him straight in the eyes.

"It was Captain Hanley, he planned it all, and he killed that man."

"But why, lass? Why would he do that to you?"

Bea began from the first day both Hanley and Joshua had come into her life. She watched as her words brought on a wave of emotions in her Da. He paced between the narrow walls. She told him how Hanley had first attacked her as he walked over to the wall, leant his forehead against it, as though unwilling to hear more. She told him of the rape, holding back as much detail as possible, for both their sakes. Then she recounted how Hanley had told her Joshua had challenged him and wounded him.

"That is why I think he has done this, to pay me back somehow." Bea hung her head.

"Why didn't you *tell* me, lass?" He rubbed her back in a circular motion like he used to when she was young. "Why did you not?" His voice became childlike itself, full of sore confusion. Her breathing quietened.

"I was afraid what you might think - what the town would think. I was foolish, I just wanted to escape from it all, I thought you would be angry, as you were . . . I'm so sorry Da!" She turned her head away from his gaze.

"Lass - the town disputin' of your character is better than you bein' on trial for murder – and God knows I'm sorry for the way I was toward you."

Bea stiffened in his hold. "What will happen next?" Her voice was distant, reflecting on the grim possibilities stretching out in front of her.

"There is to be an inquest tomorrow, in the courtyard o' The Globe. If they charge you, it will be there." Bea started suddenly.

"Da - the march – it..."

"Not here, lass." He leaned in and whispered. "Charlie is next door."

"I am sorry, Da." They sat silently for a minute.

"We can't have much time left, but... could you do two things for me?" He nodded, tilting his head in a question. "Would you get me a dress from home? I cannot wear this; they will condemn me as soon as they see me."

"Aye - good thinking, lass. And?"

"Will you tell Joshua what has happened?"

"Is that a good idea?"

"Please Da, he has a right to know - I need him to know – then it is up to him if he walks away."

For the first time he saw the love his daughter had for the man he had never met. Both fell into silence as they heard the footsteps coming towards them.

TWO DAYS HAD PASSED since Joshua's encounter with Hanley at the duel. Slowly, the feeling of dread had crept away as Hanley's silence flowed through his hours. The young merchant wasted no time. That same day, he sent out enquires for vacancies in Bristol and Liverpool. Reaching out to former friends and work colleagues, he carefully chose people outside of his father's own contacts. He had intended to wait until after they were married and during their honeymoon, petition by letter. But now, time was not on his side. Day after day, the relentless heat bore into his patience. He could not recall a time when this part of the country had been so hot. Rays of light shone through the large window, casting a spell over the dust as it danced in the golden air. His mind raced over endless lists in his head. He rolled onto his side, watching the sun rise above the trees through the gap in the curtains. The image reminded him of Bea, and the thought of soon waking up with her as his wife lying next to him filled him with a strange, light-headed joy. In a week, they would consummate their relationship, and he could love her wholly as a woman should be loved. His body stirred at the idea, his mind tracing the lines of her lips, remembering her taste, her hair, and the curves of her hips. Endless delightful daydreams of Bea, however, were not, in fact, what occupied his agenda. He had promised his father he would travel up to the mine to check on production, and the day was already running away from him. Dressing himself, he could feel the sweat trickle down his back with the heat of the day only just beginning. Slowly, he made his way through to the morning room for his first cup of coffee and a cigarette.

"Master Mason."

"Butterworth".

"Good morning sir - this was delivered for you first thing." Butterworth held out a small, neat envelope in his hand.

"Thank you."

"Anything else I may assist with, sir?"

"That will be all thank you." Joshua studied the handwriting on the enticing letter, struggling to find anything familiar in it. "Wait - is my father still in the house?"

"Mr Mason left at eight for a meeting, I believe sir."

"Thank you, Butterworth."

"Very good, sir."

As soon as the butler had departed, Joshua eagerly cracked the crimson wax and opened the single sheet of thick cream paper.

"DEAR MR MASON,

I was delighted to receive your recent letter - congratulations on your happiest of news.

I am pleased to be in a position to communicate that an opportunity has arisen to be part of a newly formed scheme, in a situation that would suit you, I believe, here in Bristol.

The pay is modest, but there is scope for advancement, along with rapid growth, under your leadership. We would require you to start in no less than two weeks' time, and I propose that should the offer be agreeable to you, I will arrange a house for you and your wife myself, at my earliest convenience.

I await your reply in readiness

Kindest regards,

Mr Spencer"

Joshua read over the letter twice before considering the prospect fully. He poured himself another cup of coffee hoping to focus his thoughts in the way of a normal day, as he weighed up the arguments for and against. He had held Mr Spencer in high regard whilst under his direction as a fresh graduate three years ago. His Father had wanted him to gain experience with the merchant guild, but he had deliberately made the acquaintance of Mr Spencer on his own initiative, keen to prove to his father that he was no idle student. He puzzled over the substance of the scheme to which Mr Spencer referred. Would the outcome be worth the risk if the venture had so much room to expand? With two thousand saved of his own money, Joshua knew they had enough to support themselves until they became settled somewhere, but there would be no second chances; the first choice had to be the right choice, on his part. He smiled to himself; what he loved about Bea was that she would jump at the chance of an unknown and challenging prospect, while others would step back. They would need to leave in a week, allowing time for his reply to reach Mr Spencer. He had arranged a small ceremony at a parish church he rode past so frequently in Spark Bridge. After the wedding they could travel down to Bristol for their honeymoon, taking in the sights and planning their future as they lay enclosed together in bed. He allowed himself a hazy imagining of Bea walking down the aisle towards him in her bridal gown, and then both of them riding hard away - from Ulverston, the judgement of his peers, and Captain Hanley, forever.

He would speak to the Reverend Phillipson on the way home from the mines, to confirm all the preparations were well in hand. Joshua became giddy. In the past, he had been almost fearful of this moment, unable to conceive a life away from his family. Now, he was excited at the prospect of forging an alternative path for himself and for Bea, and perhaps the children they would one day call their own. He gripped hard onto the thoughts of this new future, and left the room, bounding back up the stairs two at a time towards his room. Sitting at his desk, he wrote two letters: one in reply to Mr Spencer, and the other to Bea, with news of their imminent beginnings, sealing one with wax, and the other with a kiss.

MR LIGHTFOOT TOOK THE best jacket he could find, and pulled tight the heavy woollen fabric, buttoning himself up as though into a suit of armour. Ever since he had seen his daughter in her cell that morning, he hadn't been able to shake off a dispiriting coldness, aching through his bones even on such a hot day. He brushed off a few stray pieces of hemp and hay, nervous at the prospect of meeting a member of the gentry under such a cloud, let alone the man who wanted to marry his daughter. He tackled the horse to the cart, sending Matty home to collect a dress for Bea. The thought of a grilling from his wife was not one he wished to contemplate for the moment.

He told his men to monitor the boys while he went to show some samples to a couple of interested merchants and discuss potential orders. None of them seemed to know about Bea, and he wanted to keep it that way, until the last minute. Gossip would spread through the town quickly enough, and it was only a matter of hours before he would lose the advantage of a disinterested workforce. Within the half-hour Matty came bounding back up the track.

"Is Bea... alright?"

"She will be."

Mr Lightfoot wrapped the dress in a spare piece of fabric and placed it on the front seat. He grabbed the reins in his right hand, and hauled himself up with his left, giving the horse a gentle whip as she happily kicked off. He made his way into town, giving his usual nods to the familiar townsfolk, and preparing what he was going to say to Mr Joshua Mason, wondering all the while what his prospective son-in-law would be like. His train of thought sank further, reflecting on the highly anticipated march; a failure before it had even begun. He had heard that Charlie had been missing but hadn't expected to see him in the cell next to his daughter. What did that mean for the Reformers? How much would he tell them?

One challenge at a time, he thought. First, he had to save his Bumble Bea, and then tackle what was left of The Cause. Bob Lightfoot was well-aware that if his childhood friends and neighbours knew his now-disgraced daughter was connected to the Mason family, everyone would shun him. Nevertheless, Bea needed him, and she needed hope. His task was simple, and the rope-maker was in no doubt that his first-born now came before everything else.

BUTTERWORTH GUIDED Mr Lightfoot down the backstairs and to one of the more unused sitting rooms with obvious distaste by the starched butler. He almost sat down but thought better of it. He knew that this house, and the family it belonged to, as well as their staff, would never have opened their hearts to Bea. He had always known that she was better than the life they had given her; clever, kind-hearted and yearned for more. It had saddened him to watch her become lost, even somewhat hardened by their family life, thanks especially to his own embittered wife, but seeing her today, how alone she had looked; there he had truly failed her.

"Can I help you?" Joshua stood at the door with a questioning look.

Mr Lightfoot studied the well-dressed gentleman before him. He realised that this man was only a boy himself, full of youth, with a kind, energetic face.

"Mr Joshua Mason?"

"I am?"

"I'm Bob Lightfoot, sir, Beatrice's father."

Realisation and panic flashed across Joshua's face. He walked closer to the man in the centre of the room.

"Mr Lightfoot, you must believe me: my actions towards your daughter have been completely honourable - I wanted to speak to you myself, before we... made our decision, but Bea insisted, she would do it alone -"

"I am not here about that."

"Then, why... - is Beatrice alright?"

Mr Lightfoot was pleased at least that the young man's concern seemed genuine.

"I do not know how to tell you all that's passed, sir, so I'll speak plainly." He paused for a second and considered the difference the next few moments might have on Beatrice's future, and the slim chance of her ever gaining even a small share of happiness. Looking Joshua straight in the eye, he began; slowly at first, then in his usual measured tones, as his strength of character carried him through the retelling of things he didn't want to admit what had happened even to himself. "...But then, it was my rope knife used to stab the man. That falls hard against her. Though to my mind it shows more that someone *wanted* my lass to be thought guilty above all others..."

Joshua gripped tight the polished wood, not knowing if he should sit on the chair or stand, his face drained of all colour. He gazed at his father-to-be with grief-stricken eyes, then let out a deep moan.

"I should have shot him through the heart."

Bob put out a hand to steady the young man. It was taken warmly, and the two men stood looking at one another, so different, yet inextricably united.

"She shall not face this alone." Joshua's voice was full of determination. The colour had returned to his skin, and the rope-maker could see his thoughts coming together again, the need for action taking over.

"I must see her. We must see her. Will you allow me to go with you? Then you and I may think what we can do to fight her cause."

Mr Lightfoot nodded. If seeing her betrothed gave her fire for the ordeal of the following day, then so much for the better. Nothing less than Bea's life was at stake now, and they both knew it; any slight chance of giving her hope was worth the risk.

"Follow me – we'll go directly. And thank you, sir, for trusting my feelings in this. I only hope your daughter can do the same."

Chapter 29

The Globe was full to the brim with eager onlookers, hoping to glean some exciting titbit of gossip. During the course of the previous day, rumours and gossip had engulfed the town like wildfire about the murderous lace-maker Beatrice Lightfoot. Already the rows of chairs were filled with all varieties of town folk, ready to cast their own personal form of judgement upon the proceedings and their protagonists. Mr Lightfoot nervously made his way up the side-aisle, his eyes scanning around the makeshift courtroom. The purpose-built stage held a large, dominant table and chair for the legal presider. To the left of the stage was the podium, crafted for the sole purpose of containing his daughter. Positioned opposite this were the twelve seats for the jury. Bob Lightfoot loved his hometown, and its people, but trusting them with the life of his first-born? Never.

Joshua gently placed his hand on the rope-maker's shoulder and felt him sigh.

"Aye son – sir - I'll be fine".

For Joshua's part, he had not known true nerves until this morning. He had spent the night at the club, unwilling to go home and receive the talk from his father. His churning stomach threaten a revisit of his morning cup of coffee as the sensation crawled up his throat, causing his breathing to become slow and jolting. He had a layperson's knowledge of how such proceedings were run, having attended a few cases with a friend at Cambridge who was studying the law, but as to the details and the specific risks that would need to be overcome, he was no more knowledgeable than Mr Lightfoot. He had often thought in those days to study the law, if it had not been for his father's wishes for him to continue in business. And look how that had turned out, he thought to himself bitterly.

After seeing Bea yesterday, he had sent an express letter to his friend, Peter Livingston, now a barrister in London. The evidence was stacked against her. Seeing the small, crumpled figure cowering in the corner of the cell, forced to wear her bloody dress for days on end, the dress in which she had been... It was killing him slowly. He had never felt more powerless. She had refused any kind of contact, recoiling at his touch. She almost feared him, Joshua had realised, stunned. Hanley had taken more than her innocence when he had forced himself inside her; he had broken her spirit. He had taken her trust, her fearlessness, and worst of all, her heart. She was closed off for now, though he hoped that one day he would be the one to reverse that evil. Guiltily, he couldn't shake away the feeling that he too had been robbed. Her first experience of making love had been unspeakable, a tearing of the soul, tainting all future physical contact with the memory of pain and powerlessness. In the bleak lamplight, he could see her swollen eyes, and the blue bruises smeared across her face. He wished he had the power to exchange places with her. If he had only aimed better that day, she would still have been his entirely, willingly, in body and mind. The rising noise of the crowd as the magistrate threaded himself through the crowd brought him back to the courtroom.

Mr Forester banged heavily on the table to call for silence. "I will take charge of proceedings today..."

"Is that proper?" Joshua thought out loud.

"...Judge Copperfield has been taken ill. Are all present that should be?"

"But he's already decided about Bea." Mr Lightfoot turned to Joshua, fuming.

"Mark my words -" Joshua broke off as they escorted Bea out of a side room.

With the iron shackles tightly fastened around her slim wrists, the larger of the two deputies dragged her out. They had transported her over to the holding room at dawn today, shunted from one dark space to another. She blinked around her, searching for any familiar faces. But the blinding light from the sun was too much for her starved eyes, and she lowered her head. The heat at least felt good, thawing out her frozen body, and the magistrate had allowed her to change into the light woollen dress her father had brought her to minimise any reaction from the onlookers. She felt an overwhelming pressure rolling off the crowd, like an angry tide.

"Order!"

Mr Forester bellowed, followed by the small wooden hammer banging against the table. Everyone continued to shout, either at their neighbour or at Bea. "*Silence*!" A gentleman holding an armful of loose scrolls took his seat at a small table situated below the stage, as the twelve jury members filled their places one at a time: farmers, butchers, shopkeepers, and a man of the cloth. Joshua was thankful not to notice any seamen amongst their number. Mr Lightfoot eyed each of the figures warily. He knew a handful by name; some he trusted to be fair, others he suspected were not.

"*We have come here today to discuss the death of the late Mr William Gregson on the night of August eighteenth, year of our lord 1831. Your duty as the twelve jury members is to pronounce a verdict on this regrettable incident, and whether the person held in custody before you today, Miss Beatrice Lightfoot, should be taken through to trial. Would the first witness, a Mrs Kerr, please step forward.*"

A large, wide-eyed woman squeezed through the seats and made her way up to the front. Her ample cheeks blushed like apples as she waited for her audience to quieten.

"In your own words, please can you explain to the jury what you saw on the night of the eighteenth?" Mr Forester gestured to the silent twelve.

"I was turnin' in for the night, when I 'eard a terrible scream. I waited a minute, to see if it would 'appen again or if it was just a fox, like... but, I 'eard it again, someone yelling out... so me and my boy – Henry 'e is, sirs - went out searchin'. Well, I could not find a thing, but then Henry came running up, fast as y'like, sayin' something about a man and woman, dead. So, I followed him, and what should I find but *her*, on the ground, passed out cold, with the dead man layin' on top of her!"

The crowd began tittering. The magistrate waved an impatient arm.

"Quiet, please - Mrs Kerr: continue."

"Well, I did not rightly know what to do at that, and then Mr Campbell turned up, and said that the boy should fetch the magistrate. She stirred a bit, I saw 'er eyes blinkin', she were tryin' to move and get free most likely, but she could not lift him. I said to meself at the time, she should have thought of that before – well!"

A roar of laughter swallowed up Mrs Kerr's broad voice.

"Thank you, Mrs Kerr, you may sit down now. Could the second witness please come forward; a Mr Campbell?"

Mr Forester intoned across the crowd. Mrs Kerr took her exit, smiling delightedly at the audience. In a few strides, Mr Campbell stood waiting in front of the magistrate. He looked worn out, with his crinkled paper-thin skin hanging loosely on his face. Standing in his Sunday-best, he stole a glance at Bea. But there was no animosity towards her in his manner, rather his eyes seemed full of pity.

"Mr Campbell; in your own words, could you please describe to the jury what you saw that night." The tired-looking figure stood a little straighter.

"I was making my way home back to Sandside from The Bay Horse - had a couple of beers after work, y'see - when I saw Mrs Kerr and little Henry standing in the road, looking at something. I recognised the lady at once as bein' Miss Lightfoot, on account of knowin' her Da. She was in a real state, hurt badly. I wanted to stay to make sure no harm came to her, while Henry fetched yourself, sir. She tried to move, but I told her to stay quiet. She was repeatin' that she did not do it, over and over."

"On your way back from the public house, did you see anyone else on the road? Any strangers?"

"No, sir, I didn't see anyone else on the path until the poor young lady."

"Thank you, Mr Campbell, you may return to your seat now. A Dr Phillips? Please step forward".

On the opposite side of the aisle, a man stood up, dressed all in black. His powdered wig was slightly lopsided as he trembled with nerves.

"Dr Phillips, you have examined the body, have you not?"

"Y -yes", the physician stuttered.

"Please can you inform the jury, from the evidence, how Mr Gregson died?"

Dr Phillips coughed loudly and straightened his jacket.

"Upon examination of the body, I found two stab wounds on his chest situated below the breastbone. One puncturing the left lung and the second puncturing the left ventricle to the heart, the latter resulting in instant death". The crowd muttered to one another sullenly.

"Would you say they cause these stab wounds through panic or were deliberate?"

"By the force and position, the person would have known these stab wounds would have been fatal, to be able to reach under the ribs like so." His right hand suddenly thrusted out in front of him, gesturing to the audience the move the killer made, followed by a gasp from the crowd.

"I would like to take this opportunity to show the jury this knife, which was discovered at the scene." Mr Forester gave the knife to the clerk, so that he could exhibit it along the row.

"In your professional opinion, could this knife have made those kinds of injuries?"

"Yes. I have examined the knife carefully, and with no doubt, taking in the blade's length and angle of the teeth, it was this weapon which killed Mr Gregson." The crowd instantly broke out into a discussion about the recent evidence, throwing narrow glares towards Beatrice.

"Thank you, Dr Phillips, you may take your seat. Mr Lightfoot, to take the stand."

Immediately the crowd fell silent. Bob Lightfoot let out a long sigh, avoiding Bea's gaze, rose to his feet and moved forward.

"Mr Lightfoot, do you recognise this knife?" The whole courtyard was watching him.

He shifted on the spot, his hands fidgeting with his cap.

"Aye, I do - those are my initials on the handle, I use it to cut the hemp."

"Without any doubt whatsoever, you say this is your knife." He pronounced every word slowly and clearly, so that no one could mistake what he was implying.

"Yes, this is my knife." There were jeers from the crowd directed at Bea. She could not look at her Da, saddened beyond words to see her quiet, hardworking father forced to bring his own name voluntarily into disrepute in the courtroom.

"Can you recall any reason why your knife should be at the crime scene?"

"No, sir. I noticed it were missin' the day before, but as I wasn't needin' it at the time, I put it to the back of my mind, thinkin' to find it at home, mislaid, so to speak."

"Take a seat Mr Lightfoot - Today we will not hear from Miss Beatrice Lightfoot." Bea leant against the newly crafted banister, holding herself upright as her knuckles turned white. The crowd jeered. "May I remind everyone; this is in fact an inquest to determine whether Mr Gregson was murdered, or if in fact it was indeed a circumstantial or accidental circumstance. Miss Beatrice Lightfoot is not on trial today but is assuredly the prime suspect, therefore: if the jury deem Mr Gregson was murdered, I will have no other choice but to charge Miss Beatrice Lightfoot with murder."

Joshua felt Mr Lightfoot boil in anger beside him. He turned to the older man in anguish.

"How can they possibly know whether this is a case of murder if they don't hear from Beatrice herself? She represents at present merely a girl of loose morals; why should they deem she has acted in self-defence if they aren't party to her side of the story? And what of Captain Hanley, why is he not here?"

"What about Captain Hanley?" Mr Lightfoot blurted out, in echo to Joshua's complaint, across the Globe.

"Mr Lightfoot, you have had your turn; please don't shout out across the crowd. But to answer your question, I have already made enquiries: Captain Hanley was partaking in a local public house - The Sun, I believe - between the hours of nine in the evening and four in the morning on the night in question, as it seems to me most sea-faring men are. There are several witnesses who can vouch for him."

"No... That cannot... that cannot be!" Bea declared, but no one could hear her over the ensuing commotion.

"I suggest the jury take a short recess and consider a verdict on the cause of death for the late Mr Gregson." The twelve members exited into one of the side rooms behind the stage, while two lackeys remained either side of Bea.

"It does not look well for my lass, does it?" Mr Lightfoot murmured in broken tones to his companion.

"I..." Joshua looked helplessly at the rope-maker beside him and saw for the first-time small similarities between him and his beloved Bea: the prominent chin, and the fierce, almond-shaped eyes. He resisted the urge to drop his head into his hands and instead tried to stay strong in front of Mr Lightfoot and the darting glances that surrounded them. Their agony was not prolonged.

The jury slowly filed out of their room after only five minutes of deliberation. The crowd cheered one by one, as they noticed the men resuming their seats, each clutching a newly gained tankard. Mr Forester stood up.

"Mr Thomson, has the jury returned with an unanimous verdict?"

"We have concluded, sir, that Mr Gregson died from the two deliberate stab wounds inflicted by the knife you have there as evidence, and that being so, Miss Lightfoot there must stand trial for murder."

The courtyard burst into an uproar of enthusiastic booing and cheering. Mr Forester nodded calmly and made a sign to the two men either side of the podium as they dragged Bea to her feet with a hand wedged under each armpit.

"...and it is therefore my duty to inform you, Miss Lightfoot, that I charge you with the murder of Mr William Gregson, and will stand trial in Lancaster Castle on Monday next". The words suddenly brought Bea back to life.

"*I didn't do it... You have it all wrong!*" she screamed.

"No... They can't do this!" Joshua blurted out.

The two men dragged her back towards the holding room once more as she fought to be released. Mr Lightfoot stood up quickly, white-faced, and made his way to the exit, Joshua followed hastily. As they emerged into the courtyard, a cloaked man brushed past them almost immediately, jostling the rope-maker, then skirting back into the shadow of the high wall.

"How does it feel knowing it will be one of your own ropes that tightens around her pretty neck?"

Mr Lightfoot spun round, a look of horror on his face. Joshua darted forward and tried to pull the hood from the stranger's head, but he was already mingling with the onlookers flooding out from the warm, sweaty courtroom. Bob was about to charge forward when Joshua grabbed him by the shoulder.

"We must save Beatrice. Causing a scene here will do no good." He glanced around at the throng. "Leave Hanley to me, I will not fail a second time."

Chapter 30

A guard barged into her cell before the sun had risen, placed the iron shackles over her wrists and shoved her wearily out into the alleyway below, nudging her right shoulder roughly every few steps toward Kings Street. She could tell dawn was coming soon through the dense, early morning sea mist. There was a heat in the air, and the day ahead would be a hot one. The small thin man with his slick hair and unmoving stare stood waiting beside the panelled wooden box, with its worn edges, imposing wheels and flaking black paint designed for crossing the sands to Lancaster.

She had watched other wayward travellers many a time, and until recently, had thought she would be crossing herself as a new bride, with Joshua by her side, and the excitement of their shared prospects filling her thoughts. Instead, she was about to be transported like just another criminal in the back of a magistrate carriage, facing trial for murder at Lancaster Castle. She heaved herself up, climbing into the dank space as the padlock clicked shut behind her, caging her inside. How much she had wanted to escape from this town, to find adventure, and had risked everything for that dream... Had she asked for too much? She could hear the stallholders readying their displays to secure the early buyers, oblivious to her dread. She prayed that this would not be the last time she would see Ulverston, that somehow, in a few weeks' time, she would be acquitted, and Captain Hanley would be locked away, unable to mark her life any further...

She bit back tears, knowing that even as she allowed the thought to manifest inwardly, there was no chance of it coming to pass.

The sound of iron shoes sparking against the cobbles crept closer. She could hear Mr Forester issuing orders to the men, as the sound of more horses joined their group. With a sudden jerk, the carriage heaved forward, causing its inmate to tumble backwards. She scrambled upright again, clinging to the small bars of the window, and watched how the growing light solidified the mist coating the coastline, creating a denser, murkier atmosphere. As they grew closer to The Bay Horse, a bustle of whispering voices seemed to surround her. A congregation of fellow passengers and voyagers formed at the side of the bank, waiting for the signal. Then, as though sensing he was expected, like a sea creature rising from the depths of the waves, a mucky figure with a sodden beard, stringy hair and bulky coat stepped silently out from the mist. Using a notched staff, he checked the shifting sands underneath his feet. From the inside pocket of his coat he plucked a worn leather pouch, from which he drew a clay pipe and a pinch of tobacco.

He let out a long puff of smoke with a raspy cough.

"I am Twed, Guide of the Sands." He took another puff of his pipe and continued: "Before we begin, I have a few rules. First: do exactly as I say, my family have been crossing the sands for generations, and we know what we are doing. Second, stay to the right of the wooden markers. I have placed out the first five and will judge the rest as we go. The mist makes it hard to see, so go slow, and go steady. If you stray from the markers, I cannot guarantee your ground. The sands are continually shifting, and new spots of quicksand will develop. If you find yourself sinking, don't struggle - it will only cause you further trouble. Call for help, and I will come. Remember, there will also be channels of water to watch for. Now the tide is at its lowest, and we only have a couple of hours to get to the far side before it comes all the way in again. Follow me."

Turning his back on the crowd, he strode forwards across onto the sand, grinding his pipe between his teeth. People scrambled about, picking up their belongings and taking flight after him. With another jerk, the horse sprang to life and headed down on to the sand. The rhythmical motion of the carriage, fusing with her exhaustion, lulled Bea into a strange restless sleep, and she surrendered to the next few hours without protest.

THE SUDDEN JUMP FORCED Bea awake as the carriage rocked and shifted on the new, craggy ground. The brilliant white light faded away, revealing patches of green. She could hear the horse clattering over stone underneath, as she felt the carriage rise at the back, the green merging into what looked like fields. Bemused, she thought that perhaps they had made it across the sands already, and she had slept away the hours.

Squinting out from between the bars into the grey dawn, she saw a signpost: *"Bell's Drapers of Flookburgh"*. Her heart sank, for she knew exactly where they were. They had crossed only the small bay, making their way over the short distance through Flookburgh and Allithwaite; then back onto the sands once more across the larger bay to Lancaster. Climbing high above the fog, Bea looked down on the wispy low clouds engulfing small pockets of land one at a time. The straggling party quickly made their way through Allithwaite, then Bea felt the carriage shift as it started making its way down the hill, back towards the sands. A hushed peace descended on her, transporting her amongst the cloud as if the mist itself already saw her future, and wanted to keep her hidden safely away.

A sudden lurch brought her out of her trance; the carriage had come to a stop. The box drifted to one side slightly, as though it were floating. She moved over to the small window, but there was only mist, out of which rang alarmed voices, followed by splashes drumming against the side of her small wooden cabin. A hurried discussion was obviously taking place outside, and Bea felt the box shift again, but this time, further down, into the sands. A horrified realisation sparked in the dim light; the carriage was stuck, and it was sinking. She leant her head against the wooden wall, trying to make out what her escorts were saying.

"Fetch Twed; tell him the back-left wheel is lodged in a channel," came Mr Forester's voice. "Right, the rest of you, get ready to push! Brown, on my command get the horse to pull as hard as he can." She heard a low muttering between the men.

"Right, *go*."

The carriage lurched forward a fraction as the men panted and moaned under the strain, but the horse gave way, and the carriage slid back, even lower this time. Water dripped through the thin cracks between the door panels.

Panic bubbled away in Bea's gut. "What's happening?" she choked out through the iron bars, in a voice she barely recognised as her own. The muttering continued amongst the men. "Please, tell me what's going on?"

Mr Forester boomed out once more: "Give it another go. - Brown - on my command - now!"

The carriage lunged forward again as the men strained harder, but the stubborn wheel refused to spin. With a chorus of frustration, they allowed the carriage to tumble backwards once more. Like a sinking ship, the box angled deeper into the channel of water. The drips became engorged, pooling together to form a fluid stream. A salty pond took shape in the corner by the door.

"Water is coming in." she announced, unaware if anybody was listening. She waited for a response. "Hello?"

"What?" a frustrated voice snapped back.

"Water is coming in!" she repeated, leaning her head against the bars, but no one responded.

The stressful atmosphere, accompanied by the rising water, agitated the horse, and he called out and shifted around, attempting to break free from his tack. His sudden jerking made the carriage slip back further. The sands displaced again, and the forceful ebb which had drawn back the waves, sucked in again, stronger and broader. The rising water seeped rhythmically through the hinges of the door frame, causing the pond to grow, reaching out to her skirts.

"Stop! Stop what you are doing!" Twed's gruff voice cried out to the men.

"We need to get the carriage out."

"Did none of you listen? You will only sink it faster. The tide is coming in, you must abandon it, and fetch it when the water goes back out again." He unbuckled the horse. "You have minutes to make it to land before the tide engulfs you all..." There were more muffled sounds from outside the carriage. "Take what you can and follow the rest of the group."

"Please, let me out?" Bea called, her voice rising with a hint of fear. She climbed to the back of the shrinking box as the pond grew to the size of a bath. The frustration of not knowing what was happening filled her with anxiety. Her rapid heartbeat and shallow breath seemed to make the walls close in ever faster. "Hello? What's happening out there?" she shrilled to anyone who might be listening.

"QUIET... Right, John, you follow Twed to the front of the group... Once you're on land, go to the Castle directly, and fetch back another carriage, anything suitable to transport her in – Go, then... The rest of you, get the horse loose, and I will release Miss Lightfoot, and carry her on my own."

Bea heard the turning of a key in the lock as she made out the image of Mr Forester in the small aperture.

"Oh, thank you..."

"Hush, woman - the carriage is sinking, you will have to travel the rest with me." He forced the door open, pushing back the water. The tide flowed through the gap, instantly filling the small wooden box, its weight pushing the carriage lower into the sands. Bea reached her shackled hands out to him, and in one move he pulled her out into the body of water.

He dragged Bea forward. Her head went under as her feet failed to find the sand underneath. With his free hand, he grabbed her around the waist and heaved her back up. She coughed as a long gulp of air filled her lungs and her head broke the surface. Keeping her tight next to him, he climbed out of the channel, each footstep sinking into the sands below. He let Bea down as he grabbed the reins of his horse, and she shivered as the waves crashed around her hips. Mr Forester scanned the horizon for the group ahead but saw nothing. Not only that; he saw no markers either.

"Come with me."

She fought against the aggressive tide as the growing waves crashed in around her. The salt made her retch after days of little food.

Mr Forester surveyed the men, nodding to the one holding the carriage horse. He glanced down at Bea; she was not making a sound, neither shouting nor crying. In that moment she seemed younger, and almost childlike. He wondered for the first time if she was truly capable of murder. But it was too late to be thinking along those lines. The jury would surely find her guilty, and the evidence was stacked against her. But he still could not shake off a new feeling of doubt.

"Gary - help her up."

"Thank you," Bea breathed through chattering teeth.

Gary grabbed her around the waist as Mr Forester kept the horse still with one hand and heaved her up with the other. The soaked dress clung to her like a second skin, and Gary's hand slid down to her buttocks and around the top of her thighs, groping as she moved. "Don't touch me!" Mr Forester noticed the instant fear in her face, and the shudder in her body as Gary snatched his hand away, sneering.

"Keep your hands to yourself," snapped the magistrate.

The horses fought against the current as they made their way to the shore, battling and shifting as they struggled through the relentless onslaught of the waves. The party curved round, following the shape of the land, and Bea suddenly made out the end of the group, forging their way on to the shore as the last of the mist faded.

The front man in their party tumbled from his saddle. Fighting as one, horse and rider both tried to swim, their heads barely visible above the waves.

Realising what had happened, Bea screamed.

"Stop!"

Mr Forester pulled hard on the reins and spun round.

"It is another channel..." Her shackled hands pointing forward.

The tall man surveyed the scene ahead, wishing he still had his eyesight from twenty years past.

"Alright men; you must get down and help your horses to swim across."

"You need to undo my chains..." Bea declared, holding out her wrists.

"No!"

"I will not run off, am I? I'll not get very far... I cannot swim with these on, so, either take them off or carry me alongside - you cannot arrive at Lancaster Castle without me."

He muttered underneath his breath as he pulled out the keys from his pocket. With a click, Bea felt the instant release from around her wrists. The magistrate jumped down first with the crashing waves, almost knocking him off his feet and attempted to steady himself as he helped Bea slide off the saddle. Her feet failed to find the sand bed as her head went under once more. In one kick and a stroke of her arms, she broke the surface.

Silently, she thanked her Da for teaching her how to swim when she was young. She glanced back at Mr Forester, who was losing a battle with his horse. Frightened, the animal was locked in a stationary position, head back, eyes staring. Mr Forester strained on the reins as he gradually became engulfed by the continuous onslaught. The more he pulled, the more the horse fought back, terrified of the noise and the weight of the water. Bea hesitated for a moment. Less than a week ago, she would never have given it a second thought. But life was different now; she had no security, and no open heart. Kicking furiously, she swam back towards him.

"What are you doing? Head to the shore!" he yelled over the top of the deafening waves.

"Take off your jacket... Just do it, trust me." The magistrate obeyed instinctively; their roles reversed in the furious alien landscape, where nothing was clear, and all lives became equalled.

"Place it over his head, so that it covers his eyes. Now, gently stroke his diamond with one hand to calm him ... Good. That's it." Instantly the horse stopped kicking and shuffling as his ears relax back into place. Bea motioned him to pull the reins just a little in the right direction. Without any resistance, the horse followed his owner into the channel.

"Thank you."

Their only enemy now was the turbulent sea, pushing them further off course, and away from the shore. Exhausted, Bea's legs cramped up under the strain of swimming; they had crossed the channel, but the sea had risen too high to allow any of them to stand. Mr Forester watched Bea struggling to keep her head above the waves. They tried to press downward toward Morecambe shore, but the sea was forcing them upwards and outwards. Realising they had no chance of fighting the current when all three of them couldn't last much longer, the magistrate made a rash decision. He directed them straight ahead, towards Hest-Bank, only forty feet away. Suddenly he heard Bea cry out and turned to see she had gone under. Waiting, he held his breath, watching if she would come back up.

Fearing for the worst, he glanced over at their horse, who seemed to carry on independently to the shore, then dived under the waves, scanning the murky waters for a glimpse of her. Coming up for a quick breath, he dived deeper. The salt blurring his vision; he reached out to a large shadow in front of him. Gripping what seemed like an arm, he kicked away at the seabed and fought his way to the surface. Placing her onto her back, he swam as fast as he could towards the bank, dragging her behind with an arm round her shoulders. The current finally on their side, he made the shore within minutes. Gasping for air, he hauled her lifeless body onto the stone beach. She lay there; white, motionless, and limp, and in a surge of panic, he grabbed her shoulders and shook her. The magistrate checked for any sign of breath as he held his hand over her open mouth and nose, then tilting her head back, he took a deep breath and pushed all the air he had in his lungs into her mouth, fear lending him strength. He took another deep breath and tried again, this time with a garbled prayer. As he panted for breath, ready to bend over her again, her body jerked, convulsed, and retched up the dark depths of the bay from her lungs. Turning her a little onto her side, Mr Forester fell back heavily onto the pebbles. Her eyes peeled open as her mind stirred.

"Do not move, rest -", he panted, himself exhausted, and a little shaken.

She lay there, the biting breeze stinging against her chilled body. She shook uncontrollably: she just wanted to sleep, now and forever. The magistrate knew they needed to keep moving if she were to have any chance of surviving. He stumbled over to the horse and backed him towards Bea. With his encouragement, she reached up, and placed her arms around the horse's neck, and clambered up to lie heavily across the animal's mane, watching the gorging turbulent sea as though in a dream, and the strange party staggered its weaving way towards Lancaster Castle.

Chapter 31

September 1831

"I wanted to make sure you received the blankets." Mr Forester stood at the cell door holding a soot-smeared lantern, dispelling fragments of light against the murky walls of the castle cell.

"Yes, thank you." Bea stood to one side of the door with the moth-bitten mantle wrapped around her shoulders.

"I also wanted to thank you for what you did yesterday with the horse – I've had him since he was a colt, and his mother before him." He coughed and studied the opposite wall, unsure how to act or what else to say.

"It was nothing, just something I had seen other men do before." An awkward silence fell between them. "Thank you – for saving my life – I hope it wasn't in vain," she added as a quiet afterthought, following the words with a small sad chuckle. The man sighed.

"...As I said, I wanted to make sure they had afforded you the blankets. I've heard my fair share of stories about the jailer here; some deserve his treatment, while others do not."

He turned his back and made his way to the door.

"I didn't do it you know – everything I told you was the truth."

"That's not up to me now." He said, reaching his hand up to knock, pausing.

"I know - but I wanted you to know that you didn't save a murder's life – just a girl who trusted the wrong man."

He turned back round to face her now, holding the lantern in her direction.

"If that is true, the court will judge you kindly."

Bea took a step closer, anger reflected in her voice.

"That's not true though, is it? - The men in that courtroom will see me like you did, like everyone else did that day. A working-class girl who has resorted to whoring – a rumour spread by the Captain himself - cornered with a knife and a dead sailor... If they raped me, in your eyes, then I was asking for it – is that not so? And I would only have carried a knife that night because I wanted to kill someone... They never suspect, of course, that a man with Captain Hanley's reputation would have a horde of sailors willing to vouch for him, in fear of their own lives! To them I am nothing, worse than that; I am someone to be made an example of. Is that not true, sir?"

She stood in front of him now as he held the lantern up higher, highlighting her sad, stricken face. She had a spark in her that remained alight, even after all she had been through. Perhaps she was telling the truth, but the evidence was certainly stacked against her.

"No – it is not... Nevertheless, the evidence is what it is."

"It is how you *say* it is."

"I cannot help you now – I am sorry." There was nothing more he could do; only pray that she had a fair trial. He turned again to leave.

"I understand. I just wanted you to hear the truth."

He paused for a moment before knocking to exit.

"I wish you luck, Miss Lightfoot."

A trepidation built inside as the door slammed shut behind him.

THE NEXT THREE DAYS, they locked her up in one of the old dungeon cells in the castle's basement, encased in darkness except for a few shards of light let in by cracks in the broken rock-face. She attempted to prepare her mind for the days ahead, listening to the different footsteps travelling up and down the long-enclosed walkway to her cell, and trying to measure the time, her efforts thwarted alternatively by exhaustion and hunger. She opened her eyes as one pair of steps came unmistakably closer, right up to her door. The reverberating thud as they pulled the bolt back sent her scurrying to the far wall. The door creaked forwards as Joshua Mason entered quietly, holding a lantern.

"Beatrice? Bea?"

He spoke her name as if this wretched creature standing before him wasn't the same woman he loved, the same woman who had taught him to see the world and its people in a different, truer light.

"Joshua?"

The small pool of warm light illuminated his face. Tiredness and fatigue made him look older now, Bea thought blankly, than since their last meeting above the shoreline. He placed the lantern on the floor and approached her slowly. Bea recoiled as he attempted to touch her; the thought of a man's hands on her, all but her Da's, was too much. She hated Hanley with a cold, sickening fury for taking that from her. All she wanted to do was to fold into Joshua's embrace and let her head fall into its familiar nook. She was still his, wasn't she? But as his fingers touched her bare arms, her body shuddered, and she stepped back against the wall.

"How long do we have?"

"I bribed the guard with a guinea, we have an hour."

Two more figures walked in behind him, into the now cramped space.

"Da?"

"Aye lass, I'm here."

"Bea, may I introduce to you Mr Peter Livingston," Joshua gestured to the second man now standing stiffly beside him.

"Miss Lightfoot," the other responded lightly, bowing slightly.

Bea could just make out that a pristine handkerchief in his left hand, which he was struggling not to place in front of his nose, to guard himself from the putrid smell that now pervaded her home.

"Bea, Peter is my friend from Cambridge. He is a barrister in London, and I sent word to him when you were being held back in Ulverston. He would like to defend you at trial tomorrow."

"So, it is tomorrow then?"

"Yes, love." Her Da stepped in. "Mr Forester told us before we came to see you what 'appened at the crossing," he whispered. "If anything could make me prouder of you, lass, then his telling of that day has done so."

Bea let her head fall but held out a hand for her father. He stood beside her and took it warmly, stroking the back of her hand, knowing without needing to be told, that she didn't wish to be touched.

"Are you all right? Were you hurt?" Joshua tried to move a little closer.

"Shall we get down to the trial, we only have a certain amount of time to talk." Mr Livingston spoke kindly but brusquely, placing the linen square back into his jacket pocket, and taking out a sheet of paper adorned with copperplate notes. "Due to the timing of all this, they have scheduled your hearing for tomorrow morning - to mark the end of the two weeks assizes' season. A couple of days later and you would have had to wait another four months in this... so we are fortunate in that respect. However, it does not give us a lot of time to prepare. Your father and Joshua have told me all that they were able. Nevertheless, I would like to hear it from yourself, to confirm my personal appraisal of the best way we should proceed. If you would, Miss Lightfoot."

He gestured Joshua to stand beside him and hold the lantern at an angle so he could compare his notes to Bea's testimony.

"Where would you like me to start?"

Bea did her best, feeling his gaze on her at every word. But the act of confessing to an impersonal party, there to support her, released a little of the pressure that had built up inside her mind. She felt a slight weight lifting as she raised her head to the three men.

"And yet, the magistrate said at the inquest that Captain Hanley has an alibi for the night in question?" Mr Livingston clarified.

"Yes - his own seamen vouching for him," Joshua snorted.

"Yes, yes, most probably they are," Mr Livingston agreed. "Our difficulty is that if they call him as a witness, I will have no option but to twist his story back onto itself until he reveals his own lies. This is no mean feat, especially with a man bent on revenge, as your Captain seems to be. If we do not summon him, I will have a greater chance to discredit the testament. But we shall not know this until the trial itself."

"So, you will be able to prove he is lying?" Bea sounded almost hopeful.

"Not necessarily. It sounds to me as though he has ensured that..." his voice trailed off. He coughed. "That's to say, if he has taken this much time and effort to conceive such a malicious campaign to my reckoning, he will not be leaving tomorrow to chance. You have witnessed him murdering a man," he paused for a moment, thinking how to phrase the next statement. "Forgive my frankness, Miss Lightfoot, but, if he does not finish the job he started, then he leaves himself wide open to being placed in a similar position. You do realise that, if the trial tomorrow does not go our way, you are most likely facing the noose."

"Peter -!"

"He is right. I have thought about it but... I had not truly accepted it until you said the words, just now."

"Well, we won't let that 'appen," her Da added.

Joshua smiled at her. "You are innocent, my love."

"And that is what we are going to press upon," affirmed Livingston.

"Tomorrow you must trust me, and allow me to do my job, whichever direction I may seem to take."

Bea nodded her head in agreement.

"Do you have a strategy?" Queried Joshua.

The lawyer smiled. "I always have a strategy."

After a few more questions were asked and answered, their allotted time was up. Bea bid farewell to her Da but as the three men made their way to the door, she reached out.

"Joshua -?"

He turned immediately.

She waited until they were alone and gestured him closer. "Promise me... if tomorrow does not go our way...." She watched him as he shifted forward, ready to protest. "If it does not go to plan, that... you will turn your back on me and walk away."

"I cannot do that, and I will not do that!"

"I will be facing death and disgrace, I do not want you to see that, or be part of it. You need to think of your own future and leave me far behind."

He cradled her face softly between his hands.

"I have no future without you in it. We should have been married by now and starting our new life together." He smiled kindly at her.

She tried to reply, "I know", but the lump in her throat prevented her.

"Hanley took that away from us," he continued, with a hint of anger. "But he cannot divide us any longer."

"Joshua -" she uttered, the salt from her tears stinging her dry, cracked lips.

"No more talking, my love, tomorrow is not yet here, who knows what will come to pass." Kissing her hands and then her lips tenderly, he breathed a little warmth back into her chest. She relaxed her breathing, almost imperceptibly.

"Time," a voice called in through the darkness.

"I love you." Joshua spoke the words clearly and calmly as he made his way to the door.

"I love you too!"

He could hear her sobbing in the darkness as it diminished his own resolve, and the guard slammed the door shut.

Chapter 32

The chattering commotion deafened her as they thrust her into the Crown Courtroom. Instantly the cramped audience turned their heads in her direction and started heckling her like she was a court jester. With only six tiny windows up high near the rafters, the court relied on the light from hundreds of candles. Every part of the room was richly furnished, from the grand throne for the presiding judge, to the two small thrones on either side, and the elegant oak cage into which she was adroitly placed. The fine craftsmanship in the wood panelling reached to the vaulted ceiling, as though a monument to justice. She tried to find her Da and Joshua in the sea of faces, catching a glimpse instead of Mr Livingston looking polished in his long black robe and immaculately powdered white wig, strangely stiff with its curls balancing on each side. Watching as he confidently weaved through the crowd, her heart pounded in her chest; Joshua had looked so full of sorrow the night before – had they given up already? She could tell by the tenderness of her neck, and the bruises on wrists that the full impact of the attack and the battering from their crossing was clear, feeling the shades of blue, black and yellow smeared across her body. Would her appearance help or hinder her cause, she wondered?

She gazed at her feet, willing Joshua to hear her thoughts. *I am sorry for entering your world, sorry you had to be so strong for my sake, sorry for all you have lost through our love, sorry that you don't walk away when I know you should. But I am not sorry you love me, nor that I love you.*

Mr Livingston made his way over to the table nearest to Bea and gave her a curt nod. First the jury members entered, followed by the clerk calling out for the crowd to stand as the three judges strode into the room to complete the ensemble. Everyone was then permitted to sit save her, as the clerk recited.

"Beatrice Lightfoot, you have been charged with the murder of Mr William Gregson on the night of August eighteenth, 1831 in Ulverston. How do you plead?"

"Not guilty your honours," Bea responded, as Mr Livingston had instructed her.

"Very well, proceed."

A tall man with a long sallow face stood gracefully in front of the jury members, looking at each one before he started.

"Gentlemen of the jury, throughout this proceeding you will hear the evidence I put before you, which will demonstrate and illustrate how this woman intended to seek out the late Mr Gregson for money in exchange for services, and murdered him when he became violent towards her. You will hear how her character has drawn men into disrepute previous to this incident. You will be presented with the murder weapon, found at the scene of the crime, and owned by her father. Last, you will learn how she was discovered by three witnesses, alone, save for the dead man still on top of her, and the knife at her side."

He finished proudly, gesturing to Mr Livingston to do him better. Mr Livingston gave a sharp cough as he rose from his seat.

"Mr Williamson, the prosecutor, wants you to believe that this crime was pre-meditated; planned to the smallest of details. I say to you it was – but not by my client." A low murmur slithered through the court.

"Miss Beatrice Lightfoot is a hard-working lace-maker and a daughter of a Master rope-maker, who lived with her family, supporting them fairly with her own income, and raising her sisters while her father and brothers attended to their own business. I put to you it was in fact Mr Gregson himself who sought out Miss Lightfoot - who attacked her, conspiring with another, and attempted to assault her before his accomplice killed him. This crime was an act of revenge, staged exclusively to condemn her, and to cast a shadow over her family."

There might still be a chance of hope after all, Bea thought to herself, as the members of the jury turned to one another and exchanged surprised glances. Disgruntled, the prosecutor sauntered over and took his place in front of the judges.

"For my first witness, I would like to call Mrs Kerr to the stand."

Mrs Kerr made her way to the witness box, smoothing down her salmon-pink dress, which clung to her in all the wrong places. She checked that her straw bonnet was positioned straight, nervously fiddling with its pink ribbon, whilst Mr Williamson repeated the same questions as Mr Forester had several days earlier, resulting in an identical response. It was then Mr Livingston's turn to cross-examine Mrs Kerr.

"Mrs Kerr, you told us you heard a scream – that it was this very cry that caused you to become aware of the plight of Miss Lightfoot. Could you possibly describe for me, and for the rest of the court?"

"Yes, sir - t'was a chillin' sound, it almost sounded like a vixen's call; bloodcurdlin' so it was, sir!" Mrs Kerr nodded feverishly.

"So, you heard Miss Lightfoot's fearful call out for help, and it chilled your blood. Have you considered since that night that a woman who is in the process of killing someone secretly, in the dead of night, does not produce a bloodcurdling scream for help?"

"I- er– well, if you put it like that... I suppose not...?" Mrs Kerr blushed in embarrassment and hesitated.

"Whilst you stood waiting for the magistrate to arrive, did Miss Lightfoot say anything to you?" Mrs Kerr looked put out and shuffled her feet. Her fingers moved automatically to her bonnet-strings once more.

"She said... that she wanted 'elp... and that she were innocent... She said, someone else had killed that man - but there was no one else around, I checked!"

"That night was particularly dark, with no moon in the sky - is it not possible that someone was concealed within the tree line? Did you or your boy search the surrounding area?"

"No, I mean to say, there might've been... but I didn't 'ear 'em." Mrs Kerr appeared fearful at the suggestion.

"Thank you, Mrs Kerr; no further questions." Mr Livingston bowed politely to the townswoman and to the judges before he retook his seat.

Bea saw Mr Forester in the crowd below, looking up at her with an injured expression, but the magistrate swiftly shifted his gaze to the man approaching the witness stand.

Mr Williamson called Mr Campbell as his next witness, the poor man exhibiting an even more rueful countenance than on his first appearance. Mr Livingston's cross-questioning continued, impassive and steady.

"Mr Campbell, you remarked you knew who Miss Lightfoot was when you saw her, owing to your professional relationship with her father. How would you describe that family?"

"The Lightfoot's are a long-established family, Ulverston born an' bred. They are well thought of - people listen when Bob Lightfoot talks. They run their business well, an' keep to themselves."

"Would you think it likely that they would be associated with scandal?"

"No sir, I was indeed shocked when I first saw Miss Lightfoot there layin' on the ground, her dress all torn, covered in cuts and bruises... she kept saying she did not do it, nor did it look like she 'ad."

"Thank you, Mr Campbell. No further questions."

Mr Williamson next called the magistrate to the box. Mr Forester held his head high as he responded to the questioning.

"Mr Forester, you are the magistrate for the Ulverston area, are you not?"

"Yes, I am."

"Can you describe for the court what happened that night?"

"A young lad came to my door saying there was a lady on the old harbour road about half a mile out of the town, with a dead man pinning her down, and much blood about them both. Myself and two of my deputies made our way to the place, where I saw Miss Lightfoot lying injured, with the deceased party on top of her. She was covered in blood and seemed somewhat dazed. She made some allusion to a second man, but since she was the only living witness, my deputies took her in."

"Can you please describe how the two people were laid out?"

"Miss Lightfoot was on her back, with the top part of her dress torn. Mr Gregson was face down, his torso over her own, and the lower half of his body between... her open legs... his trousers up. The blood appeared in the main to come from the gentleman's stab wounds, but the lady was also bleeding, from her head, and.." Mr Forester gave Bea an apologetic look, "in her skirts." The crowd tittered.

"Then what happened, Mr Forester?"

"I then discovered the knife, lying close by, and we called for the doctor."

"The good doctor remarked in the inquest that the man had died as a result of two stabbings in the chest area. By the position of Miss Lightfoot under Mr Gregson, would you say that she had physically issued these two wounds?"

"It is possible, before he fell onto her, of course. They were also remarkably deep, according to the doctor's testimony; it would be unusual that a woman of Miss Lightfoot's build could inflict such wounds. However," he coughed, "it is...possible..."

"Yet she remarked that someone else stabbed this man. Did you see anyone else in the vicinity that night?"

"No."

"Miss Lightfoot insists that a certain Captain Hanley killed Mr Gregson, after molesting her - did you inquire into this accusation?"

"Yes, but Captain Hanley has ten sworn statements he was in The Sun that night between ten and four."

"So, I put it to you, Mr Forester, that no one else, on the evidence available, is likely to have committed this crime, apart from Miss Lightfoot?"

"There are conflicting testimonies, certainly, and these might point to Miss Lightfoot as a possible culprit."

"Thank you, Mr Forester."

"Do you have questions for the magistrate, Mr Livingston?" The head judge enquired, uninterested.

"Yes, your honour - Mr Forester, when you examined Mr Gregson, were there any other marks of attack?"

"There were: he bore a slight wound at the side of his head."

"Would you say it was a fresh wound? Possibly as a result of Miss Lightfoot defending herself? Or was this an old injury?"

"We discovered a rock nearby, with blood upon it, which would explain the injury – fresh, and recent, as you say."

"If she did, as you suggest, have a knife on her, then why would she use a rock to defend herself with? Why not use the knife straight away?"

"I could not possibly say."

"Two more questions, Mr Forester: upon inspection, were Mr Gregson's trousers buttoned or unbuttoned - and were there any *marks of activity* on the front portion?"

Mr Forester hesitated, "buttoned and covered in blood, I believe."

"Forgive me, but in contrast, when you examined Miss Lightfoot, you saw evidence that her person had been violently assaulted. Then, can you tell me; if Mr Gregson had not, as his clothing would suggest, committed this act, who assaulted her? Did that not suggest to you that another man had at one time during the time of the incident been present? After which Mr Gregson also tried to attack her? Does the evidence of blood from between her legs not suggest that in fact Miss Lightfoot had been a maiden before this vicious assault took place, discrediting the rumours of her being a whore, and luring one or both men deliberately to the road at night?"

The words painted a vivid image in Bea's mind, her pelvis pulsating in pain and the smell of Hanley on top of her making those disgusting sounds. She clung on tight to the wooden barrier, feeling her legs giving way and the urge to vomit constricting her gullet.

Mr Forester looked at Bea again and then back at Mr Livingston.

"Yes, it would... But maybe the murder happened after the assault on Miss Lightfoot and given that there was so much blood it was hard to tell..."

"On closer inspection, the evidence does not point to that theory. You saw what you wanted to see Mr Forester and refused to enquire further."

"But given the man Miss Lightfoot accused has been vouched for several times over, and we have no other suspects..." The magistrate looked helplessly at the jury.

"Thank you, you may step down Mr Forester."

"The next witness I would like to summon is a Captain Hanley." Mr Williamson called out.

Hanley stepped forward and climbed with ease into the box. He threw Bea a playful smile, as Mr Lightfoot attempted to calm Joshua next to him and encourage him to remain seated.

"Captain Hanley: can you please explain to me how you know Miss Lightfoot?"

"Miss Lightfoot and I stepped out together a handful of times, resulting in my proposing marriage to her. It truly broke my heart when she turned me down. I came back from a long voyage to the West Indies two weeks past; I had greatly missed her and hoped with all my heart that she had changed her mind. I asked her again to marry me, and again she refused me. Later that day, I became the laughingstock of my immediate circle, when I discovered she had been spotted a month earlier at dawn with another man, above the harbour wall. I admit my heart is still sore from her initial rejection, but I count myself now as having a lucky escape."

"Thank you, Captain. Now, can you think why the lady might blame you for this man's murder, and her assault?" Bea, along with the rest of the room, held their breath to hear the next sentence clearly in the packed courtroom.

"I can only think that... maybe she is what people say - a harlot... She was stepping out with at least two men at one time; perhaps poor Mr Gregson was the third - that we know of - She might blame me for his death because she wished for an easy scapegoat... She may not have known I was at the tavern that night, and assumed I fit the usual bill for a sailor on leave... or, simply because she enjoys seeing men like me suffer." He played the wronged lover perfectly, right down to the slight, concentrated pauses, and small facial gestures.

Bea's heart clawed its way out of her chest and into her throat. Hatred overtook misery, injuries, and regret, filling her cheeks with heat.

"Were you on the road at all on the night of the murder?"

"It is as Mr Forester says - I was in The Sun the whole night, spending a little of my pay on my men. I wanted to forget the accused. Her... rejection..."

A vision of red swept across Beatrice's eyes as she gripped the polished wooden balustrade, holding her in, trying her hardest not to make a sound.

"Do you have any further questions for your witness, Mr Williamson?" the judge asked.

"No, your honour."

"Mr Livingston, do you have questions for the witness?"

"Not at this moment your honour - but I do request permission to call upon him again."

The supreme judge contemplated this request with his colleagues. "This is quite unorthodox... however we will allow it, on this occasion."

"Thank you, your honours - I wish to call Miss Beatrice Lightfoot as the next witness." Mr Livingston stood before her with a certainty in his face. For the first time she had met him, she saw a kindness in his eyes.

"Miss Lightfoot, on the night in question, can you tell us how you came to be on the coastal path heading towards the canal, alone?"

"I had received a letter to meet someone urgently."

"Can you tell me who this letter was from?"

"It was from" she found Joshua in the crowd sitting beside her Da, who nodded at her, pleading with her. "A gentleman - who had recently proposed marriage to me, whom I had accepted. We were to be wed in secret within the week, and start a new life in Bristol, or Liverpool, wherever he could find work. But..." she hesitated, "it was not from him, as I found out later, it was from Captain Hanley there. He confessed himself - during..."

"During the events of that evening?"

"Yes."

"And what were those events precisely, Miss Lightfoot? Please address the jury."

"Sir, I received a letter from my betrothed - or so I believed – saying I was to meet him that evening at the old harbour road."

"You still have this letter? Will your young man not confirm that he never wrote such a note?"

"No... I think they took it from me after I lost consciousness."

"Then you have no proof that you did not meet Mr Gregson of your own accord. Please continue, Miss Lightfoot."

"When I heard someone following me, I ran – but I believe Mr Gregson struck me from behind, hitting my head. I was beaten and held down by another man – Captain Hanley... He... he forced himself on me.... I was trapped, I couldn't move." Bea closed her eyes, reliving the horrify ordeal, unable to look at anyone as she spoke the next words. "He forced himself into me, violated me... raped me... telling me I was his and no one else's... then afterwards I was frozen – with the pain." Tears flowed out between her closed eyes. "Then, as I tried to rise, Mr Gregson... positioned himself... trying to do the same -"

"So, you stabbed him in defence of yourself?" At Mr Livingston's question, she opened her eyes.

"No - I didn't! I hit him with a stone to free myself, kicked my legs out but Mr Gregson remarked he would kill me afterwards and at that, Captain Hanley struck him in the chest, more than once... I screamed at the horror Before I could move, Mr Gregson collapsed on top of me."

"Did the Captain say anything to you at any point?" Mr Livingston encouraged her to continue.

"He told me I had humiliated him and should be punished for it... that if he could not have me, then no one else would. After he left me, I passed out from the wounds and the breathlessness caused by the weight of... of the body."

"What do you propose the Captain meant by that statement?"

"He meant this:" she gestured to the courtroom, and the judges. Sadness exuded from her, as a haunting expression spread across her face.

"Had Captain Hanley ever showed you a sign of violence before?"

"Yes." Her voice was meek. "Yes – once before that night. On the day he returned to Ulverston, he came to me and asked me to marry him again. I refused, and he tried to force himself on me, saying, I owed him my body, that I belonged to him. He heard my Mam approaching us so he let me go and ran off into the woods." The room became feverishly animated. She turned to face Mr Livingston, and in the corner of her eye saw Hanley bow his head to her in mock congratulation.

"Thank you, Miss Lightfoot, I have no further questions." Mr Livingston's smile shone briefly before he took his seat again.

"Mr Williamson; your witness," the judge intoned.

"You have told us that Captain Hanley killed the man found on top of you, yet we have ten witnesses, all of whom say he was with them all night. How do you explain this for the jury?"

Struggling to breathe, Bea wanted only to crumple to the floor. To curl up into a small ball and close her eyes until the nightmare had disappeared. Instead she allowed the adrenaline and fury to give her strength, to keep her standing. She saw Joshua and her Da, their grey sunken faces reaching out to her.

"I cannot," she replied clearly. "I suspect he has asked his men to lie for him, but I cannot prove it. I can only speak the truth that I know."

"The word of a woman who has been out at all hours with two unmarried men, on her way to meet another, and discovered with a dead man on top of her? No more questions, your honour."

Mr Williamson shook his head as he took his seat. Mr Livingston stood up.

"I wish to call back Captain Hanley to the stand."

Amused, Hanley stood like a soldier, shoulders back, with a wide stance, hands behind and chin held high.

"Captain Hanley, we heard from Miss Lightfoot's account that it was you in fact who attacked her on the night of the eighteenth. If you loved her as you say you did, would you not be the first to suggest her character was at odds with her crime?"

"She killed my First Mate; I certainly would not have proposed marriage to her had I known -"

"I beg your pardon - you knew Mr Gregson. Why have you not mentioned this fact before?"

"I am sure I did..."

"Can you tell me then, how Mr Gregson came to be out on the road with Miss Lightfoot without your knowledge? It seems odd to me that your relationship with the deceased has not been made apparent sooner - I thought you were drinking with your men that night at The Sun – surely your right-hand man would have been one of that number?"

"He must have heard me talking about her in the snug and tried his own luck. And certainly, I have never denied knowing Mr Gregson."

"He heard you talking about marrying her, your love for her, and your sorrow at her rejection, and your first mate, then decided he would rape her? Does that not seem a rather abrupt course of action?"

"As I say, my suggestion is merely a conjecture – I have no first-hand knowledge of the event. I can only say that I have known Gregson from childhood, and he was loyal to me beyond most."

"Loyal to the point that if you asked him to assist you in attacking a young woman, he would obey?"

"That would be a convenient interpretation, sir, to be sure. You have the details of the witnesses who can prove I did not commit the murder. If at one time I harboured a deep affection for Miss Lightfoot, it does not therefore prove that I murdered William Gregson. Either way, I cannot see your line of questioning as helping the accused at present."

"You will keep your personal opinions to yourself, Captain Hanley," ordered a judge.

"I have ten bystanders to say I was drinking in The Sun at the time of the murder. I cannot help you further, sir."

"No more questions, my honours."

"If there are no further witnesses, I must ask the jury to retire to their chamber and consider their verdict. Do you find Miss Beatrice Lightfoot guilty or not guilty for the murder of Mr William Gregson? You must all be of the same mind. Thank you, gentlemen."

A STILLNESS DESCENDED body by body over the room as the jury took their seats. Bea noticed Joshua talking to Mr Livingston, unable to make out what he was saying. She braced herself and sent out one last silent prayer. The three judges finally strode in from their chamber and turned to the foreperson of the jury.

"You have all reached the same decision?"

Bea closed her eyes and pictured Joshua's face, willing him to be strong for whatever happened.

"We have," replied the foreperson.

"Continue."

"We the jury find Miss Beatrice Lightfoot *guilty* of the murder of Mr William Gregson."

It is over; all over now.

The left judge placed the haunting square black cloth over his central companion's head.

The court room stood at the clerk's demand.

"Miss Beatrice Lightfoot, you have been found guilty of the most heinous crime of murder. Therefore, it is my duty by law to inform you that on the chosen day, before the month is out, you will be taken to a place of execution and hung by the neck until dead – may God have mercy on your soul. Take her away."

Bea screamed involuntarily and pressed herself against the back panel of the podium. The guards heaved her down from the docks as they stopped Joshua from approaching her. Then the crowd closed in around her, blocking her view. The light within her faded too, as they carried her back towards her cell, taking her first steps on her journey to leaving the world behind.

Chapter 33

"May I have a word with you, Bob?"

Distracted by the sight of Bea being dragged away, Joshua failed to notice Mr Forester.

"Bob – Mr Lightfoot, Mr Mason - I realise I may not be the person you wish to see at this moment in time, but... is there anything I can do?" the magistrate enquired gently.

"I think you have done enough!" Joshua scorned.

"You have every right to be angry, and you must believe me when I say I was only doing my job -"

"You have helped to condemn the wrong person-" cried Mr Lightfoot in anguish.

"I acted on the evidence that I had, perhaps I misjudged the other party, perhaps I could have done more; she -"

"Do not blame Beatrice!" snapped Joshua, already looking over the magistrate's shoulder for Hanley.

"I do not. After witnessing the proceedings today, I now understand better why she acted as she did – perhaps that is my fault. If there is anything I can do to help, please, send word."

"There is nothing -"

"Wait." Mr Lightfoot studied Mr Forester, wondering how far his offer would extend. "Nate - D'you truly believe that my Beatrice is innocent?"

"Unfortunately, ... I do. I apologise for my failings. After crossing the sands, speaking to her in her cell, and seeing how the Captain conducted himself first-hand in the witness box: yes, I do." Mr Lightfoot took a risk.

"Then come find me at The Fox and Hound in two hours' time. You can make good yer promise."

JOSHUA GLIMPSED HANLEY slink off into the crowd, and fuelled by a foolish anger, the young man stalked after him. He watched as Hanley strode through the crowded bustle of townsfolk. Heedless of the drama that had just concluded in the Castle behind them and made his way into the nearby woods on the outer limits of the town. Leaning against a tree, Joshua felt a stream of sweat trickling down his back and temples. Taking a moment, he tried to slow his breathing, and ask himself rationally what on earth he was about to do; to force himself to make time and consider all eventualities. But all he felt, all he knew, was rage. At himself for not protecting Bea when he should have, even after learning from his own father what kind of monster Hanley was. At Bea for being foolish enough to accept his offer of silk in the first place, and at her family, for not better protecting her. Above all else, he felt a twisting, unbearable kind of anger at knowing he might never see her again, after he had asked her to be his and losing the potential future they might have had.

Joshua Mason left all traces of youth behind him in that instant and crossed the bitter line towards true independence. At that moment he knew he had no one but himself to take action and truly own the consequences.

In the distance, behind a tree, he made out a dark figure, hovering silently. He carefully crept closer as he attempted to formulate a tangible plan. He had contemplated this moment a dozen times over the past few weeks, but now, standing with the opportunity manifest in front of him, he was at a disadvantage. He had no weapon, and no way to defend himself. And yet -

"Mason." Hanley's animated, welcoming voice took Joshua by surprise.

"Hanley. I thought it was about time we finally finished this, don't you?"

"She did look rather wretched in the stands today; do you not think? The bloom has quite vanished from her now – what a pity. At least now she will hang, and the pain will soon be over."

"You are a lunatic." Joshua knew if he were to stand any chance against the Captain, he would need to control the adrenaline and the hatred coursing through him. He took a measured look at his opponent.

"You loved her, didn't you." It wasn't a question.

Hanley gave a barking laugh, and his smile vanished as he strode closer to Joshua.

"You must have heard my history, if not from your father, then from others. If you believe even half of them, you would not ask me that question. I have been told; I do not know what love is."

Joshua shook his head.

"I believe them - and yet I can still understand how you must have felt about Beatrice. There is something about her that makes those fortunate enough to know her feel... worthy, full of hope. She reaches out in a way few women do. I am begging you - spare her." Hanley's face was set into a blank mask.

"She was mine – she sold herself to me, and then to yourself. She holds no value for me now."

"You cannot buy someone - If you loved her, then change your statement - you could still spare her."

"And what - implement myself for murdering someone? Why would I do that?"

"I am not here to play games, Hanley."

Joshua craved a cigarette; he could feel his nerves ready to explode in his body. The men stood a foot away from each other, waiting for the other to pounce.

"No, you came to finish it."

Joshua's mouth became dry, and his fingers numb as Hanley produced a slim silver dagger, holding it loosely at his side, staring emptily at his opponent. Joshua knew instinctively that the deranged seaman was about to strike.

He stared at Hanley's large, muscular build. He knew he did not have half the strength Hanley had, but he was younger and faster, with a sharper eye, and he knew that whoever made the first move would surely have the advantage.

Without warning, his right fist smacked into Hanley's jaw, catching him off guard. A playful glint flashed in Hanley's eyes as he staggered upright, rubbing his face ruefully.

"Don't tire yourself out, lad!" Hanley laughed.

Before the last word had left his lips, he darted forward and hooked Joshua's jaw, thrusting his other hand out with the blade held firm. Joshua caught a flash of silver, and knew, without really processing the thought, that he had to roll with the punch to avoid the same fate as William Gregson. He used the momentum of Hanley's force to spin himself round to the Captain's exposed left and slammed his elbow in a backward stab as hard as he could into the lower part of his ribs. Hanley reacted instantly, thrusting his clenched fist into Joshua's stomach, causing him to momentarily double over. Before Hanley could take him into a headlock, the young merchant spun away, missing the knife blade by inches as it slashed upwards past his tilted chin. Angrily, Hanley swiped at the younger man again, and Joshua felt his abdominal muscles tighten as he arched his entire body back in on itself to avoid losing his guts to the woodland floor. Again using the taller man's momentum against him, Joshua grasped the wrist that held the knife, and thrust it back unnaturally over Hanley's shoulder, twisting the Captain's whole arm round behind his body in the same movement, pushing it up towards the shoulder blades. Hanley yelled and loosened his grip on the knife handle, and the blade fell to the ground.

Joshua kicked it away, but in doing so lost his balance slightly. Hanley felt the young man's grip soften, and took his chance, wrenched his arm free and punched him full in the face. Joshua's vision exploded, blood filled his eyes, and he staggered, dazed. His eyes wide with fury, Hanley threw a second punch, taking Joshua to his knees, but as he aimed a kick at his collarbone, Joshua grabbed hold of his foot. Hanley fell back with a cry, and Joshua lunged for the knife.

Slithering over the now churned-up mud of the clearing, his mind was empty save for a single thought as his bloody fingers found the handle. He felt Hanley's hands on his ankles, and let out a bellow of rage and desperation, thrashing around with all his strength to stop the other pinning him face down to the earth. He heard a dull crack, and a cry. Without stopping to breathe, he instinctively spun round, thrust the knife upwards and outwards. Like a skewer through a ripe peach, the blade gradually sank into Hanley's shoulder. He fell forward, his face halting within inches of Joshua's own. Joshua watched the bright, warm blood creep down the side of the hilt and onto his hands. Hanley looked a little confused and sat backwards onto the woodland floor like a toddler failing to stand, trying feebly to remove the blade. Joshua heard himself gasp. It sounded strange and disconnected, as though from a distance. He shuffled backwards as the colour drained out of the Captain's face, his mouth remaining strangely red.

Joshua checked to see if anyone had appeared during the struggle. Panting, he glanced back at Hanley. Perhaps fate might step in and claim him... or should he finish the job, as he had so often wished to do? But even now, after his irreparable violence and malignant cruelty, Joshua knew he was incapable of killing another human being in cold blood.

Instead, he placed the decision in God's hands, staggering to his feet, Hanley still failing to remove the blade as the blood flowed from his wound. *I pray I never see you again.*

As he walked away, he heard Hanley splutter in unfamiliar tones behind him: "*You always were a weak one, boy... I should have drowned you like a pup...*"

Chapter 34

A fragment of light broke through the rock-face, like sunbeams through the clouds, teasing Bea with a snatched memory of life outside. Bea stretched her arm out, dappled with tiny bite marks and patches of raw skin from being in the cell for days, weeks; alone, but not alone. She watched shadows form across the floor and remembered how she used to play shadow puppets for the girls in the old loft. Had it even been her, the bright, auburn-haired girl, weaving her hands around in strange contortions, keeping one eye on the delighted faces of her audience, ready to rock the lantern and make them shriek? And then she heard it, the drumming sound becoming louder against the stone, dimming out the light, casting her back into darkness.

She pulled herself upright, clinging to the crumbling sandstone, and shuffled sideways until she felt the large licked-out groves, and waited, trembling. A few drops of water trickled over her fingertips, and her parched mouth salivated as she leant forward, reaching out with her tongue. There was a thickness to the water as it soaked into her sponge like tongue, with tiny shards of stone which ground against her teeth and a bitter taste of salt. Lowering herself down, her eyes flickered shut, her body gave way to exhaustion as she slipped out of consciousness again.

BEA HEARD THE CREAKING sound of the door through the darkness, and the iron clanking against iron from the keys swinging from his belt. She knew what she had to do: their evening routine, and she pulled herself up and stood to attention. From the dim glow of the candle in the passage, Bea could make out the broad silhouette of her keeper. He stood in front of her and dropped the metal plate deliberately on the floor, as though for a dog. She knew it would be the same stale bread and mouldy cheese, or a lump of rotten meat, followed by the bowl of water, most of it splashing onto the earthen floor. He took a step closer to Bea and brushed the hair away from her face. She held her breath as his hand wandered from her neck and hovered over her breasts, before resting at her waist.

"Eat," he mumbled, pushing to the floor.

Bea tensed away from his touch and fell to her knees, feeling out for the piece of bread. The hard crust was sour in her mouth, as she felt her gums bleed. And yet she was thankful, and her stomach grumbled at the taste of any food. She quickly took another bite, then another, whilst the man stood over her, watching curiously, and panting. Finishing the meal did not take her long. She picked up the bowl. There was enough water for two mouthfuls today. The jailer let out a grumble, scraped up the plates, and made his way back to the door. Bea waited for the clicking of the lock before curling back into a silent ball, tears rolling down her face as her body shook with grief.

Leaning her forehead against the wet stone, void of hope, she now knew for certain that there was nothing left. In the blind darkness, she wondered blankly: if she could have reversed only one aspect of her story, would it have changed this ending?

THE CLASHING SOUNDS echoed in the passageway again. Bea instinctively crouched low to the floor and scurried into the corner, wrapping her arms around her legs and pulling her head in tightly. She rocked back and forth as the keys turned in the lock and the bolt slid sideways. She could hear two lots of footsteps enter the room and feared they had finally come for her.

"Five minutes," a familiar voice growled.

She listened, terrified, as the door slammed shut, her head down.

"Oh god, Beatrice? Bea? Lass?"

Bea scrambled backwards on the spot, attempting to get smaller, to escape into the walls.

"Lass, it's your Da."

"Da?" her voice was barely audible. She kept her head buried in her knees; it must be a trick of some sort. She had finally lost her mind.

His heart broke at the sight of her. The air was putrid, and it caught in his throat. What had become of his daughter?

"Yes, lass," he spoke gently, as he edged a little closer.

She slowly lifted her head and as he came closer, she could smell a hint of hemp in the air.

"Da!" She crawled out of the shadow like a creature from the murky depths of the canal. Was it him, could it be him? The lamp light highlighted his grey beard and tired eyes. She scurried a little closer, the light making her eyes squint. "Da?"

"I'm here, lass."

In a sudden jump, she flung herself through the air and into his arms. He stroked her soiled hair and clung to her frail body.

"Da, they are going to kill me, they are going to kill me . . . I don't want to die . . . they are going to kill me, Da!"

"It's alright lass, hush now."

He cradled her like a child and let her mutter away.

"Why did you not come earlier? How long has it been since the trial? I can't tell in here anymore..."

"It's been three weeks, pet - I wasn't allowed to come earlier, not until all was ready."

"When... when will it be Da?"

"Tomorrow."

Tomorrow and it will all be over. She wasn't ready to die, to say goodbye to everything and everyone she loved.

"Da – I'm sorry, - I'm so sorry..."

"You've done nothin' wrong, my girl. Hush, just you let me hold you."

"I don't think- that is- I'm not ready to die!" Her eyes were wide and full of fear. "Will it hurt? You hear stories – of what happens; will that happen to me?"

She felt her father's body tense.

"Nothing bad will happen, Bumble Bea."

Wrapping their arms around each other, they cried. Then she rested her head against his chest, listening to his steady heart and breathing in his familiar herbal scent. After a while, they broke apart.

"The girls send their love and say they miss you, poor lambs."

"Do they think bad of me?"

"All they know is you're gone, but they don't know why."

"When they are old enough, tell them truth... tell them how much I loved them..."

"I will, lass."

"I love you, Da."

"I love you too, lass."

There was nothing more to be said after that; they could have talked about all the tiny details of life; instead, they merely held each other silently until it was time for him to leave.

Chapter 35

"Is it all in there?" Mr Lightfoot asked, patting the heavy tarpaulin.

"Aye – be careful, Bob. If this should go wrong..." Uncle John handed him the reins and shot him a warning look along with them.

"Look after the family whilst I'm gone." Mr Lightfoot ignored the glance and gave him a pat on the shoulder. He sluggishly climbed up to the seat with his cargo stored neatly in the cart behind. "I better be off if I'm goin' to make that last crossing."

"Da, tell Bea -" Matty couldn't finish the sentence, but his father smiled at him with a fierce expression in his eyes.

"I will, lad. Now, do me proud, and keep helpin' your Uncle John."

THE MORNING FELT LIKE any other morning; it didn't feel like this was the day she would die. She had wished there had been some paper so that she could leave letters to express her final thoughts. She particularly wanted to say goodbye and thanks to Alice, and to tell her she understood why her father had refused to allow her to attend the hearings. Bea hoped Alice would find happiness and courage with Mr Woodhouse and not be fearful to fall in love. Love: to think all this happened because of such a beautiful, burning emotion. But he had not come to say goodbye. She had hoped to have seen Joshua one last time, even though she had told to leave her behind and all the words she would have said to him, had been said already. The pain of goodbye would quite possibly have proved too much regardless, knowing she would have to leave him behind, having been so close to the type of happiness that she had never thought possible.

She paced around the edges of the cell, familiar to her now, muttering out her goodbye letters into the void. The streams of light broken through more insistently, and she knew it was almost time. She sent out her last prayer, beseeching God not to judge her to harshly when she stood before him. And then she waited, the minutes like hours. The jailer's footsteps followed the beats of her heart, and at the sound of the iron sliding back, she knew she was ready.

AS HER BLACKENED FEET stepped onto the small wooden platform, a wave of noise hit her, jeering her towards the noose. The early morning light bleached her squinting eyes, and she suddenly felt as though she was back, high above the harbour wall, with the gulls screaming and calling, the crashing of the waves roaring distantly below, and the undertow dragging pebbles down the beach in an inexorable foaming rush. The sharp biting wind tunnelled its way through the tight street and forced itself through her. The smell of rotten food and excrement wafted upwards, bringing her sharply back to the moment.

A firm push in the small of her back hustled her forward; stubby fingers thrusting into her, forcing her up the narrow wooden steps. The words were becoming clearer, a few hateful spectators throwing angry accusations. But she no longer cared what the people said, what they thought, or who they were. Like a child scraping the moss at the edges of an empty well, her moribund existence would soon evaporate, leaving behind a tainted stain.

As she reached the platform, three men stood waiting. The largest was cloaked in darkness, his black hood a blessing of anonymity. Like a raven standing above the dead, he stood back, ready to feast on her remains. The smaller elderly man on the contrary seemed proud to show his face in his long robe and distinctive white collar, staring at her with disdain in his eyes. The third was the Judge.

A deathly holy trinity, thought Bea.

"Anything you would like to say?"

Bea glanced out into the crowd in a daze and wondered if they had come. As the last seconds counted down, the only words she wanted to say were for them and them alone. She scanned the horizon and saw Joshua and her Da, standing side by side. She looked at Joshua; he had come to say goodbye. She was sorry for so much, but never how much she had loved him. His harrowing expression ripped away the seal on her mouth and forced her to speak the only words that mattered.

"I," she stuttered, her voice catching in her throat. "I - love – you."

"Time!"

In a single moment, the world turned black as the cloth slid over her face. A voice nearby muttered words in another language as a haunting silence descended over the audience. The dam broke and her tears flowed, washing her clean, allowing the sorrow to consume her as the weight around her neck tightened. She tried to think of happier times, a joyful thought to transport her through to her next life; but the images were already fading away. Nothing came to her, only a cold, biting fear of the unknown.

In a split second, they tore away the world.

Her stomach lurched...

She was falling.

Chapter 36

Joshua and Mr Lightfoot braced themselves as they watched the black hood being placed over Bea. Joshua nodded at Mr Forester, who stood at the corner near the Judge, overseeing the day's events as Mr Lightfoot listened carefully to the surrounding crowd, unable to take his eyes off his daughter. The few seconds felt like a lifetime as they watched Bea shake with pure terror. Then it happened, the floor opened, and the rope descended. They strained against each other's grip, watching to see if their planned had worked. Out of the usual commotion of the spectators, Mr Lightfoot heard distant screams followed by the sound of marching drums. For a moment he thought he would have to watch his daughter hang, but in the same second that the trap doors hit the underside of the platform, the rope snapped. Joshua signalled to Mr Forester as the crowd gasped in shock. They needed to work fast. Mr Lightfoot made his way to the back of the crowd and looked for a sign of his men. The drumming and sounds of chanting were getting closer.

"It's an act of god!" shouted Joshua clearly above the dull chatter of the onlookers.

He heard some crowd agree with him as he shouted louder.

"God has forgiven her sins." Someone else in front of Joshua pitched in.
"She is blessed!"

Another shouted as the hangman stared at the rope in disbelief.

"Excuse me your honour," Mr Forester was already on the platform, and had approached judge.

"Can it wait man; we have to deal with this... situation..."

"I am sure you are already aware of this, my lord, but by law you cannot rehang this woman." Mr Forester's voice rang out far louder than usual across the crowd, as much to them as to the judge.

"Nonsense, we have found her guilty... Of course, we can hang her." The Judge gestured to the executor to fetch more rope.

"Not if the rope breaks - this is deemed an act of God, a ruling by a higher authority, my lord. An old law, but it still stands today."

The Judge stopped what he was doing and turned to face Mr Forester.

"We had found her guilty of murder; are you now telling me she must be now be freed?"

"Yes - you have carried out the sentence, but god has granted her freedom."

A nearby member of the public overheard the tail-end of their conversation and passed it on to their neighbour.

"God has granted her freedom!"

In the background, the screams had become markedly louder, with the sounds of war drums and the chant: *'The Reformers are coming,' 'Join us,'* breaking through the noise of the crowd.

"Did I hear that correctly? I thought you had dealt with the rebellion, Forester?" The judge seemed somewhat at sea. "That the ringleader is currently in our cell and is about to hang next."

Mr Forester studied the crowd for Mr Lightfoot; he hadn't been made aware of this part of the plan.

The sound of people jeering and joining in the song of the marchers seeped through the courtyard and the streets that surround the Castle.

"We demand to be heard, to vote for what is right and not what this corrupt government deems fit!"

"*AYE!*" The workers shouted as one.

"They trample down the working man and woman..."

"Tear it down..." declared a man in the crowd.

"I will attend to it, sir – I suggest we disperse the public here as quickly as we are able."

Mr Lightfoot stood further up the street, shouting back observations towards the crowd, and repeating the Reformers' words for all to hear.

"They are callin' out for support; callin' for all men and women to revolt against the government... To fight back against the rich man, the mill owner and the landowner - all them that command, that judge us common men; we shall take back our country and our livelihoods! Who's with us?"

The onlookers went wild, half turning their backs on the gibbet and pointing at the advancing parade.

"Reform!"

"Let's take back our land..."

"Let her go, God has spoken..." Joshua called out, hoping someone else would bite.

"Aye, let 'er go!" came a call from the middle of the throng.

"Let her go, she 'as been saved from their sacrifice..." Another cried.

"You are not greater than God, he is my ruler."

"Your honour, for your safety, I think you had better leave before this gets out of hand. I will send for the soldiers."

"But what about the girl, surely she must hang?"

"My lord, if you grant it as an act of god - it will please the masses - perhaps buy you some time to leave... I fear what might arise in the wake of this... surge of this rebellion..."

The mob swarmed closer to the gallows, pushing against one another, attempting to get closer. Joshua was already at the foot of the platform, hidden in shadow.

"Do you think this is an act of God?" the judge asked the frightened clergyman standing at the back of the platform.

"I believe so sir – and if it means we can leave before..."

"The people of Lancashire are rising up with the Reformers, it is time to shake the foundation of this corrupt court and so-called Castle..." Mr Lightfoot had no fear left now; his heart was full of hope.

The mob was sparking with anger, and the Judge saw he had no other choice if he wanted to save himself. He stepped forward hastily and tried to make himself heard over the commotion.

"Ladies and Gentlemen, I have a statement to make – it is with due consideration that I have abode by the old law, that being: if the rope should break, it is indeed an act of god, and Miss Lightfoot shall not be hanged again by this court. It is therefore within my power today to allow this woman to walk free – and may god have mercy on us all."

The crowd rejoiced at the populist sea-change.

"The people have spoken..."

"The power of the workers!"

The Judge gestured for the baffled jailer to release Bea as he disappeared hurriedly towards the main doors. Joshua battered frantically on the small door in the side of the wooden stage before the jailer could get there first, broke through, and removed the black hood and rope around Bea's neck. He lifted her, limp and terrified in his arms, and carried her quietly through a side-gate.

With the noise of the crowd soaring to a crescendo, the Reformers could be heard coming closer, heading towards the doors of the Castle. One by one the men and women began filtering towards the new crowd, joining with the new wave of excitement, while the frayed ends of the hemp rope swayed gently in the breeze.

Chapter 37

"Joshua, what...?" Bea struggled to talk; a red and purple line seared across her neck.

"Don't speak, love, I will explain once we are safe."

He guided her down a side street, keeping their heads down as they passed by one or two people. The rest of Lancaster was bare, void of trade and townsfolk, as those who had not joined the march stayed hidden behind locked doors, fearful of the wrath of the soldiers. Bea struggled to walk; her legs were weak, and her starved body was dizzy from the light and movement. Nestling her head on Joshua's chest, Bea let her mind fill only with his rapid heartbeat and deep breathing; believing it was all a dream, a last-minute hallucination before death claimed her.

They arrived at a guest-house for travellers on the edge of the town, and made their way to a shabby room, where minutes later Mr Lightfoot joined them, relief sketched across his face: the first half of the plan at least had worked. Joshua had gently lowered Bea onto a long, low chair, sitting beside her and pulling his arms tightly around her small body. Her father joined their embrace briefly and then stood back.

"What happens next?" asked Bea, barely audible, not sure she wanted to hear the answer.

"We have the room for the night. But you can't stay in Lancaster, it might not be safe. You are free for now, but we can't risk them coming looking for you."

Joshua knelt next to her.

"Boston – America. We can start again; I can get work with some people, good people, who have moved out there." He gently took hold of Bea's hand. "If, of course, you will still have me?" Bea squeezed his hand and nodded in disbelief. "Tomorrow, we will make our way to Liverpool. I have booked us a passage on a large cargo ship. On the way there, we will stop off in Preston

I will make you Mrs Mason." He gave her a light kiss on her forehead before letting her go slowly and stood upright at her father's side. "But for now: rest. You have this room; we have another next door. A girl is to come up and prepare you a bath; there are clean clothes in the trunk." Bea reached out unthinkingly, fearful of being alone.

"We are close by, lass – I'll come and see you in an hour, with a bit o' food." Mr Lightfoot called for the girl, paid for her silence, and left Bea alone to wash away the last month grime in peace.

BEA WOKE SCREAMING, clutching at her throat. Joshua, who had been asleep on one of the armchairs in the corner of the room, ran to her side. Still immersed in the nightmare, she kicked out, emitting strange grunting noises. He tried to hold her to him, pulling her back to safety, but she scurried across the bed, scared the man was back.

"It's Joshua, my love... You are safe – I am here."

Hearing his voice, she stopped. Her eyes still closed, she shook, unwilling to believe him. He lowered himself on to the bed and allowed her to come to him. She shuffled into his arms and placed her head on his chest. He felt his chest become wet as he stroked her hair, rocking her back and forth, lulling her into a calmer sleep.

Mr Lightfoot tiptoed back out of the room, satisfied his son-in-law was the best person chance could have sent their way to care for his daughter.

THREE DAYS BEFORE THEIR wedding, in a little parish church on the outskirts of Preston, where their names would not matter, Joshua, Mr Lightfoot and Bea took up residence in an inn, and took a timid Bea to a dress shop. For a brief time, she allowed herself to feel like a true bride. The dress was simple, smooth-lined, in cream silk, with a floral lace veil.

Bea still couldn't shake off the feeling that these events were a dream, nor the abiding fear that each night would be her last, before facing the sun atop the scaffold once more. Worse, she occasionally found herself convinced she was dead, and this was some kind of blessed hell, tormenting her with the life she could have had.

She had prepared her mind for death, she had felt the rope around her neck, the piercing pain as it tightened as she fell. That had been real; that had been true. How could all this now be real too? How could she be getting ready on her wedding day?

Each time she closed her eyes, her mind took her back. It filled her nights with terror, but she always woke to find Joshua's patient face above her, and curling up in his arms, she dozed away the small hours, somewhat reassured. The rope-burn around her neck was turning yellow, and she saw how the staff looked at her every time her scarf slipped. Joshua added extra coins to their pockets accordingly as they made their way to and from the rooms.

Bea was many things; bewildered, tired, irritated, and guilty, but she felt no excitement, except a small flutter of hope each time she traced the lace trim on her dress. Aside from that, all she wanted to do was to sleep, and to forget.

SHE SAT AT THE EDGE of the bed on the morning of her wedding and wished for no one but Beth and Alice. She loved Joshua with her whole being and wanted to spend the rest of her life with him. She was grateful for the second chance they had granted her. But part of her had wished in this very moment, her sister and childhood friend would be standing beside her, laughing and giggling at the rumours of the wedding night and the happiness of the future to come. Instead, alone, she stood there staring at her bruised skinny body filled with the sorrow that clung to her every movement and thought. Sighing, she stepped into the voluminous underskirt and pulled tight the corset as far as she was able with a quick hand from the chamber girl; her frame had lost all shape. She fastened the last of the buttons and tied a piece of lace around her neck to conceal the bruise. In the corner of the room was a standing mirror, in which she studied her reflection distantly, pinching her cheeks for some colour, smoothing her skirts, and pinning the veil into place. She remembered how she had felt the night of the May dance, the night her life had changed.

The clock chimed 10, followed by a small knock on the door.

"Come in."

Mr Lightfoot gasped at the sight of his daughter. In less than a week, he couldn't have imagined the difference. "Lass you look . . .", he cleared his throat. "I'm proud of you . . . I've never loved yer more. And I think you picked a good 'un - even if he is a gentleman." He winked and placed a light kiss on her forehead. "Shall we go?"

"Yes," she smiled bravely, and took his arm.

THE SERVICE WAS SIMPLE and discreet, and in less than an hour Miss Beatrice Lightfoot became Mrs Beatrice Mason.

"It wasn't how we imagined it, Bea my love, but it was perfect because you are now my wife, and that is all that matters. I love you, beautiful lady."

"I love you too." It was the first time they had kissed since they had freed her, and since the attack. It was not as painful as she had imagined, and relief flooded through her at the gentle comfort of his warm mouth. When they returned to the Inn, for a couple of hours Bea forgot her ordeal, happily watching the easy, friendly conversation between her Da and her new husband: opposites becoming friends. After they had drank their ale jug dry twice, Joshua and Bea climbed the stairs to the bridal chamber.

He gently kissed her, pulling her closer to his body.

A flashback of being touched down there, and the pain of that night flashed into her mind. She pulled out of his hold, shaking slightly. She was not ready for the immediate, intimate part of their relationship.

"Sorry – I am so sorry..." she wept.

"My love, you have nothing to be sorry for. We have the rest of our lives to be together, that is enough for me."

She looked at him with wide eyes, then kissed him solemnly on the mouth, holding his face with both hands. "I love you."

TEN DAYS INTO THEIR journey across the great sea, Bea felt slightly sick. She blamed it on the storm that had passed through a few days previously. A sensation of nausea sat in her throat, always threatening but never arriving, as she sat at the little wooden desk in their room and wrote out letters for her Da, for Beth and Alice. They would dock at Boston in a day or two and wanted to have them ready for the returning post.

She had been in awe of the Liverpool docks; so much busier and bigger than she had imagined. The ships scattered about everywhere she looked, with flags hailing from countries and merchants across the globe were three times the size of those she had watched trailing into Ulverston. They had only stayed in Liverpool for a few hours, as their things were loaded onto the ship, and she bade farewell to her Da, she could not shake off the fear of being watched, as if Hanley would suddenly emerge from the shadows below the pier and claim her one last time. Joshua had told her how they fought, that he had gravely wounded the man, but they saw nothing in the papers to enlighten them as to the eventual outcome. Was he lying dead on the woodland floor, prey to small animals and insects, or alive, and nursing an even greater hatred than before? In Boston at least, he couldn't find them, Bea hoped.

She sighed, confused. It had been seven weeks since it had turned her life upside down. Seven weeks since Hanley had attacked her and claimed what he had always wanted. She paused. Seven weeks. No... it could not be seven, surely... It had been the storm. She had not bled, certainly, but that was the trial; the hanging and the trauma. Seven weeks. He had raped her; he had discharged his seed into her, and the memory of it still sent a shudder down her spine. But it had only happened once; surely God wouldn't have blessed that... *union* with a child. Seven weeks. She placed her hand over her lower belly without even thinking about the gesture.

Could there be a baby growing inside? A part of Hanley growing inside her? She had survived so much, and Boston would be their fresh start, where a new life could begin properly, far away from the past. But would Joshua... would their relationship, which had overcome so much already, endure this too? She could tell him in a month, and wait to see... but surely, he deserved more from her than lies. She paced around the cabin. She did not want a baby like this. Not *his* baby... She wanted Joshua's baby, their baby... Not a constant reminder of everything she had lost, every second of pain and madness she had endured...

Bea continued to pace back and forth, the swaying of the ship not helping the sickness. She heard footsteps coming down the corridor. Fear surged through her, but she knew what she had to do.

Joshua took one look at her.

"Bea? Beatrice, what is it?"

"Take a seat, my love... I have something to tell you."

To be continued...

Saving Grace
Deception. Obsession. Redemption

Book 2 in the Ropewalk series released on 11th May 2021

Beacon Hill, Boston. 1832.

"You are innocent. You are loved. You are mine."

After surviving the brutal attack and barely escaping death at Lancaster Castle, Beatrice Mason attempts to build a new life with her husband Joshua across the Atlantic in Beacon Hill. But, as Beatrice struggles to cope with the pregnancy and vivid nightmares, she questions whether she is worthy of redemption.

Determined to put the past behind her after the birth of her daughter Grace, Bea embraces her newfound roles of motherhood and being a wife. Nevertheless, when she meets Sarah Bateman, their friendship draws Bea towards the underground abolitionist movement, despite the dangerous secrets it poses. Whilst concealed in the shadows, Captain Victor Hanley returns, obsessed with revenge and the desire to lay claim to what is his, exposes deceptions and doubts as he threatens their newly established happiness.

Now, Beatrice must find the strength to fight once more and save Grace, even if it costs her life.

Don't miss out!

Visit the website below and you can sign up to receive emails whenever H D Coulter publishes a new book. There's no charge and no obligation.

https://books2read.com/r/B-A-LLNM-XZEMB

BOOKS 2 READ

Connecting independent readers to independent writers.

About the Author

Hayley is a teacher and whilst living in Ulverston, loved to spend the weekends walking the Ropewalk and the harbour edge and becoming inspired by the stories and legends of the area.

Read more at www.hdcoulter.com.